# MAFIA WAR

## L. STEELE

# 1

---

Michael

"You are bleeding."

Massimo's voice cuts through the silence in my mind. I raise my hand to my brow and my fingers come away wet. "It's nothing." I stare at the redness. The same blood that runs through her veins. The scarlet that had pooled around her body which had been thrown clear of the car in the blast.

Thank *Santa Maria* I had insisted on installing an ejector seat, as well as a protective shell around the driver's seat which would deploy in case of something just like this.

I had ordered the specially-made Maserati for myself, but had gifted it to her when she had asked for a car. Thank god I had. For when I had seen her trapped under the ejector seat, something inside of me had awakened. I've never been a believer in god, but at that instant, as I had jumped to my feet from where the blast had knocked me down and raced over to her, a part of me had reached out to that higher power. I had beseeched him, had pleaded with him, had asked him with every breath that I had drawn to spare her. To let her live. To allow her to survive this incident, one that I could have averted by being more vigilant. As long as I live, I'll never forgive myself for what happened.

I had leaped across the distance, reached her, sunk to my knees, and released the seatbelt. I had caught her, then lowered her gently to the ground. I had touched her brow... Cold; she had been so cold. Dirt smeared her face, her hair was in a cloud about her shoulders, and she seemed uninjured, as if she were simply sleeping, except for a cut on her arm that was bleeding. I had held her close, turned toward the car to find the flames leaping from the vehicle. That was when Christian had driven up in his car, followed by Massimo and Seb.

Christian had jumped out of his car, taken one look at us, then at the burning car, then back at us.

"Xander," I'd croaked, "Xander."

Some of the sparks had rained down on my Maserati, and Massimo had jumped into the Maserati and driven it a safe distance away. Meanwhile, Christian and Sebastian had run to the burning car. They had dragged Xander out and stamped out the fire on his coat, but it had been too late. The blast had dislodged a piece of metal which had struck through his heart. My *fratellino*, my youngest brother with the face of an angel, the talent of a genius and the disposition of a man who was so good that no-one could come in contact with him without being affected by his charm, his humor, his good nature... And his smile... The sheer goodness of it would melt the most hardened of hearts, would make all of the women around him swoon and want to throw themselves at him willingly and ask him to bed them... That man will no longer tease me in that drawling voice of his, he'll no longer be around to banter with his twin, and be the voice of reason that the rest of us most often need.

Xander, my brother, is gone and she... I had glanced down at her still form in my arms. She'd seemed to have gone paler in the last few minutes, her eyelashes a dark fan against her cheeks. The circles under her eyes had seemed so much more prominent. She'd seemed too fragile, so breakable. My heart had thundered in my chest and my stomach had been in knots as I had surveyed her features. She'd seemed still, too still...but she couldn't die. No way, was I going to let her leave me.

The wail of an ambulance had sounded in the distance. Seb had walked over to me. He'd told me that he'd called the ambulance. He'd stayed with me as I had held her, never taking my gaze off of her features, as first one ambulance, then another had pulled up the driveway.

I had watched as they'd checked Xander, declared him dead. They had placed a white sheet over the body and... My brain had frozen. My brother...was dead? My little brother was gone?

I had held onto her. I had refused to let go of her, until Seb had gripped my shoulder. He'd reminded me that they needed to get her to the hospital. I'd managed to loosen my grip on her enough for the paramedics to sweep into action. They'd placed an oxygen mask on her face, checked her vitals, run an IV into her vein, even as they had strapped her into a stretcher. They'd carried her into the ambulance and I had paused. Torn between wanting to follow her and to stay with Xander, I had paused. That's when Seb had told me that they needed to keep Xander here until the cops—who are on our payroll — had time to gather evidence. He'd reassured me that Christian and Adrian would stay with Xander while he and Massimo would follow us as I rode with her to hospital. Only then, had I gotten into the ambulance. I'd clasped her hand in mine for the entire journey.

Within seconds of reaching the hospital, she had been admitted and a team of doctors and nurses had swarmed over her. I had followed until a nurse had stopped me, told me they needed to operate on her.

I had raged and asked her if she'd recognized who I was. That I had half the hospital on my payroll. That I was not letting go of her. That's when Sebastian and Massimo had burst into the hospital with Antonio hot on their heels. They had stopped me, reasoned with me to let her go. I had watched in a haze as she had disappeared, with the doctors in tow, behind the double doors. Someone had pushed me into a chair in the waiting room across from them, and there I had sat and waited. Someone had pushed a cup of coffee into my hands. And I had drunk it. At some point, I had torn my gaze from the double doors long enough to ask them about Christian.

Christian, who had lost his twin, the soul who had been with him from the moment he'd been conceived. Sebastian reminded me that Adrian was with him. The two of them had accompanied Xander to the mortuary, where his body had been taken for a post-mortem.

"They need to release the body." I had risen to my feet, only for my legs to give way, and I had slumped back in my chair. "I need to go to Christian," I had murmured, and tried to stand up again, but Seb had stopped me.

"You need to stay here with her," he'd told me.

"She'll want to see you when she regains consciousness," Massimo had added, and I'd known that they were right. I wanted to be here with her, but at the same time, I wanted to be able to comfort my brother, to mourn my youngest sibling Xander. I had balled my fingers into fists as I had stared at the double doors. I could not allow her to also leave me. I would not allow the same fate to befall her.

I continue to stare at the doors, willing them to open. I lean my head back against the wall. Every time my eyes close, I jerk myself awake. Antonio gets all of us coffee, which I sip before placing the half-filled cup aside. At some point, Sebastian brings me something to eat, and my stomach lurches. I refuse the food, lean forward in my seat as I keep my eyes glued to the door.

Suddenly, the sound of the doors opening has me snapping my eyes open. I spring to my feet and my head spins. I square my shoulders, dig my booted feet into the floor, and track the progress of the doctor who walks toward me. Around me, my brothers, too, stumble to their feet. Massimo and Seb flank me as the doctor halts in front of me. His scrubs are blood splattered, his hair awry and shadows encircle his eyes. His jaw is set and his features wear an expression of stoic patience? Of resignation?

I falter and Seb grips my shoulder. "Steady, *fratellone*," he murmurs, "stay strong."

"How is she?" I croak, then clear my throat. "Tell me," I demand, "how is my wife?"

"She's still unconscious." He holds my gaze, "It's difficult to say anything until she is awake."

The next thing I know, my fingers are wrapped around his collar and I have hauled the doctor up to his tiptoes. "She has to make it," I growl. "She cannot die."

"We are doing everything we can," he says in a calm voice.

Anger thuds at my temples. "Do better," I snap. "If anything happens to her, I will not let you live."

He doesn't blink. Either the man's a fool or he's got the balls to face up to my anger. "Do you hear me?" I demand.

He holds my gaze, then nods.

I tighten my hold on his collar, and Massimo touches my shoulder. "Not going to help if you kill him, brother. He's treating her; he's on your side."

I glare at the doctor, then release him. He steps back, his features impassive.

"I'm sorry," he murmurs, "but we couldn't save the child."

*The child. My child. Our baby.* A hot sensation stabs at my chest. The pressure behind my eyes builds. I swallow down the ball of emotion that clogs my throat. "I don't need your sympathy," I growl. "If she dies, you die; remember that."

Seb shuffles his feet next to me.

"Do you understand, *doctor*?" My eyes bore into his before I turn away, stalk toward the door at the end of the corridor.

"Don't you want to see her?" the doctor calls after me. "It would help her if you sat with her for a little while, maybe spoke to her."

I set my jaw. It's because of my negligence that she is in this situation. How can I stand in front of her, when I have failed her? I failed to protect my own wife. She deserves so much better than this. Since I first saw her, all I have done is screw up her life. She's better without me.

I slow my steps, then glare at him over my shoulder. "No," I snap, "I don't want to see her." I turn to Massimo, "You stay here with Antonio. Make sure you protect her."

"With my life, *fratellone*," Massimo replies.

I wince, then set my jaw, "Seb, with me."

I stalk out of the hospital, Seb on my heels. He doesn't say anything as I head for my Maserati, which one of my clan must have parked in the hospital parking lot. As I approach it, Seb hands over the key fob. I beep the car to unlock it, open the door and slide inside. I glance around the car, a twin to the one that she had been in.

One in which her blood had been spilled. Xander is dead, my child is no more, she is injured and I... I am responsible for all of it. I tighten my fingers around the steering wheel, press the ignition button, shift into gear, and the car jumps forward. I slam on the brake and the car stops millimeters from crashing into the wall in front.

"You okay, brother?" Seb turns to me, "Maybe I should drive."

"No," I throw the car in reverse, peel out of the parking lot.

We drive in silence for a few minutes, then he glances sideways at me, "Why didn't you want to see her, brother?"

"None of your business."

"You can't blame yourself for what happened to her."

I step on the accelerator and the car leaps forward.

"It was because you had a protective plate installed around the driver's seat and it worked like an ejection seat, that she survived."

"I should have known that it was too risky to gift her the car. I shouldn't have tempted fate by giving it to her. I should have, at least, test driven it first before allowing her to climb into it."

"Your actions saved her, Michael," he insists.

"It's my actions that put her in danger, in the first place... If she had not survived...I..."

"But she did."

"Whoever rigged that car got past me," I growl. "I'll never forgive myself for that."

"The bomb was rigged wrong. Only the ignition blew; she survived, Michael."

"We lost our brother, Seb," I take the next corner without decreasing speed and the tires screech in protest. "Xander's no longer with us and it's my fault." I slam my fist into the steering wheel and the car fishtails. The back of the vehicle rises off the road as the

Maserati circles in a wide arc, once, twice, before I slam on the brakes and come to rest on the side of the road.

A truck blows it horn as it whizzes past, then silence descends.

I grip the steering wheel, staring ahead as my chest heaves.

Seb sits silently as more vehicles pass us at a more sedate speed.

"Not seeing her is only going to make it worse, Michael."

"You don't understand," I growl.

"Oh?" He turns on me, "Make me. Tell me what you're thinking, Mika. This once, confide in me so I know what's going on in that screwed up mind of yours."

I shake my head, "You won't get it."

"Try me."

"I love her," I snap. "Do you understand? I love her, and already, I have put her at risk. The only way to protect her is if I keep her away from me."

# 2

## Michael

Twenty minutes later, we are parked outside the building that houses the mortuary. I stare at the door that leads inside. If I get out of here and walk in, if I see his face, then nothing will ever be the same again. *Nothing is ever going to be the same again.*

"Michael," Seb murmurs, "you don't have to do this."

I stare straight ahead, unable to take my gaze off the goddam door. Another door that leads to another loved one who is lying there...stretched out...cold. Another of my flesh and blood I have failed. Another sorrow that I will carry around for the rest of my life. Oh, Xander, why did it have to be you? Why couldn't I have protected you? How could I have allowed this to happen to you?

"Michael?" Seb touches my shoulder and I jerk. I shove the door open, climb out of the car. I step into the coolness of the building and a shiver runs down my spine. I walk down the corridor, turn right... knowing where I have to go.

This is not my first visit to the morgue; it's the first time I am here to identify the body of someone I loved like he was my own child. Xander was born when I was nine years old, and I had felt more like his parent than his older brother. And Christian? Even though Christian was only a few minutes older, it was Xander who had been the cheekiest, who could get away with anything. Who is now dead... Because I hadn't been able to protect him. It should have been me.

My footsteps echo in the empty corridor. The two men at the end of the corridor turn to watch me approach. Christian's gaze tracks me as I walk toward him. I stop in front of him, reach out for him. He evades me, then swipes out and buries his fist in my face. I absorb the hit, and the next, as he sinks his fist, this time, into my shoulder, then on the other side. He raises his arm again and his big body sways. He crumples and I catch him. I wrap my arms around him, rock him as his shoulders shudder. His chest rises and falls, as he tightens his hold on me and weeps. I rock him, even as the band around my chest tightens. The burning sensation behind my eyes intensifies and my nose starts to run. Adrian and Seb flank us as I squeeze my arms around my brother. I stay that way until he calms down somewhat, then step back.

Christian rises his red rimmed eyes, and I hold his gaze. "We'll find who did this," I vow, "and when we do, I will wipe out his entire bloodline."

Christian swallows, then steps back and wipes his face.

Footsteps approach us. I turn as a man pauses in front of us, "Who's going to identify the body?"

"I will," I brush past him, heading for the doors that lead to the morgue, when a woman bursts into the corridor.

"Xander," she gasps, glancing between us. "Is it true, what I heard about him?"

She glances between us, then her gaze settles on me. She marches over to me. "Xander," she swallows, "I need to see him."

"I don't think that's advisable." The coroner scowls, "He's not in good shape."

"Yes." She shudders, then shakes her head as tears squeeze out of the corners of her eyes, "I must see him with my own eyes. I don't believe you."

"Theresa?" Sebastian murmurs. "It's not a good idea."

Xander's childhood friend sets her jaw. "I don't care. I am going to see him, whether you like it or not. Xander... He...he can't leave me like this." She turns to me, "Michael, please." Her voice cracks.

I peer into her features, take in the determination reflected in her eyes, then jerk my chin.

"Thank you," she whispers as she wipes the tears from her face.

I move forward and she follows me. The coroner marches forward and falls in step with me. He leads us down another corridor and pauses in front of double doors.

He opens it, and next to me, Theresa stumbles. I grab her arm and steady her. "Easy," I murmur.

She squares her shoulders, then nods, "I am ready."

We step in together and the doors snicks shut behind us. The scent of antiseptic, combined with a sickly-sweet scent that I can't identify, overpowers me. My hackles rise and my pulse begins to race. Theresa's steps falter and she tightens her grip on my arm. There is a big glass window which separates us from a smaller room in which there is a covered body on a gurney.

Theresa must spot it at the same time as I do, for she draws in a breath. I sense the nervousness vibrating off of her as I steel my shoulders. The coroner asks us to wait while he goes to the other room. He walks around and stops behind the gurney. "Are you two ready?"

His voice sounds over the speakers.

Theresa flinches, then nods. So do I.

The coroner raises the sheet on the face of the body. My heart seems to stop for a second. I take in the pale features, the wide forehead, the high cheekbones, the dark hair that curls about his shoulders. It's my little brother. It's Xander, all right, and yet... It isn't.

Gone is the life that animated his every movement. Aside from sleep, which he never seemed to require much of, I've never known him to be still for a second. Not when he was a child; not when he was older... Nor even when he was painting, when he seemed to use his entire body as he dragged his brush across a canvas. He focused on the colors he chose to animate his art, focused on his plate as he relished his food, on women...and men...as he danced with them, flirted with them... As he fucked them... Even as he held back his emotions and how he felt from the woman who clings to my arm like it is a lifeline. Her body grows heavy and she slumps. I catch her before she can hit the floor.

I scoop her up in my arms, jerk my chin at the coroner, then walk out.

Adrian straightens as I stalk over to him and hand Theresa over. "Take care of her. Xander felt...something for her, so she is under our protection."

I turn to Seb, "We need to find those behind the explosion that killed him and my child, and wounded my wife. Pull out all stops. Ask our men to hunt down every single one of their contacts to find out who is behind it."

"Is that wise?" he asks.

Christian turns on him. "How could you even ask this question?" He snarls, "Someone killed our brother, and instead of seeking out vengeance, instead of returning that favor a million-fold, you choose this time to question why we'd do it?"

"Michael's spent his life building up his reputation among the five families. He's worked his entire life to attain the position of Don," Seb retorts. "If he screws it up, he'll only regret it later."

"Are you saying that you'd rather he not do anything about what those *stronzos* did to him...to our family? Our brother is dead, Seb. Dead." Christian's chest heaves, "Or is it because Xander wasn't your brother, that he was only your half-brother, that makes you so uncaring about his death?"

Seb pales. "Take that back," he growls.

"That's it, isn't it?" Christian peers into his face, "You've always wanted to be one of us. You couldn't stomach the fact that you were a bastard. That no matter how much you tried, you'd never be a true heir to the Don. It's why you don't care that our brother's body lays there lifeless. Instead, it's why you are more concerned with avoiding vengeance... Which, by the way, would mean that we also lose face with the rest of our clan, you—"

Seb rears forward and smashes his head into Christian's face. Blood blooms from his nose, and with a roar, Christian charges him. He shoves Seb into the wall, gets an upper cut in. Seb's body jerks and his head snaps back. He growls, grabs at Christian's shoulders and I snap, "Stop."

Seb glares at Christian, who glowers back at him.

"Back the fuck up, the both of you," I order.

Seb pauses; Christian snarls. The two stare at each other, anger pouring off of both of them in waves.

"Control yourselves. I won't remind you again."

Seb shakes his head, seems to get a hold of himself. He releases Christian, who takes a step back.

"Sorry," Seb rubs the back of his neck, as he shoots me a sideways glance and mumbles, "you know I mean well."

Christian turns to me. "So, what's it going to be, Capo?" he says through gritted teeth. "You going to let this go, or you going to hunt down the men who did this?"

I jerk my chin in Seb's direction, "I appreciate your counsel. I know you only have the best interests of the Cosa Nostra at heart, but you know what I have to do."

Seb jerks his chin, "I am with you whatever you decide, Boss."

I turn my attention toward Christian. "Shake hands with Seb," I order and Christian glowers at me.

"Now," I snap.

He stiffens, then turns and holds out his hand and Seb shakes it.

Christian instantly pulls back his arm, then brushes past me, "I am going in search of the motherfuckers."

"You are not going anywhere on your own."

He stalks forward and I call out, "I've lost a brother. I don't plan to lose another."

Christian pauses; his shoulders heave. I stalk forward, wrap my arm around his neck and pull him to me. "I know it hurts," I swallow, "I know how much he meant to you... To all of us. We won't let this go unpunished."

Christian tries to shake off my arm, but I don't let go. "Cry, go punch a bag, do what you need to do to let off steam. Then, when you're thinking straight, come find me and we'll finish this."

Christian avoids eye contact. He pulls away and I release him. He stalks off and I turn to Adrian, "Stay with him. See that he doesn't hurt himself... Or get himself killed."

Adrian follows him while Seb draws abreast with me. "What now, Capo?"

"Now we track down the bastards," I square my shoulders, "but first, I need to see my wife."

"You took off without seeing her, now you want to go back?" Seb shoots me a sideways glance, "What's happening with you, brother?"

"None of your bloody business," I growl at him.

He frowns at me and I blow out a breath. "I wanted to get here and make sure that Xander was..." I squeeze my eyes shut, "that he was okay. That Christian was able to deal with the grief. That he..." I swallow down the ball of emotion in my throat, "wasn't going to do something crazy."

"You mean, like kill himself?" Seb says in a low voice.

I turn on him. "Don't fucking say that aloud; don't even go there," I warn him as I try to deny my own fears. I bunch my fingers into fists, "I will do everything in my power to keep my brothers, my family...to keep all of you safe, you feel me?"

Seb jerks his chin, "You're a good Capo, and an even better brother and husband, but—"

"But?"

"You can't control everything, Mika. Not even you can cheat death. When it's time to go, it's time to—"

I grab his collar and shove him against the wall, "The fuck are you getting at, Seb?" I thrust my face into his, "You trying to tell me I couldn't have saved him? Or my unborn child? Or prevented my wife from getting hurt? Is that it?"

"I'm trying to tell you that it's not your fault, Capo."

He holds my gaze, his own calm and steady. Somehow, in the last few weeks he's grown more mature, more patient, able to keep a clear head while I am on the verge of losing my shit.

It comes from being too close to a situation. I understand it. Hell, I have seen men crack when tragedy came knocking on their doorstep. I'd always thought I was above that. I thought I was invincible, that even if something happened to me or mine, I'd be able to deal with it, to find a way through it. Yet here I am, unable to face my own wife, which is what had sent me running from her in the first place. And now, I can't wait to see her again, to make sure that she is safe. Apparently, I can't make up my mind about something as simple as, do I want to stay with her or stay away from her? And there is only one way to find out. By going back to her. By being in the same room as her. By finding out how it feels to hold her again, to breathe in her scent, to take in her gorgeous features, to look into her eyes and apologize for not having been able to protect her from what happened.

I release Seb, then step back. "I'm sorry," I roll my shoulders, "I know you mean well."

"And I know you love your family and her more than anything else in this world."

"Like that made a difference when it came to their welfare." I rub the back of my neck, "I am aware that not even I can cheat death." I bare my teeth, "Doesn't mean I am not going to try my damnedest."

Turning, I stalk toward the exit.

# 3

Karma

Thump, thump, thump. The muffled sound reaches me, then fades away. I glance around at the white space that envelops me. I am floating on a cloud of nothingness. It's peaceful here and so...so lonely. A chill grips me. I glance around, take in the white space that envelops me. Where am I? I try to move but my limbs feel too heavy. I try to put one foot in front of the other but my legs don't seem to obey me. The scent of something dark and edgy teases my nostrils. His scent. I glance up, spot a man walking away from me.

"Capo," I try to reach for him, but am not able to move. Thump, thump, THUMP. The sound grows louder. More persistent. It mirrors his steps as he stalks away from me. His broad shoulders, that narrow waist, those powerful thighs that flex as he puts more distance between us.

"Capo," I yell, but he doesn't look back.

"Michael," I scream as I push myself forward, but am not able to move. *Why can't I move?* "Mika, stop, don't go, Mika!"

"Beauty?"

"Mika," tears flow down my cheeks, "oh, Mika, where are you?"

"Here." Warm fingers twine with mine and I force my eyes open. Blue eyes meet mine, a burning white in their depths that echoes the white I had been surrounded by.

"No," I grip his palm, "Mika, no." A sinking sensation coils in my chest. The hair on the nape of my neck rises, "Mika, please," I whisper, my voice hoarse, my throat dry.

He leans in closer. "What's wrong?" He peers into my features, "Are you in pain?"

"No," I shake my head as I glance around the space. The scent of antiseptic assails my senses. I take in the white walls, the fluorescent lighting, the equipment pushed up against the wall, "Am I in the hospital?"

He nods, holds up a cup of water and places the straw between my lips. "Do you remember what happened?"

I pause to collect my thoughts as I swallow. "I remember seeing you..." I scrunch up my eyebrows. "Then I reached for the ignition, and the car," I swallow, "the car...it..."

"The ignition blew. The bomb placed in the vehicle was faulty. You were thrown free."

"Thrown free?" I raise my free hand to my forehead and wince.

"I had a jump seat installed, so if anything ever happened to the vehicle, the roof would open and the ejector seat would activate."

"So, I was...ejected out of the vehicle, along with the seat?"

He nods.

"And Xander?" I frown. "I remember seeing you say something to us. I couldn't understand what it was, but I think Xander did, because he turned to me, and then... I don't remember anything after that."

"I was speaking in Italian." He sets his jaw, "He probably realized that I was warning him."

"Where is he?" I glance around the room. "Is he okay?"

Michael glances away, then back at me. My heart begins to race, a bead of sweat slides down my back.

"Mika," I whisper as I tighten my hold on his fingers, "Xander… Is he…"

Michael holds my gaze, "He didn't make it."

"No." My heart feels like it's going to break and a ball of emotion blocks my throat. I shake my head back and forth, intensifying the pounding. "No, Mika, no," I gasp.

A vein throbs at his temple. I take in his mussed-up hair, the hollows under his eyes.

"It wasn't your fault, Mika," I whisper.

"Wasn't it?" He holds my gaze and his features seem to settle into a mask. I sense him withdrawing from me and my stomach drops.

He tries to pull his hand free and I hold onto him. "Michael, don't do it."

"Don't do what?"

"Whatever it is you're thinking about, don't do it."

"You're distraught," he murmurs, "still dazed from the…the incident."

"No." I swallow and try to sit up, but he places his hand on my shoulder.

"Don't try to move yet."

"I am fine." I glance between his eyes, "Thanks to you, Michael. Don't you see? You had the foresight to ensure that the car would hold up to something like this."

"I failed you," he says in a hard voice. "I couldn't protect you and our child."

"Child," I stare at him. "The baby." I release his hand and place both of my palms against my stomach. My flat…empty stomach. How could I have forgotten? Or had I already subconsciously known and hadn't been able to face up to it? "My baby," I whisper as I glance down at myself, "he's gone."

The tears that I had been holding back well up. My face crumples and he moves forward. He wraps his arm around my shoulders, pulls me close. I bury my face in his chest and allow the shock, the sorrow, the disappointment to well up and overwhelm me. I dig my fingers into the front of his shirt and allow myself to cry. He holds me, rocks me, runs his fingers down my hair. I sense his chest planes flex under my cheek and glance up. His features are hard, but his eyes? Those blue eyes of his blaze with an inner emotion... Grief? Anger? A mix of the two, maybe? He holds my gaze, neither of us speaking as I reach up and flatten my palm against his cheek. "Mika," I swallow, "I'm so sorry."

"I am the one who should be sorry." A nerve flares at his temple, "I'll never forgive myself for this."

"It's because of you, I am alive, Mika." I frame his face with my palms, "It's because of your foresight that I am here."

"But he isn't." His voice is dull, "Xander is gone, and so is our child. I should have seen this happening. I should have known that as soon as I allowed myself to feel for you, that as soon as I fell in love with you —"

He firms his lips, attempts to pull away, but I grip his lapels. "You love me?" I whisper. "Of course, you love me. I knew it, Mika. I knew it...even before you told me."

"Past tense," he grabs my fingers and detaches them from his shirt, "I loved you."

"Wait, what?" I blink. "You don't mean it."

"Don't I?" His lips twist, "Now that you're no longer the mother of my child, I don't see any reason for this arrangement to continue."

Something hot stabs at my chest. I gaze into his features, and of course, he stares back. He allows me to read the intention in his eyes. The decision he's made is clear in the cut planes of his face.

"Don't do this, Mika. Don't push me away. Not now; not when I need you; not when we need each other."

"I don't need you." His fingers squeeze mine as if he's imprinting the sensation of my skin against his, then he releases me.

"I don't believe you," I reach for him and he steps back.

"Believe it, Karma." He straightens. "I never should have taken you from London, should have never married you. If I hadn't, you wouldn't be in this situation today."

"You need to let go of the guilt, Mika, and look forward. Xander is gone, but I am still here and I love you, Mika; I do."

He winces, then squares his shoulders. "It doesn't matter anymore." He balls his fists at his sides, "All that matters is tracking down the men who did this and making sure that they pay for it."

"You need revenge. I understand," I tip up my chin, "but that's not going to bring back Xander or our child."

"A few weeks of being with me and you think you know me?"

"I know what's going to hurt you, Mika, and this…this quest for vengeance will destroy whatever you have left. It will destroy us."

He chuckles, "There is no more us, Karma, can't you understand that?"

"No," I tuck my elbows into my sides, "but what I do understand is that you are hurting and lashing out. And you think if you sever your connection with me—which, by the way, you can't—but you think if you cut all ties with me, I am going to be safe, and you're wrong."

"Oh?"

I nod, "It doesn't work that way, Mika. It's not you, it's the life-style you are in that was bound to backfire on you some day. And it did."

He scoffs, "You going to lecture me about my beliefs and my values now?"

I shake my head, "No, of course, not. If anyone can understand the pull of the dark side, it's me, Michael. It's why we are so well-suited."

"It's why you are lying here on a hospital bed, having lost our child."

I squeeze my eyes shut. "You are trying to hurt me, Michael, and it's because you are in so much pain right now. Why can't you share it with me? Why can't you lean on me? Why can't you allow me to lean on you, when I need it the most right now?"

"Because. I. Can't." His voice is so anguished, so full of torment that I snap my eyes open.

"Michael, please don't do this," I beg. "Don't leave me; not now."

"You are free to go back to your family." He looks everywhere but at my face. "I'll make sure to tell Antonio to help you with any arrangements."

He turns to leave and I call out, "I am not going anywhere."

He freezes.

"You heard me, Michael. This is my home, I am your wife, and I am not leaving. Not when you need me more than anything. Not when we need each other."

He shakes his head, "Your choice. If you prefer to stay in Palermo, that can be arranged too."

He stalks forward, and I stare at his retreating back. Shit, shit, shit, what do I do now? How can I make sure to have some form of contact with him? What can I do to make sure that he doesn't just disappear after this?

"The Christmas party," I cry out, "I want to go ahead with the event."

He turns abruptly and his gaze bores into me. "Xander is gone and you want to go ahead with the festivities?"

I flinch. "He'd have wanted it. He'd have hated for us to be unhappy and mourning him."

He hesitates. "In Sicily, we mourn for at least a month in the period following a death. Celebrations are normally cancelled, or at the very least, conducted in a somber setting."

"I understand," I glance away, then back at him. "We needn't have a party on the scale I'd planned for, but maybe something in a smaller setting? Xander would have wanted us to celebrate his life." I tip up my chin, "You know I am right, Mika."

Michael jerks his chin. "Fine," he tilts his head, "you can stay until the Christmas party, and then I am sending you back home."

And then he's gone.

# 4

Michael

What the hell is wrong with me? I had wanted to haul her into my arms, comfort her about our loss, hold her close and tell her that it was okay, that she was still alive and that's what really mattered. But something inside of me had hardened, and I hadn't been able to lower the barriers enough to tell her.

It's as if Xander's death crushed every last emotion that had sprung to life since I met her. He is gone, my child will never be born, and the only thing that matters to me now is to make sure that she is safe. It's why I want to send her away, far from here, away from my influence, where my presence can't taint her, where the company I keep can't endanger her. Where my way of life will no longer cause her harm. It is the only way to ensure that she will never have to go through this kind of loss again.

She deserves better than me. She deserves someone who is on the right side of the law, who can give her security and safety, and keep her shielded from the darkness in which I spend so much of my time. She deserves more, so much more. Everything that I can't give her. It's why I have to let her go.

And yet, when she'd asked me about the Christmas festivities, I hadn't been able to refuse her. She'd been right—Xander would not have wanted us to grieve his absence. He'd have wanted us to remember him with happiness, wanted us to have a good time as we indulge ourselves in his memory. It's why I had given in to her request, and the Christmas party will take place as planned...

First though, I have to get through the funeral.

It's been three days since I left her at the hospital and returned home. I'd gotten on the phone and made arrangements for Xander's funeral. My brothers had offered to help but I had refused. This is something I have to do by myself.

Despite all of my influence within the police department, I hadn't been able to prevent them from conducting an autopsy on the body, which had delayed the funeral by a few days. But it had also given me the time to arrange for a funeral of the kind that befits Xander.

I straighten my cuffs, stare at my reflection in the mirror.

The eyes that look back at me, the features that fill the mirror are so like Xander's. It should be me in the casket... It should have been me in that passenger seat and not him.

The only way to get through this tightness that claws at my chest is to find the bastards who did this and kill them... That is one thing on which I will not compromise. That is the only thing that keeps me focused... Avenge him, that's the only thing that can restore the balance...somewhat. I knot my tie around my neck, tug on it until it hangs straight down. Then I turn and head for the doorway to my bedroom.

Her door opens at the far end of the corridor and she steps out. Clothed completely in black, from the veil that flows over her eyes and covers the bandage on her forehead, to the gown that draws across her narrow shoulders and down to her feet, which are clad in black stilettoes, she resembles a goddess who has come to stake her claim on the souls of us mortals.

She approaches, her movements slow enough to indicate that she is not completely healed from the incident.

The day on which I had lost, not one, but two of my children. If something had happened to her as well... I never would have been able to live with myself.

As she walks toward me now, all the pent-up emotions threaten to boil over. My fingers tingle and I want to wrap them around the nape of her neck, haul her close as I lick her lips, slide my fingers up her skirt and shove aside her panties to cram them inside her channel, which I have no doubt will be soaking wet.

She comes to a stop in front of me, and her scent... That luscious scent that is so Beauty fills my senses. My cock swells and the blood rushes to my groin. I widen my stance, glare at her as she tips up her chin. Her lips tremble as she parts them, and damn, if I don't want to lean down and thrust my tongue inside her mouth and feast on her, and draw from the comfort that she can offer me.

But I won't. I owe it to Xander to hold back. Xander, who is dead and who will never know what it is like to be married, to father a child, to see his paintings displayed in the best museums in the world, to grow old with his woman by his side, to see us take over the Cosa Nostra, to feel the wind in his hair as he drives with the top of his car down, to cuddle up with his wife, to hold his newborn... Fuck. I close my eyes, fold my fingers at my side. *Oh, Xander, how am I going to get through the next few hours? How am I going to bury you...my heart?*

Soft fingers curl around mine, and I glance down to find Beauty has clasped her fingers around mine. She flattens my hand between her much smaller ones. They almost seem like a child's in comparison to the width of mine. Her pale skin is like ivory against my tan. I stare at the contrast. So fragile, yet so strong. So breakable, yet so... Tenacious. She is a study in contrasts. The yin to my yang. The other part of me...and yet...

I can't keep her with me. This one time, I need to be selfless. I need to let her go so she can survive. So I know that she is safe... Wherever... Whoever... She is with.

The breath hisses out of me and I hear her intake of breath. I glance down to find I've wrapped my fingers around hers and have squeezed. I loosen my hold, but she doesn't let go.

"You didn't hurt me," she insists.

"You shouldn't come to the funeral," I snap.

"We've been through this, already." She firms her lips, "Now is not the time to pull back. Now is when I appear by your side. Now is when we show the world that they didn't strike us down. That I am still alive."

"And mark a target on your head again?" I growl.

"I'll be safe as long as I am with you."

"You'll only be safe when you are away from me."

"I beg to differ."

"Why are you so stubborn?" I growl.

"Why are you so...so...pigheaded?" she snaps back.

I scowl at her and she flushes, but doesn't look away. Her eyes blaze with that inner fire that has attracted me to her from the beginning. That I need to resist if I have any hope of letting her go. I take a step back. "Just this once, I am allowing you to have your way," I set my jaw, "but make no mistake, once Christmas has passed, you will return home to London."

I release her, begin to walk away.

"Twice," she calls out behind me. "That's twice you've let me have my own way."

I stiffen. *Minchia!* She's right. First, I allowed her to continue with the Christmas festivities, and now, I've acquiesced and allowed her to come to the funeral. Goddamn it, she's getting to me and I am not even aware of it. The faster I get her out of my sight, the faster I can go back to being how I was.

Alone. Focused. This time, on revenge. It's the path I have chosen for myself; the path I should have never allowed her to sway me from.

I turn away from her, then walk down the stairs and open the door for her. We step outside where Antonio, Sebastian, Christian, Adrian and Massimo wait for me. I slide into the driver's seat of my Maserati. Sebastian holds the passenger door open and she slides in next to me. He slips into the back seat, along with Antonio.

Massimo follows behind in his car with Christian.

We complete the fifteen-minute drive to the chapel in silence. The last time I was here, I had faked my own funeral. This time... It's real... More than real.

I ease the car into a parking space in front of the chapel, push open the door and step out. I walk around to open Beauty's door. I hold out my hand and she places her palm in mine. I tuck it into the crook of my elbow, then walk forward. Sebastian follows me, and within minutes Christian, Adrian, Massimo and Antonio fall into line behind me. We walk into the chapel and every person turns to watch us. The place is packed, as is to be expected. I walk to the front row, guide her to our seats, when she stiffens. I glance over as Nonna rises to her feet. She closes the distance between us and holds out her hand.

"Nonna," I take her hand and kiss her fingertips. Her fingers tremble. I glance down into her face, take in her anguished eyes. Her features are composed though. I wouldn't have expected anything else.

She grips my fingers as she gazes up at me. "Mika," she swallows, "I hope you are going to hunt them down and teach every last one of them a lesson."

I bend my head, and she kisses my forehead. She releases me and turns to Beauty. Something unspoken seems to pass between the two women. My Nonna nods. She steps back, takes her place next to my father, who turns his face away from me.

Typical. In times of crisis, you can count on my father to retreat into that stony place inside of him where none of us can reach him. *Like me. Che cazzo.* Where did that thought come from? I am nothing like him.

I will not let myself become like him. I am far more focused, have more empathy for my brothers, for my clan. Hell, if it weren't for that, I'd have gunned down every single head of our rival clans, and all of the other families. I'd have shot first, then asked the questions.

Instead, I have my men searching, identifying who was behind it… Then, I'll begin the killing. Which is only fair. An eye for an eye; a tooth for a tooth. The death of their entire family for the death of my brother and my unborn child. Yeah, that's only right.

There's a commotion behind me. I turn to find Luca prowling up the aisle.

# 5

Karma

I glance around to find Luca stalking over to Michael. What the hell? What is he doing here? Michael stiffens, his nostrils flare, and color suffuses his features. His shoulders seem to grow even bigger in size, stretching the material of the suit-jacket. He pivots, closes the distance to Luca, then smashes his fist into Luca's face.

There's an audible gasp from the congregants as blood spurts from Luca's nose and drips to the floor. He staggers back, then straightens. He makes no move to defend himself as Michael plants his fist in his left shoulder, then his right, then slams it into his stomach. The breath whooshes out of him and he drops to his knees. He bunches his fists at his sides, bows his head almost in supplication as he waits...and waits.

Michael raises both of his fists as if to bring them down on him and I scream, "Stop!" I lunge forward and every bone in my body seems to protest. My head spins at the abuse I am subjecting my already battered body to, and I grab hold of Michael's jacket. "Stop," I pant, "please, don't do this."

There are more gasps from the mourners. Behind me, I sense Nonna and Michael's father rising to their feet, but I ignore them.

"Get away from me, Karma," he growls. "Get out of my way before I hurt you."

"You said you'd never hurt me, Michael," I hiss. "You promised you'd never allow anything to happen to me."

His shoulders bunch. Thick waves of tension vibrate off of him and his muscles jump under his skin. His entire body tenses and I am sure he is going to shake me off and complete what he'd set out to do, but he pauses. One by one, he forces his muscles to unwind. He lowers his arms to his sides and I release the breath I'd not been aware I was holding.

"Karma," Nonna calls out to me in a low voice. I turn to her and she glances at Michael, then back at me. She shakes her head. Something in her gaze reaches out to me. I can't understand what she's trying to tell me...but something inside me insists that I obey.

I release my hold on Michael and stumble. Michael pivots so quickly that he seems to blur. He grips my shoulder, holds on until I have regained my footing. He eases me back into my seat, then points a finger at me. "Stay," he growls, before he stalks over to where his brother has risen to his feet.

The two men glare at each other. Luca's features are pale but his gaze is clear. Defiance is evident in his stance, but his eyes reflect regret and hope and love... I swallow, turn to Michael, take in the hard set of his features.

He jerks his chin and Luca holds up his hands. "I am sorry," he says in a voice low enough that only Michael and his family can hear. "I am truly sorry, brother."

Michael blinks and his features twist as if he's torn between forgiving him and hitting him again. Then he seems to compose himself.

"I forgive you," he snaps, "but you will have to pay your dues, Luca. What you did can't go unpunished."

Luca draws himself up to his full height, "I would expect nothing less."

Michael nods, "Then welcome back, *fratello.*"

Luca holds out his hand. Michael ignores it and winds his arm around his brother's neck. Luca grips his shoulder and the two embrace.

A palpable murmur runs through those assembled as Michael claps Luca on his back. Luca does the same, then both step back.

"I am so sorry," Luca murmurs. "It was my mistake to go after something that belongs to you."

"And mine that I never trusted you enough to let you in on our inner workings." Michael steps back. "But let's discuss that later." They both turn to look at the open casket.

"Fuck," Luca swears, "fuck, fuck, fuck." He balls his fists at his sides, "I should have been here protecting our family. I failed you, brother, and for that, I will never forgive myself."

Michael stays silent. The two stare at Xander's body for a few seconds more. Then, Luca walks around and to the other side of the pew. He sits down next to Christian who glares at him before he looks away.

Michael walks toward the front of the church, then turns to face the audience. A frisson of fear runs through the gathered people who instantly fall quiet.

It's unusual that he'd be the first to speak. I'd have thought the priest would read from the Bible, but he's the Capo, so I guess Michael makes his own rules, even at a funeral.

He glances around the assembled people and silence envelops the space.

"Alessandro Donatello Domenico Sovrano was more than my brother. In many ways, he was my son. My flesh and blood. The child I brought up and protected and made sure he never went to bed unhappy. He was the most talented of us. He had the face and the heart and the temperament of an angel. He was the youngest, and yet, he was the thread that held our family together. Now that thread has snapped and it falls to me to avenge whoever took him from us." Michael glances around the room.

I don't need to look over my shoulder to know that he's making eye contact with the different heads of the families who've gathered there. I imagine the leaders of rival clans are also there. At least, I think I saw Nikolai among them.

The silence stretches as Michael continues his silent assault on the audience. Someone coughs, someone else shuffles their feet, a baby cries and is shushed. The sound of someone sniffing reaches me. I glance over to the other side of the aisle, and find a girl clutching a handkerchief in her hand as she glances in the direction of the coffin. Her shoulders shudder, her features seem to crumple. She jumps to her feet and runs out. I spring up to go after her, but Nonna grips my arm and hauls me back.

"Leave her be; she needs time to come to terms with what has happened," Nonna murmurs.

I sink back onto the seat, "Who is she? Did she know Xander well?"

"Her name is Theresa," Nonna replies, "she is Alessandro's childhood friend."

Just then, a book drops to the floor with a thud that echoes around the room. I jump and Nonna places her hand on my leg. Her touch is reassuring. I glance toward the front where Michael hasn't moved from his earlier stance. The silence stretches once again, a beat, then another.

"What is he doing?" I whisper. "Why isn't he speaking?"

"He's making sure he gets his message across to all those who are present, making sure they'll take the message out to whoever was responsible for what happened."

Nonna firms her lips. She pulls her hand away and I stare straight ahead.

Michael sweeps his gaze over the audience, then nods. "I will hunt down the murderer who was responsible for my brother's death, and when I catch him... Not even God will be able to save him from what I have planned."

Goosebumps pop on my skin. He returns to his seat and the priest takes his place to read from the Bible.

. . .

Two hours later, I glance around the living room of my husband's home.

For all practical purposes, we are still married and I am still in the role of the Capo's wife... A role I am hoping to keep for a long time, despite Michael's insistence to the contrary. Fact is, I can't see myself anywhere else; can't see myself with anyone except him.

If I'd had any doubts about this... If I'd held onto any notion of escaping from him before... The car incident completely wiped all of it out of my mind. Somewhere between sleep and wakefulness, where I had floated after being ejected from the car... When all my barriers had dropped and I had sunk into the depths of my subconscious mind... At that point, I had shed all of my inhibitions, all of my fears, all of my insecurities, and I had embraced what I truly want. Him. I need him as much as I need the air I breathe. I yearn for him as much as I wish for a place to belong. I hunger for him, thirst for him, covet him with a passion that comes from somewhere deep within.

I ache to know him fully, completely. I hanker to have a family with him, to carry his children, to envelop myself in that sensation that I only get when I am with him. When I am secure in the knowledge that he belongs to me and I to him... That our darkness cancels out that of each other, that our hearts and minds and intentions are in sync... Maybe because I had lost the child I had briefly carried, because I had almost lost my own life, I know now what I am meant for. To not only embrace my art as a fashion designer, but to also embrace my heart's calling to be a mother, to embrace my soul's purpose to be his other half, to be the Beauty to his Beast, to be his.

There's a touch on my shoulder, and I turn to meet Nonna's shrewd gaze.

"You're in love with him," she declares.

I half smile, "Am I that obvious?"

"You wear your heart on your sleeve." She peers into my face. "It's why you took a knife to him... It's why you now follow him with your gaze, in the hope that he'll recognize what almost anyone else can read from your expression."

*Shit.* My shoulders slump, "I *am* that obvious."

"Except to him," she glances toward where Michael is speaking with Seb.

Christian and Luca are glowering at each other, while Massimo is speaking with a woman I don't recognize.

In another corner, Nikolai Solonik, stands quietly sipping his vodka—yes, Michael had provided for everyone's tastes. Nikolai's two brothers stand on either side of him. None of the three are speaking. With their imposing height and wide shoulders, not to mention the tattoos that peek out from under their collars and from the edges of their shirt sleeves, they should seem threatening... But somehow, the feeling that emanates from them is more of curiosity as they follow the proceedings.

In a third corner, a tall, broad-shouldered man sips his whisky. His lean features are striking, and there's a tightly leashed sense of power about him.

"That's JJ Kane, head of the Kane Company," Nonna offers.

"The Kane Company?" I wrinkle my nose, "Why do they sound familiar?"

"They are the most powerful organized crime syndicate in England."

Of course. I have read about him in the news. "And he's here, why?"

"He wants an alliance with the Cosa Nostra to grow his presence beyond the UK."

"I thought Mafia men don't share their business dealings with women?"

Nonna chuckles, "But then, I am not just any woman. I am the Nonna of the Capo and the mother of the Don." She turns to me, "Besides, I have my sources."

"You mean you have spies within the clan?"

"Also, people who owe me who keep me informed of all important developments." Her eyes gleam, "Of course, if I were to ask my son and grandson, they wouldn't refuse to share information with me, but this way is more interesting, don't you think?"

"Interesting?" I open and shut my mouth, "You really are quite a woman, you know that?"

After the funeral, Michael had driven me here. We hadn't exchanged one word the entire way. Hell, he hadn't even directly looked at me for the duration of the trip. It's almost as if he's trying to avoid me.

"So why is he avoiding you?" Nonna's voice interrupts my thoughts.

*What the—!* Is she reading my mind or what? I blink, turn my attention to her, "Who's avoiding me?"

She clicks her tongue, "Don't try that with me. You know who I am talking about."

I blink rapidly, then bite the inside of my cheek. If I thought the Sovrano men were overwhelming... Well, Nonna is, undeniably, far ahead of them. "If you mean Michael, it's because he feels responsible for the explosion and for..." I clutch at my glass of wine, "And for the baby, and for what happened to Xander."

"Ah," she takes my arm and guides me to a chair, "sit."

"I am fine." I frown.

"You're not fine. You just left the hospital and you've been through an emotional rollercoaster, not to mention the physical impact of the car blowing up."

I flinch.

"It hurts to hear it, huh?"

"You know it does."

"It's better to talk about it than to keep it all bottled up inside."

"Is that what you did with them when they were growing up?"

She draws in a breath, then urges me to sit down. I sink into the chair, then glance up at her, "Did you?"

"I wish I had," She straightens, and glances across the room at the faces of the Sovrano brothers. "I wish I had been more open with them. Wish I had taken them from under their father's care earlier... but I was weak."

"You, weak?" I laugh, "Not quite how I see you, Nonna."

She glances down at me. "I come from a traditional Sicilian family. I was married at sixteen, pregnant at eighteen with my first child."

"Don Sovrano?"

"Don Sovrano," she nods. "I had four other miscarriages after him. Gave birth to a girl who didn't live."

"I am so sorry," I whisper.

Her lips twist, "It was a long time ago."

"Does the pain...ever go away?"

"It...fades a little with time," she draws in a breath, "but it never leaves you. It settles in your heart, becomes a part of it, so you occasionally take it out and glance at it. You try to get over it but it doesn't really leave you. It becomes a part of you. And much as you want to take the story out of you... Some resonance of it always remains."

"Oh," I blink back my tears, "that's...profound."

She glances away, then back at me, "I know you've been through a lot in the short time that you've known Michael, but the two of you are lucky."

"We are?" I stare, "How can you call us lucky? He kidnapped me. I tried to kill him. He married me because my father promised me to him and he... Ah...hasn't exactly been nice to me since."

"He saw you, saw something in you that he wanted; he took you, wedded you, and despite the fact that you stabbed him at his wedding, did not kill you."

I bite the inside of my cheek.

"You escaped him, only to return to him."

"Only because I thought he was dead."

"He faked his own funeral, knowing it would entice you to come back to him."

I shuffle my feet. "I still wanted to escape him," I whisper.

"Only you were foiled by the car-bomb."

"Now he doesn't want to acknowledge me anymore. He is convinced that my being with him puts me in danger. He wants me to return to London."

"Are you going to?"

"No," I swallow. "No," I say with more vehemence, "if he thinks he can snap a finger and I obey him, then he has another think coming."

"If that isn't true love, what is? He is worried about your safety and you are worried about him. The two of you found each other." She raises a shoulder, "The circumstances were a little, what you English might call dodgy, but that only adds to the excitement, I am sure."

"Nonna," I open and shut my mouth, "you can't say things like that to your granddaughter-in-law; and at a funeral too."

"You're right."

"I am?"

"I am not nearly as drunk as I should be at the funeral of one of my favorite grandsons." She glances around and a waiter materializes with a tray of drinks. She snatches up a snifter of whiskey, then holds it up to me, "To Alessandro."

I opt for the wine, then raise my wineglass, "To Xander."

She drinks from her own glass, then stares into the depths of her whiskey, "He wasn't what he seemed you know?"

"Xander?" I frown, "Are we talking about the same laid-back man who loved to paint and who was the most charming of all the brothers?"

"He was all that, and brilliant at his painting too. A genius ahead of his time, some would say." She takes another healthy swig of her whiskey. "I loved him more than anyone else, maybe even Michael sometimes." She glances around the room, "And the boys know it. But what they didn't realize was that he was also confused."

"Confused?"

She glances at me, "Let's just say, he felt something for Theresa, but never told her so. Not because he couldn't, but because he wasn't sure if he loved her. Because she wasn't the only one he was interested in."

I straighten in my seat. "You mean there was someone else he loved?"

"Not one…" She stares at me meaningfully.

"Oh, so you mean he slept around?"

"He did," she glances away, then back at me, "and not only with women."

"Oh," I take a sip of my wine, "which is normal, right? People are attracted to both men and women sometimes."

"Not in Sicily, they aren't."

"Oh, please," I scoff. "Sicilians are not exempt from who they are drawn to, and I don't understand why you are speaking like this about Xander, considering we've just come from his funeral."

"When you are old like I am, you are always only one step ahead of death, and you never know when it's going to catch up with you."

A shiver runs down my back. "That's…"

"The truth," she cuts in. "I've learned it's best not to fuck around when you have something to say."

I laugh, then turn it into a cough, "Didn't expect you to use that word." I take in her determined features, "You're a force to be reckoned with, Nonna."

"So are you."

"I am?"

She tilts her head, "You'd have to be for the Capo to marry you. You do realize that he broke the norm when he did so."

"And that's a problem…?"

She raises a shoulder, "I'd have been happier if he'd married a nice Sicilian girl, who'd have stayed home and given him kids, but it wasn't to be."

I glower at her.

She raises her hand, "I hope you don't mind I'm being honest with you. I feel like we've gone beyond the need to hide things from each other, don't you think?"

"By all means," I tighten my hold around the stem of my wine glass, "go ahead and tell me what you're thinking."

"Ultimately, though, I am coming around to the fact that you are good for him."

"You are?"

She nods, "Clearly, the two of you are in love with each other, and as I said, it's rare to find that, so…"

"So?"

"So, you'd better play your part and make sure he comes around to accepting you now. And I do hope and pray that you get pregnant quickly again. Nothing like having a man's child to completely change things and ensure that your marriage is on rock solid ground."

"And here I thought you were ahead of your time."

"I am." She smiles sadly, "It's why, after going against my son and ensuring that I moved the boys to LA and took them out of his grasp, and after holding my own against the men of the Cosa Nostra, one thing I have realized is that it's best not to make things too difficult for yourself."

I frown, "I am really not sure what you are trying to tell me."

"That what you did earlier, when you tried stopping Michael from attacking Luca in front of everyone else... Don't do it again."

"Excuse me?" I snap. "I'll do what I want, when I want with him. He's my husband."

"And the Capo of the Cosa Nostra."

"I know that," I scowl.

"Do you, though?" She looks me up and down, "You are the wife of the most powerful man in Europe. Which means your position comes with certain responsibilities."

"Oh, please," I scoff. "It's not like I am married into the bloody British royal family."

"Isn't it?" She arches an eyebrow.

I blow out a breath, "Can you please stop playing games and just tell me whatever it is that you are trying to say?"

"You tried to stop your husband from beating up his younger brother in front of his rivals and in front of the people who look to him as their leader. The same brother who helped you escape earlier. At the worst, it looks like you were trying to cuckold the Capo—"

"Oh," I gulp.

"—at the best, it looks like you were trying to defy him."

"O-k-a-y," I flush.

"Either way, you made him lose face in front of his clan and his business rivals. And the fact that he didn't turn on you, but actually listened to you, revealed that he places a lot of faith in you."

"What's wrong with that?"

"Haven't you been listening to anything I have been saying?" She scowls, "You showed yourself as being his weakness—"

"—which means I made myself a target all over again? And that it's probably only a matter of time before they try to get to him through me again." I slump my shoulders.

Nonna half smiles, "Knew you were smarter than you look."

"Gee, thanks." I twist my fingers together. "So, what? I need to be more careful how I come across with him in public."

"Among other things." She purses her lips, "Can I share something else with you?"

"Please," I raise my hand, "don't stop now."

"I didn't get along with my mother-in-law, at all, god rest her soul," Nonna crosses herself, "but she did give me one piece of advice which stood me well."

I eye her warily, "And that is?"

She leans in closer, "You need to be a feminist at heart and an independent woman to the outside world, but when it comes to your husband, you want to be his mistress in daily life, and his whore in bed."

# 6

Michael

I look over to find my Nonna engaged in conversation with my wife. They seem to be getting along. Nonna says something and Karma chokes on her drink. I take a step forward when she places her drink on the table and composes herself. She glances at Nonna, who smiles at her. The old bat actually smiles... And it's one of her rare genuine smiles, too. What the hell?

What are they talking about? And why do I care about it, anyway? I turn my attention back to Sebastian, "It's time." I jerk my chin at him, then pivot and walk out of the living room, down the corridor to my study. My father follows me and closes the door after him. I walk to the bar in the corner, pour whiskey into two glasses. My father walks over and accepts a glass from me.

We each take a sip in silence, then my father turns to me, "It's a mistake, accepting Luca back. He's turned on you once; he can do so again."

"Didn't ask for your advice, father."

He bares his teeth, "She's making you weak. This is what happens when you think with your dick. If you'd only killed her as you'd originally planned instead of marrying her, Xander might still be alive today; she—"

"That's enough," I snap.

My father's eyebrows rise up. "Don't raise your voice," he growls.

"Don't talk about my wife. Not now, not ever. Next time you do so, I'll—"

"What, kill me?" He bares his teeth, "You'd kill your own father over a whore?"

"Shut up," I snarl, "shut the fuck up."

He laughs, "You're losing your ability to think straight."

"And you..." I tighten my grip around my whiskey glass, "are overstepping the line."

"I am your father." He chuckles, "I am meant to overstep the line."

"You're nothing to me," I growl. "The day I consolidate my power with the rival clans, I will take over as Don, and then... You will be nothing to anyone in the Cosa Nostra."

"I look forward to that day."

I snort, "You expect me to believe that?"

He looks me up and down. "You may find it difficult to believe this, but I am your father, and nothing would give me more pleasure than my oldest son succeeding me."

I place my glass on the bar counter, "If that is all—"

"Xander was a liability."

"Excuse me?"

"He wasted all his time painting."

"He had a gift."

"He fucked men."

"I am aware."

The Don stiffens, "You knew it and you didn't do anything about it?"

"He was entitled to do as he pleased."

"Not when he was my son."

"I am not going to stand for you talking shit about him," I growl.

"He's better off dead. At least, his funeral provides a stage for you to turn up the pressure on our rival clans. Now is the time for you to act, to take assertive action that will allow you to consolidate this hold over our rivals, to increase the influence of the Cosa Nostra, to—"

I throw up my fist and catch him in the jaw. He stumbles back, and the glass slips from his grasp and crashes to the floor. "The fuck?" he growls. "How dare you raise your hand to me?"

"I'll do more than that." I straighten as the door to my study flies open. Seb rushes in, followed by Massimo, Christian, Luca, and Adrian. They pause when they notice the Don bleeding from his mouth.

He levels his gaze on me. "You are making a big mistake, boy," he murmurs, "you don't want to make an enemy of me."

"You became my enemy the day you raised your hand to me."

"It was the only way to ensure you grew up to be a man."

"I grew up, all right... To hate you. I don't want you anywhere near my wife or my brothers."

"They are my sons, too."

I turn to the men. "Choose, then," I snap, "him or me."

They glance at each other, then Seb turns to me, "We're with you *fratellone*. You've been more than a father to us, more a parent than the Don has ever has been."

My father chuckles. He glances over the faces of the men, then laughs again. "You leave me no choice then."

"Leave, father," I jerk my chin toward the door, "you have your answer."

"You are going to regret this, each one of you."

Seb walks over to the door and holds it open. The Don turns and stalks over to the exit. He pauses, then turns to glare at us, "When you need help, don't bother coming to me. When you lose everything, including that pretty new wife of yours, you remember that it was I who was behind it."

Turning, he leaves.

The door snicks shut.

"What the fuck?" Christian explodes. "What the hell was that about?"

"He wasn't very complimentary about Xander," I rub my fingers across the back of my neck, "It was inevitable."

"I mean, what did he mean by that threat?"

"That?" I raise my shoulder, "Who the fuck cares?"

"He's not one for idle threats, brother," Massimo cautions.

"Neither am I." I snatch up my glass, drain it, top it up again, then walk over to take my seat behind the desk.

"Out," I jerk my chin at the door, "it's time to cut this bullshit short."


Ten minutes later, I lean back in my chair as I take in Nikolai and JJ. The silence stretches as none of us speak. Neither JJ nor Nikolai shuffle in their seats nor look uncomfortable. Their faces wear the same expression of patience that I assume my features reflect... At least, I hope it does. I glance between them, then consider my drink.

"Revenge," I finally say, "is a powerful emotion. It can make or break a man. It can galvanize you to do the kinds of things you didn't think you were capable of."

"And you need revenge," JJ ventures. "Hell, I would too if it were my brother who was killed in an explosion, and my wife who was hurt."

"She was pregnant," I growl. "My wife was pregnant."

Silence descends, then Nikolai murmurs, "I am sorry, brother. How can we help you?"

"By helping me track down the bastards behind this."

"I'll spread the word... Hell, if your speech earlier hasn't gone viral within the underground network...in a manner of speaking, that is," JJ offers, "I'll make sure I alert all of my sources. It's only a matter of time before the perpetrators are found.

I jerk my chin, "And you, Nikolai?" I train my gaze on him, "What are you thinking?"

"Whoever did it was, clearly, after your life."

"That's no secret. He's the Capo. Hell, they want him to step down from becoming the Don." JJ frowns. "They were trying to finish him off before he took the position."

"Is that all it was?" Nikolai drawls.

"What else could it be?" JJ replies.

"You tell me," Niko holds my gaze, "you sure you're looking in the right place, Michael?"

My heart begins to race and my pulse pounds at my temples. I lean back into the chair, and the handle of my knife that's tucked in at the small of my waistband digs into my back. "You're implying—"

"That it may have been one of your own." Niko nods. "Don't tell me the thought hadn't occurred to you?"

It had, but I am not going to own up to it. "You let me take care of what happens with my clan." I tip up my chin. "I simply need you to spread the word among your men and their contacts. I want the culprits to be brought to heel before Christmas."

JJ whistles, "That's only a few days away."

"More than enough time, if the two of you get behind the effort."

"You threatening us, Michael?" Niko asks in a soft voice.

"I am..." I glance between them, "reminding you that when we embarked on this partnership, it meant that you prioritize my... request before anyone else's."

"Your brother was killed; it's like my own was taken from me." JJ raps his knuckles on the table, "Consider it done."

I turn to Niko whose gaze narrows. He seems like he's about to say something, then changes his mind. "I'll get my men on the job."

I rise to my feet and so do they. JJ turns to leave and Niko follows.

"Nikolai," I call out and he pauses, "I am counting on you."

He glances at me over his shoulder, "Partnerships are almost as important to me as family." He touches his forefinger to his forehead then stalks out.

I walk toward the bar and pour the rest of the whiskey into my glass. The door opens and her scent reaches me. I stiffen, then place the now empty whiskey bottle down on the counter. The door snicks shut and footsteps approach. I sense her pause behind me. She touches my arm and I pull away. I walk over to my chair and sink down into it.

"What are you doing here?" I ask as she stands there, still dressed in that black dress that outlines her every curve. She reaches up, removes her hat with the netting and places it on the bar counter. Instantly, my gaze is drawn to the wound on her forehead. Her features are pale, her frame too slim. There are dark shadows under her eyes, and fuck, if she doesn't look like she's going to collapse any moment. As if on cue, she sways and I curse. I slam my glass down on the table, then lunge forward. I reach her just as she puts out a hand to steady herself.

I swing her up in my arms and she protests, "Put me down, Michael."

"Not a bloody chance."

She chuckles, "You're swearing like a true Brit."

"God forbid," I snap as I walk toward the door.

"Where are you taking me?" she asks in a soft voice.

"To bed, which is where you should have been all day."

"I couldn't have missed the funeral, Michael," she protests. "Xander was my friend... maybe one of the only friends I have made since I came to Sicily."

"What about Cassandra and Aurora?"

"They are my friends too, but Xander... He was special, you know?"

A ball of emotion clogs my throat. I increase my pace, until I reach the steps. I take them two at a time and reach the landing. I stalk down the corridor to her room, then shoulder my way inside. Her cat meows, then brushes past my legs. I stumble, right myself. "Bloody cat," I swear, and she laughs.

"Yep, my influence is rubbing off on you, Capo."

I reach the bed, lower her down onto it, then reach over and pull off her stilettos. "What was the need to wear these god-awful things? You could have worn something that did not put so much pressure on your back."

"Worried about me, Capo?"

Her soft voice coils in my chest. My heart stutters and my groin hardens. Every sense in my body seems to focus in on her. I straighten, take in her pale features. "Painkillers," I growl. "Where are your painkillers?"

She nods toward the bath and I walk over, rummage around in the shelves behind the mirror until I find them. I walk over, hand them over to her, then pour a glass of water from the carafe on the bedside table. She swallows down the pills with the water, then sinks back. I take in her dress-covered body, "Why don't you take that off? You must be uncomfortable in that."

She hesitates and I scowl, "I've seen everything there is to see, Karma."

She looks like she's going to protest, then nods. She sits up and I grip the hem of her dress. I drag it up and she raises her hips, then her arms so I can pull it up and off of her. I drape the dress over the chair, then take in her pale body. She's wearing a black bra and panties, and I take in the marks on her shoulders, across her chest, the small bandage across her belly button where they'd had to perform a keyhole surgery to stop the internal bleeding. My heart thuds in my chest. My gut twists. I sit down next to her on the bed and touch the bandage. She flinches and I pull back. "Does it hurt?"

"No," she whispers, "it's...just difficult seeing it, that's all."

I flatten my palm across her belly and goosebumps pop on her skin. "Are you cold?"

She shakes her head. The cat pads over to me, brushes against my leg again and mewls. "He wants to come up on the bed." Karma says softly. I bend, pick him up, place him next to Karma. The cat instantly curls into her side and purrs. She drags her fingers down his fur and smiles. I take in the way her fingers slide across his skin, how he stretches, then coils in on himself and closes his eyes. Lucky cat, to be able to press into her body and fall asleep with not a care in the world. Fuck, how can I be jealous of a bloody cat? And since when have I started using 'bloody' to swear? Maybe she is right. Maybe more of her influence has rubbed off on me then I'd care to admit. I rise to my feet and she reaches up and grabs my wrist.

"Stay, Michael," she implores. "Please, just for tonight. I don't want to be alone."

I glance away, then back at her. "You need to leave, Karma," I finally say. "I can't do what's needed if I'm constantly worried about you. It's best you return to London, to your family."

"You're my family, Michael. You and your brothers. I am one of you now."

I shake my head, "I can't justify putting you in so much danger."

"If you think my leaving you will help lessen it, then you are wrong." She sits up and the cat protests, then rises up on its feet and stalks away to the other side of the bed. "You know I'm safest when I am with you."

"I know no such thing."

"Why are you being so cold, so withdrawn? Why can't you see what's in front of your eyes?"

"Karma," I warn her, "I don't want to argue with you about this."

"Then don't." She stares at me and I hold her gaze. The silence stretches, then she sighs, "There's no talking you out of this, is there?"

I shake my head.

"Fine, then." She glances away and her chin wobbles. A tear slides down her cheek and my chest tightens. I sink back onto the bed, gather her close. She coils into me much like the cat had done earlier and sniffs. "I wish I hadn't lost the child, Michael. I hadn't thought I was looking forward to the birth of the baby, but I was, more than I'd ever imagined. I mean, I'd never thought I'd become a mother, and now it's all I can think of."

I wrap my arms around her, pull her closer. A shudder grips her as I run my hand in circles over her back. "I'm sorry, Beauty. Truly, I am."

The tears drip from her face, wet my shirt as I hold and rock her.

"I... I am also sorry that I interfered earlier today," she hiccups.

"Interfered?" I scowl, "What are you talking about?"

"When you went after Luca, I tried to stop you. I swear, I had no idea how that could be interpreted by the guests. I simply wanted to ensure that you wouldn't hurt yourself."

"I can take care of myself, Beauty," I press my lips to her forehead, "but your concern is much appreciated."

"Oh," she peers up at me, "so you're not pissed off that I made you lose face in front of everyone?"

"Maybe a little," I lie. "As you're aware, I don't take kindly to being told what to do."

"Not even by your wife?" She flutters her eyelashes, still spiky from her tears, and my heart stutters.

I peer into her face, then half smile, "You're learning how to get your way with me, hmm?"

"Me?" she sniffles, "I'm doing no such thing," She snuggles into me, "I simply want to make sure that I am not treading on anyone's toes without realizing it."

I draw in a breath, "Nonna's been talking to you, I take it?"

"A little bit," she mutters. "She does have a point. I really don't want you to lose face because of me."

I notch my knuckles under her chin so she has no choice but to meet my gaze, "I'll never lose face because of you, Beauty. And you don't have to change yourself in order to be by my side..." I hesitate.

She frowns, "But? There is a but isn't there?"

"But, you still can't defy me—not in public, and not in private. I am not a man who can be ordered around."

"You don't say?" She widens her gaze, "I really hadn't noticed that about you, Capo."

I can't stop the chuckle that rumbles up my chest. I grasp the nape of her neck, bring my forehead to hers, "So damn sassy." I brush my nose against hers, then press a kiss to her mouth, before tucking her head under my chin.

She nestles against me, as I rub circles over her back.

Her body twitches, and I glance down to find her eyes shut. I hold her a little longer, until her breathing deepens. Then I place her onto the bed. I pull the sheets up and tuck them under her chin. I glance at the cat, who pads over and settles in beside her. "Keep watch over her," I murmur as I bend and kiss her forehead.

I straighten and watch her a few more seconds. I take in her now flushed features, those slightly parted rosebud lips, the slender length of her throat. When I leave, I know what I must do next.

# 7

Karma

A knock on the door wakes me up. I open my eyes and grimace. A dull headache knocks at my temples, and my eyes feel swollen. I turn over on my back, and glance around the shadowed room. The curtains have been drawn... and I normally leave them open before I go to bed. That way, I know approximately what time it is when I wake up. Which means someone else must have drawn them... Michael... He must have done it before leaving. Had he stayed last night? Had he watched me sleep? I remember clinging to him, asking him to stay and then I had started to cry, damn it. I had clung to him and wept, and he had drawn me close to him and held me, and then, I don't remember anything. I must have fallen asleep in his arms. When had he left?

Next to me is Andy. He walks to the edge of the bed, jumps off, then pads over to the door. He turns to me, then glances back at the door. I swear, that cat can talk without saying a word. He's way too smart for his own good.

The knock sounds again. I sit up, call out, "Come in."

Cassandra shoulders open the door and Andy darts to the side. She walks in holding a breakfast tray. Andy follows her. She places the tray on the table near the window, draws the curtains open. The sunlight streams in and I wince.

"Good morning," she choruses as she looks me up and down. "How do you feel today?"

"Sore," I cough, then throw my legs over the side of the bed. I stand up, and every muscle in my body feels like it has been put through the wringer.

Andy walks over purring loudly; he brushes against my calf. I glance down, remember I am still in my bra and panties. I glance around for a robe or something to cover myself with.

"Here," Cassandra hands me the robe she grabbed from the chair near the bed. Andy prances away as I walk slowly into the bathroom, feeling every bit of the hard fall I took when I was ejected from the car. To think, I could have very easily died... Like Xander... Poor Xander... Like my child.

A shudder grips me. I walk over to the sink in the bathroom and grip the edge, take in a deep breath. Another. I need to stop circling back to what happened. Need to somehow focus on the now, the present... On proving to my husband that I would be safest by his side. I open the faucet, hold my palms out under the flowing water. I splash the water onto my face, brush my teeth, comb my hair back. By the time I step out, I am feeling a little better... At least, more collected, at any rate. I walk over to the tray of food on the table and take a seat. Cassandra pours a mug of coffee for me.

"Why don't you join me?" I ask.

She seems like she's about to refuse and I shake my head, "Please, I insist. I really could do with some company right now."

She hesitates, then nods. Pouring herself a cup of coffee, she sits down opposite me. I reach for one of the plates that had covered the dishes. I turn it over, pile it with scrambled eggs, toast and bacon, and push it toward her.

"Oh no, I can't," she protests.

I scowl. "I bet you haven't eaten breakfast today."

She blinks.

"Well, have you?"

She shakes her head.

"Come on, then." I nod toward her plate.

"There's only one set of cutlery," she points out.

"We can share," I reach for a fork and push my spoon toward her. She grabs it and for a few seconds the sound of cutlery hitting the plate fills the space. When I have polished off almost everything on my plate, I place my fork down, "Is the Capo working from his home office today?" I ask.

"He left very early and told me he wouldn't be back for dinner."

"Oh," I blink, "guess he's working from his office at Venom, then."

She glances up at me, "He told me to help you in any way needed with the Christmas party."

I hold her gaze, "Guess you're thinking that it's in bad taste to hold a celebration so soon after a funeral?"

"I think it will help bridge the rift between the brothers."

"You mean between Michael and Luca?"

She nods, "And Sebastian and Christian."

"What's up between those two?"

She raises a shoulder, "I am not sure, but they seem to always be fighting."

"Hmm," I toy with my fork, "I'm hoping some kind of event to commemorate Xander's memory is what they need to lower the barriers between them and talk."

"More like talk with their fists," she snorts. "Those brothers have been known to fight at the least provocation."

"Really?" I frown. "They always come across as so suave and sophisticated."

"It's all a front." She shrugs. "When they were younger, they got into scraps all the time. It drove Nonna crazy."

"Nonna," I chuckle, "that woman is formidable. I guess she'd have to be to survive so long in this family of men, but still... I don't know whether to be in awe of her or to hate her."

"The former." Cassandra reaches for her coffee. "You have her on your side and it will be easier to win over everyone else in the family."

"Not that I want to have anything to do with Michael's father." I shiver. "That man gives me the creeps."

"The Don is dangerous," she admits, "but I don't think you have anything to worry about from him. Michael will make sure that the Don keeps his distance."

"I sure hope so," I murmur, "especially since they are both coming to the Christmas party."

"You also need to reach out to Theresa."

"Xander's friend?"

She nods, "If it's an event to celebrate Xander's life, it would be incomplete without her."

"Can you help me reach out to her?"

"Better than that, I've already asked her to come to meet you later today."

"Why can't I go to meet her?"

"Because the Capo has left instructions that you are not to leave the house."

I blow out a breath. He doesn't want me to leave the house and yet...he doesn't want me to stay with him. The man is seriously making my head spin.

"What's wrong?" Cassandra peers into my face, "Everything okay?"

"Peachy," I murmur, "what time is Theresa coming?"

# 8

Michael

"Capo."

I glance up as Luca strides into the room. He glances around at the assembled faces. Sebastian and Christian are sprawled in chairs in front of my table; Adrian leans against a wall; Massimo is seated in the middle of a settee on the far side, with his bulk taking up most of the space. All of them stalk him as he comes to a halt in the middle of the floor. He meets my gaze head on. "Is this going to be an inquisition?" he murmurs.

"What do you think?" I lean back in my chair. "Our father thinks it's a mistake that I took you in."

"And you?" He folds his arms across his chest, "What do you think?"

I rise to my feet, lean forward and place my palms flat on the table, "I think it would be a mistake if I didn't."

His chest rises and falls, "I am sorry, Michael." Luca looks around at his brothers. "I never meant to hurt any of you."

"And yet, you did." I curl my lips, "I am not interested in your apologies, Luca."

"What then?" He shuffles his feet, "What else do you want from me, Michael."

"Information."

"Ah," his forehead smoothens, "of course, you do. I should have known that this, too, would be a transaction for you."

"You didn't think I would simply let you walk back into the *famiglia* without paying a price for your indiscretions."

"Of course, not." He chuckles, "There's more of the old man in you than you'd like to admit, Michael."

I set my jaw, "Who was behind the attack, Luca?"

He blinks. "You think I know who was behind it? Don't you think I would have stopped him, then?"

"I don't know, Luca, would you have stopped him?"

He shakes his head, "Do you really have to ask me that question, Michael?"

"You tell me, Luca." I look him up and down. "Last I knew, you were helping my wife escape. You watched, you even encouraged her to take the oar to my forehead."

"I saw my opportunity and took it, Michael."

"Why would you do that?" Christian springs to his feet, "Why would you go against one of us? You showed our enemies that we are not invincible. You exposed a chink in the armor. It's why they dared place a bomb in the car. It's why they dared try to harm us. You are responsible for Xander's death as much as the person who actually planted that bomb."

Luca's jaw tics. He lowers his arms to his sides, "I would have done anything to protect Xander. I never would have hurt him, or one of you."

"And what do you call what you did to Michael?" Christian glares at him. "How can you stand there and claim what you did wasn't to hurt us when all the evidence points to the contrary? In fact, how dare you think you can simply walk back in and pick up where you left off, after everything that happened?" He lunges toward Luca, but Massimo jumps up to his feet, and with a litheness that belies his bulk, Massimo grabs Christian around his chest and yanks him back. Christian growls, strains in his hold, but Massimo doesn't let go.

"Take him out, until he's cooled down," I order and Christian snarls.

"Let me get my hands on the bastard. It's he who's responsible for what happened to Xander. When I get hold of you, I am going to kill you, you motherfucker!"

Massimo tries to steer Christian away, but Christian resists. The two grapple. Adrian leaps to his feet and grips Christian's shoulder. Between him and Massimo, they manage to maneuver Christian out of the room. The door snicks shut and I turn to Luca.

"Who were you working with?" I snap. "This is your chance to come clean, Luca."

His shoulders flex. He uncurls his fists at his sides and lowers his chin. "The Kane Company," he says in a hard voice. "My plan was to join forces with them, and try to take you down."

"Motherfucker," Sebastian growls. "Fucking *Cani,*" he grumbles, alluding to the Italian pronunciation of the word that translates to dogs.

"So were they behind the rigging of the car."

He frowns, "I honestly don't know."

I scowl, "You'd better know."

"I swear upon our mother," Luca thumps his chest, "I have no idea who's behind it. When I heard what had happened, all I knew was that I needed to be with my family. That I had to help you track down who did it and ensure they realize that they can't fuck with us again."

I drag my fingers through my hair. "Fuck," I hiss. "This is bloody unhelpful." I walk around the table, then stalk over to him. "What else can you tell us? What else is the Kane Company up to? You'd better have something for me, Luca, if you want to rejoin."

Luca shuffles his feet. "JJ exploited the fact that I wanted to be Capo. He offered me the chance to be his second-in-command with the understanding that I'd take over from him."

"And his son?" Sebastian frowns, "Wouldn't his son be next in line for succession?"

"His son's a tech wiz. Runs a multibillion-dollar tech start-up in Silicon Valley. He's hardly interested in following in his father's footsteps."

"JJ's not that old, though," Seb scowls. "He's what, forty-nine?"

"If that," Luca retorts. "Look, I didn't really want to take over as the head of the Kane Company. I just wanted to send a signal to you guys that you were not the only fish in the sea. That if I could not become the Don of the Cosa Nostra, there were other places I could go."

"Fuck, Luca," I glower at him, "all you had to do was talk to me, brother. We could have figured something out."

"The way you did when you went off to LA, leaving the rest of us behind?"

My heart thuds in my ribcage. "I am sorry for that; I truly am. If I could do it all over again, I wouldn't have left until I had a chance to take the rest of you with me."

"Save it, Mika." He cracks his neck. "It's water under the bridge."

"Fuck, brother, I would have done anything to ensure all of you were safe. If I had had any inkling that he'd come after you, Luca, I would have…"

"Killed him?" Luca says softly, "There's still time."

"He's our father." I roll my shoulder. "As much as I hate to say it, he is our sperm donor."

"And he'd be happy to kill any of us if he could hold onto his position as Don."

"What the fuck are you talking about?"

"Do you really think our 'dear father' will let go of his power that easily?"

I squeeze my fingers into fists, "Are you saying he was behind what happened to Xander and my wife?"

"I wouldn't put it past him."

Fact is, after how he beat our mother and drove her to an early death, I wouldn't be surprised either. And yet, I can't quite accept it. Maybe a part of me still clings to the hope that there is some modicum of love in him toward his own children? Despite what he said about Luca and Xander on the day of the funeral...

I curl my fingers into fists, "He's a bastard, and granted, he fucked up our lives...but family is the one thing that is important to him." I roll my shoulders. "He's always been clear that he wanted me to succeed him. Hell, he's the one who nominated me for Capo. It's thanks to his vote of confidence that I took over this role."

"You'd have become the Capo with or without his help, Michael." Luca's lips twist. "You have the leadership qualities, the ability to influence people, the determination and motivation to become a Don, before anything else."

Until I met her. Now all that matters is keeping her safe. No matter that it means I am going to do something that's going to make her hate me. It's better that way though. It'll make it easier for her to walk away from me.

"Michael?" Seb's voice cuts through the thoughts in my head. I turn to him and Seb takes in my features. "You okay?"

I jerk my chin, "Have we had any other information from any of our sources?"

Seb scowls, "Nothing, Michael. It's like whoever did it has buried himself in a hole and pulled the hole in after him."

Fuck, every day that goes by without us tracking down those responsible, the more the danger grows. And if it's our father who was behind it... It means she isn't safe, even in my home. It means he might still go after her, and if anything were to happen to her... This time... I would not be able to get over it. There is only one way out. To expedite my plan.

# 9

Karma

The sound of footsteps reaches me and I glance up from the outfit I've been working on.

After breakfast, I had taken a nap, then woken up refreshed. I had met Theresa, Xander's friend, and it had been clear that she had been in love with him. He'd never mentioned anything to her, and she hadn't exactly confessed her feelings to him either. She had broken down during the course of the meeting and had been so regretful about the fact that she'd never gotten to tell him how she felt.

It certainly put things in perspective. It was a poignant reminder that you have only one life and you'd better go after what you want in the time you have... Like him.

I had been emotionally drained after the meeting and had ended up eating lunch and taking another nap, from which I had woken up disoriented a few hours ago. I'd grabbed some tea, then decided to start working on this outfit—the idea had been bubbling in my mind since I had woken this morning.

It's a good thing I slept a lot today, because I feel stronger and more alert. I am determined to stay awake until Michael gets home, and God knows, I'll need all of my faculties for what I have in mind. I mean, I am going to confront him again. No way, am I giving up and allowing him to send me away. He needs to understand that it really is safest for me with him and there is no way I am leaving him... Not now, when he needs me most. So, I've been focused on my creation while keeping my ears peeled for him. Until, I hear the sound of footsteps in the corridor.

I rise to my feet, and walking over to the door, I peer outside into the corridor. Another sound reaches me from the direction of Michael's room. I step out into the corridor, reach his door, and push it. It swings open to reveal Michael sprawled out at the foot of his bed. His tie is off, his shirt sleeves rolled up. His legs, still clad in his pants, are spread out...and between them is a woman.

She's kneeling, her back to me, her hair flowing around her shoulders as she leans forward. Her shoulders move and her head bobs... What the hell? I glance up to find Michael staring at me. His features are unperturbed, almost as if he expected me to walk in on him.

Hell, he expected me to walk in on him, all right. It's why he brought her here. My heart begins to thud and my pulse rate ratchets up. I take a step forward and my knees seem to buckle. I grab the door frame and steady myself. Watch as he buries his fingers in her hair and begins to move her head forward and back, and forward. She moans and the sound snaps me out of the weird haze I'd fallen into.

"What are you doing, Michael?" I snarl. "How dare you... you...?"

"Shove my cock down another woman's throat?" He smirks, and his blue eyes seem to gleam with suppressed mirth.

"What the fuck, Mika?" I take another step forward and he chuckles.

"Do you want to join us, wife? I wouldn't say no to a threesome."

I pause, "Why the hell are you trying to put distance between us Michael? After everything we've been through, I thought you'd realize that my place is with you."

"Your place is..." he glances down at the woman between his legs, "where I tell you to be."

"Fuck this," I growl. "This is not you, Michael. You are not the macho, overbearing, chauvinistic man you try to portray yourself as."

"No?" He tilts his head, "Pray, enlighten me then about my qualities."

"You care about people, your family, your brothers. Hell, you even care about your lousy father."

He stiffens.

"You care about me, Michael. You love me."

"So?" He raises a shoulder. The woman begins to lean back and his muscles bunch as he grips her hair tighter. He pushes his hips forward and my stomach knots. A cold sensation pools in my chest.

"Stop it," I say in a low voice. "Stop it, right now."

"You don't give me orders, Beauty."

"Don't call me that."

"How about I call you the love of my life, hmm?"

"Am I, though?" I swallow, "I am beginning to think you don't really understand the meaning of the word love."

"And you do?"

I nod. "It's what I felt for the child I carried," I press my fingers against my stomach. "It's what I feel for you, Michael."

"Love," he smirks, "is overrated. It's sex that matters, and the ability to fuck who you want, when you want. Speaking of...do you want me to fuck you, Beauty?"

"I lost our child not four days ago. Do you think I want to be fucked, asshole?"

"I think," he looks me up and down, "I could take your ass. That wouldn't hurt any of the other parts now, would it?"

I snap my head back, "Fuck you, Michael. Don't do this to us, please. Just tell me all of this is an act, that you are simply doing this to piss me off so you can get me to leave."

"This," he yawns, "is me, Beauty. The real me. The man you married."

"The man I married was not only in touch with his emotions, but he also had the courage to express them. He wouldn't have put me through this..." I wave a hand at the space between us, "whatever this is."

"This is called scratching an itch. Speaking of," he cracks his neck, "you joining us or what?"

"No."

"Then you may as well leave, babe."

"You sure, Michael?" I wipe the tear that has somehow squeezed out of the corner of my eye. "Once I am gone, I won't return."

"Don't take this too badly," he gestures to the woman between his legs. "It's normal for us Mafia guys to have women on the side, you know. It had to happen sooner or later. Best you see it now, so there are no more illusions."

"You told me that you wouldn't fuck anyone else. You swore that you took your vows to me seriously."

He shrugs. "Guess I lied."

Anger thrums at my temples. I draw in a breath and my lungs burn. I take a step forward and that's when she grips his thighs, tips her head, and I can all but sense her taking him down her throat. My heart squeezes in on itself. My stomach seems to bottom out and specks of darkness blink at the corners of my vision. Damn, if I am going to faint here, in front of him and that...that...whoever that is. I spin on my feet, stagger to the door, then step out.

"Shut the door behind you, would you?"

His voice follows me out as I slam the door shut behind me. I lean against it, drawing in a breath, then another. Force myself to put one foot in front of the other. I reach my room, manage to shut the door behind me. Andy walks over and purrs as he weaves between my legs. I sink down, gather him close, and burst into tears. Fuck him, fuck the Mafia, fuck this bloody town. I am getting out of here, before he does something else that's going to humiliate me further.

His fingers had tightened on the back of her head, his biceps bulging with the effort. He dared allow her to feel the thickness of his cock? He dared let her kneel in front of him, allowed her to take the position that belongs only to me? He dared...let another woman close enough to smell him, to put her lips on him, to wind her fingers about his massive thighs? To touch what is mine?

*Fuck. This. Shit.*

I rise to my feet and begin to pack. Ten minutes later, I am done. I've only packed a couple of dresses, underwear, the essentials, and that's it. I am not going to take anything else that...that bastard bought for me. Andy rolls around on the carpet, then springs up to chase a ball of yarn that I had tossed his way earlier. How the hell am I going to carry him, though? Of course, he was given to me by Michael too, but no way, am I going to leave him behind.

There's a knock on the door and before I can call out, it opens. Cassandra walks in carrying a pet carrier with her. She holds it out to me without saying anything.

"He told you, eh?" I swallow back the anger that clogs my throat. Asshole couldn't wait to get me out of his home, apparently. I walk over, grab the pet carrier and place it near Andy who, of course, decides that's the moment he wants to run away. He darts into the bathroom and I blow out a breath.

"I'll get him, while you get dressed," she murmurs.

She walks toward the bathroom and I change into a pair of jeans and a shirt, both of which had appeared in the closet, along with a pair of sneakers. All of these things which Michael had gotten for me, in my size, and without my having to ask for anything. He'd known how much I needed to feel comfortable in those early days of my pregnancy. It was as if he'd read my mind and gleaned exactly how I wanted to be taken care of...without smothering me. And now...

He was getting a blow job from another woman? Fuck. Why the hell did he have to do that? Even if it was all an act... But it wasn't. It had seemed all too fucking real from where I was.

There's another knock on the door. I snarl at the back of my throat. What the hell is this? Paddington station, where everyone comes and goes as they want? The knock comes again and I call out, "Come in."

Adrian opens the door. He glances past me to where Cassandra has stepped back into the room. She falters and the air seems to buzz with some unsaid emotion. I glance between them, am about to speak, then change my mind. Whatever. I have enough of my own shit to deal with.

"Believe you need a ride?" Adrian murmurs.

"Took him no time to alert his cronies to the fact that I am leaving, huh?"

"The chopper is waiting."

I blink. "The chopper? That's how fast he wants me out of here?"

Adrian merely stands there without speaking.

"Not that it matters. And yeah, I'll take the chopper ride. Why not?"

Cassandra walks over to the pet carrier with Andy. She sinks to her knees, coaxes him inside. I get a glimpse of the compartments inside which carry collapsible bowls and food, water, there's even a compartment with kitty litter. Wow, that's one top-of-the-line carrier that Mika has sprung for. How can a man who takes such good care of my pet, also turn out to be so unfaithful? It doesn't make sense.

Cassandra locks the door and rises to her feet, "I'll come with you, until the chopper."

"No, thanks." I reach out and she hands the pet carrier over to me. I grab my bag in my free hand, then pause. I nod to her. "Thanks Cassandra," I murmur, "you've been a good friend."

"I am so sorry, Karma," she whispers, then steps forward and hugs me. Andy mewls and I step away from her.

"Maybe I'll see you at some point, huh?" I turn away, then pause, "Tell Aurora I'll try to reach her once I've figured out what I am going to do next."

She nods and I turn away. I follow Adrian down the corridor, past *his* closed bedroom door, down the steps, out of the house and to the chopper. The helicopter's rotors begin to whir as we approach it. Adrian opens the door, helps me up, then deposits my bag and Andy's pet carrier next to me.

Massimo looks up from the controls, "Where would you like to go?"

# 10

Michael

After she walks away from the door, I wait for a few minutes, just to make sure she's not in hearing range, then I push Larissa away.

She falls back on her ass. "Hey," she protests, "I haven't even started."

"It doesn't matter." I zip up my pants and stand up, move past her and head to the door. I grip the handle, only to stop myself. *Let her go; let her leave.* That's what you wanted, and that's what you are getting. She is leaving you, and it's the only way for her to be safe.

I sense Larissa stand up and move toward me. She places her hand on my shoulder and I shake it off.

"Let her go," she murmurs. "You and I can have a lot more fun together, like we used to. The bitch has no idea how lucky she was to have had you even for a little time. Now that she's gone —"

"Shut up," I turn on her and she stumbles back. "Shut the fuck up."

She pales. "I… I…only meant —"

"Get out," I jerk my chin toward the door, "and make sure she doesn't see you or hear you." She nods, then rushes to the door. I push the door shut, then walk to the bathroom. I glance at myself in the mirror, stare into my reflection. *You asshole. You complete idiot. What have you done?*

I blew any chance of her ever being with me again. I shattered her heart... And so soon after the loss of our child. What is wrong with me? In one swoop, I had broken her trust in me... A trust I'll never be able to rebuild. I've ensured that she'll hate me, and treat me as what I am: her kidnapper, her captor... Her husband, who had cheated on her with another woman.

*"Minchia!"* Only when my fist connects with the mirror do I realize that I have swung at it. The pain slices up my arm as blood drips down and splatters on the sink and down on the floor. I gaze at the fragments of my reflection in the shattered mirror.


An hour later, Seb and Christian arrive with Aurora in tow. When I had finally pulled my head out of my ass, I had called Seb who'd, in turn, contacted Christian, and the two had turned up with her. Christian hands the medical bag over to Aurora and she approaches me. She pulls up a chair, then unrolls the towel I'd wrapped around my hand and grimaces." I'll need to stitch this."

"Do it." I turn my attention to where Christian is positioned by the doorway watching her. She cleans and disinfects the cuts. "This will hurt," She glances up at me. "Do you want an anesthetic to numb the area before I—"

"No," I growl, "just get on with it."

Christian shuffles his feet. I stare at him and he glares back. *Stronzo* seems to have taken a shine to the fair doctor. At least, it seems to have taken his mind off of Xander. Xander...

The band around my chest tightens. The needle digs into my skin and I wince. The doctor peers up at me, and I jerk my chin at her to continue stitching. She firms her jaw, focuses on the stitching once more.

I sense Christian scowling at me, and I arch an eyebrow. He seems like he's about to say something, then firms his lips. He watches as she stitches me up. When she's done with her task, she cuts the last thread. She bandages my right hand, then begins to pack up her things.

"Thank you," I mutter.

"Try and keep it dry, and I am giving you a prescription for antibiotics to prevent any infections." She hands over a sheet of paper, then rises to her feet. "May I speak with Karma before I leave?"

"No," I say in a hard voice, and she blinks.

"No?" She scowls, "Why not?"

"Because she's not here."

"Not here?" She searches my features, "She's recovering from a serious accident, and she's not here? Where did she go? She should be resting, she —"

"*Basta,*" I raise my hand, then turn to Christian, "get her out of here."

"Get me out of here?" She firms her lips, "I am not some piece of luggage that he owns, that you can command him to move me around, you know."

"Not yet," Christian drawls.

She turns on him, "What's that supposed to mean?" She scowls, "If you think you have any claim on me, you are sadly mistaken."

"It's because of me that you and your family are still alive, make no mistake," Christian retorts.

Her face pales. She draws in a breath as he walks over and snatches up her bag, "Let's go, Doc."

She scowls at him, then back at me, "Not until I am sure that Karma is safe."

I glare at her, "She's my wife. Of course, she's safe."

"She's your wife. That's why I am worried about her."

I rise to my feet and she takes a step back. She bumps into Christian, who reaches out to steady her. She pulls away from him, tucks her elbows into her sides and tips up her chin, "What did you do to her?"

"I told you, woman. I didn't do anything to her. She's safe —much safer than she was here."

"What's that supposed to mean?"

I drag my fingers through my hair, "Look, she left for her own good. If she were here, she'd only be a target for our rival clans, or whoever it is that was behind the blast that blew up her car."

She swallows, "You...you think they are going to target her again?"

"I have no doubt they are going to strike again, and as long as she was here with me, she would have been their focus."

"That's why you let her go?"

"I told her to leave because we're done."

"Done?"

"Our marriage is done, over, *finito,* kaput," I slice my hand through the air, "and that is all I am going to say about that particular topic."

She opens her mouth, then shuts it. "How can I reach her?"

"You can't."

"She's my friend. I want to get in touch with her and make sure that she is safe."

"If you reach out to her, you'll only draw attention to where she is. Do you understand that?"

She blows out a breath, then wraps her arms around her waist, "You were wrong to let her go."

*Don't I know it?* I jerk my chin at Christian and he grips her shoulder. "Let's go, Doc," he says, his voice gentle. "As soon as I get any word about her, I'll let you know."

She turns to him, "Promise?"

He nods. Their eyes meet, hold. A flush tinges her cheeks. She pulls away from him, then walks to the door, leaving him staring after her.

Seb snorts, "Go on then. You've been called to heel, *coglione.*"

Christian scowls at him, "Shut the fuck up, *testa di cazzo.*"

Seb laughs and Christian turns to me, "You'd better know what you are doing, brother." With a last glare in Seb's direction, he follows Aurora out.

I drag my fingers through my hair, then wince when a flash of pain slides up my arm. And this is from just a cut. How much pain was she in after what she had been through? Had I been wrong to break up with her in that fashion and send her on her way? It was for her own good, after all.

So why is there a sinking sensation in the pit of my stomach? Why does my chest feel heavy? I'm rubbing the skin above my heart when Seb's phone rings.

He pulls it out, answers it, then turns to me. "We have a suspect."

Half an hour later, I enter the basement that's two stories down in the house. Luca stands facing a man who's been strung up from the ceiling. Antonio walks out to stand guard by the basement door. Purely a precaution, as the staff have been forbidden from coming down here, and the only woman who would have been nosy enough to find her way here is gone.

I clench my fingers at my sides. Fuck, I have to stop thinking about her and get on with the job at hand. The sooner I can track down whoever was behind the explosion, the sooner I can try to earn her forgiveness. Which, given how she'd left me, would be a complete miracle. What a bloody mess.

I roll my shoulders and glare at the man who watches me without any change in expression. He's in his late thirties, well built, dark-haired, and he meets my gaze. Interesting. None of my own men would have the courage to do that, which means he isn't from around here. I walk over to him, pause when I'm a couple of feet away. "You have something to tell me?" I ask.

The man's features harden. He clears his throat, then spits. The glob of saliva narrowly misses me and falls to the ground between us.

"*Figlio di puttana!*" Luca growls as he lunges forward and slams his fist into the man's side. The stranger groans and sways. Luca hits him again and the sound of ribs cracking fills the space. The man gasps, and blood drips from his mouth.

"Enough," I say mildly. "Good to know your anger issues haven't diminished in the time you were away."

Luca steps back and shakes out his hand. "Motherfucker, that hurts like a bitch."

I turn back to the man. "You have something to tell me?"

He glares at me. Sweat pours down his face, and blood blotches stain his shirt. He lowers his chin and firms his lips.

"No?" I pull out my knife and the overhead light bounces off of it. He blinks, lowers his gaze to the knife, then back at me. I close the distance between us, until the smell of his fear envelops me. He glances at Luca, then back at me, but doesn't say a word.

"Last chance before I cut off your ear, or maybe your nose... What do you say? You'll live, but look a lot like Voldemort. That might work for Halloween, but not sure you'd be a hit with the women when you resemble He-Who-Shall-Not-Be-Named, *tu mi capisci?*"

He swallows, glancing around the room again.

"No one's going to save you." I peer into his features, "Start talking or I'll start cutting."

He presses his lips together. I slash the knife down the front of his face and he screams. Blood pours out from the cut on his cheek. His gaze widens until I can see the whites of his eyes.

"Wait," he blubbers, "wait, I'll tell you."

I pause. "I'm listening."

"It was the Kane Company."

"The Kane Company?"

He nods, "I... I owed them. And the man who approached me said if I rigged the car, my debts would be forgiven."

"Who?" I thrust my face into his, "Who asked you to do this? What's his name?"

"I don't know."

"What did he look like?"

"I don't know," the man gasps out, "he...he wore a mask. I couldn't see his features."

"Fuck!" I hold the knife to his neck and he stiffens. "You're not helping me, asshole." I dig the knife into his neck and blood drips from the cut.

He swallows. "Wait," he pleads, "please wait." He licks his lips as he darts his gaze left, then right. I press the knife deeper and he wheezes, "Stop, please." He squeezes his eyes shut, "I have a daughter. I can't leave her orphaned."

"We'll take care of your daughter."

He snaps his eyes open, "Don't you dare touch her."

"Start speaking," I growl. "You have three minutes."

"He was tall, as tall as you, and spoke with a British accent."

"As does half the population of Britain," Luca snarls. "Was he old, young? How did he walk? Any tattoos? Jewelry? Anything that stands out?"

"Wait," he freezes and glances into the distance, "he had a tattoo of a flower that peeked out from under his sleeve."

Seb swears aloud, "Fucking *cani*! I knew it was them. I knew it was a mistake to be working with them."

I hold up my hand and he falls silent. "Are you sure?" I peer into the man's face. "If you are lying...." I let the words hang there.

"I'm not," he beseeches, "I swear on my daughter, I am not."

I nod, then step back, "You do realize, I can't let you go after this though."

"Please," he begins to sob. "Don't do this. I am all my daughter has."

"All I can promise is that she will be taken care of." I hesitate. If I had had a daughter, and if it were me about to die, would I regret the kind of life I had led? Given that I have lived by violence, am I bound to have a violent end? Is this how I would go too? At the hands of an enemy? Worried about my family...my wife and children, and wondering who would take care of them? Is there a way out of this for me? Do I want to leave this life of crime behind?

"Capo?" Seb murmurs and I tip up my chin. I swipe out my hand and bury my knife in the man's chest.

# 11

_____

Karma

"Whiskey, please," the man a few chairs down from me at the bar orders, "Macallan's reserve."

It's the same whiskey that my Capo favors. I glance down at my own drink. A glass of wine. I had arrived yesterday at the Four Seasons, checked in, and slept away most of the day. I'd woken up, only to get myself a quick dinner and feed Andy—who had been provided with his own food and water bowls and a designated litter area in the corner of the vast bath. Guess that's what money can get you. The red carpet treatment, not only for you, but also for your pet.

The man glances around and spots me. His face lights up with interest. His eyes gleam—brown eyes, interested gaze. "Hello, you staying at the hotel too?" He nods toward me, and honestly, he seems all right. Not creepy or anything. Only I'm not in the mood to strike up a conversation with a stranger, and certainly not, in a hotel bar. Not that I am in the mood for speaking with any man right now.

Strike that... Perhaps one man would fit the bill, one alphahole whom I want to strangle; one bastard whom I hate...and love... Damn it, I am still in love with him. Enough to still wear the wedding ring he gave me. The man's gaze lowers to my left hand and his features close.

Good. At least, it's serving some purpose, considering I had come this close to taking it off so many times since I had arrived in London. Massimo had flown me to the Capo's personal private plane in Rome. Initially, I had refused to board it, but he had persuaded me. He'd told me this was the easiest and fastest way to get out of Italy. The 'fastest' part of it had done the trick. Not to mention, the fact that Andy could travel in relative comfort had helped.

Massimo had produced a passport for Andy, and when I had thanked him, he'd said it had been Michael who had seen to it. What the—? Had he been planning this for a while then? Before I could come to grips with that thought, Massimo had handed me a check. Which I had refused... And he'd said, it was only right that I be compensated for what I had been through. That had pissed me off. I mean, could my time and emotions actually have a price put on them?

Then, he had told me not to be stubborn. That I was going to need it to get back on my feet—which was true. He said I could put it toward my fashion designing business, to think of it as seed capital, and a loan which I could return to the Capo when I was up and running.

In all honesty, I had wanted to refuse it. I didn't want anything to do with my husband's money, but Massimo had been insistent. He'd told me to accept it, that I owed it to myself. After all, I had lost time, which I would have used to grow my business, and this was compensation for that.

Well, the £100,000 check was much more than what I would have made in the past month if I had focused on growing my business. But I had decided not to argue that point. Instead, I had torn up the check He hadn't been very surprised, which had surprised me, until he'd said that Michael had warned him that this would be the probable response.

He'd pulled out an envelope stuffed with money. I had stared at it, and he had insisted I take it. When I'd refused, he'd simply said that I'd need it to feed Andy, if nothing else. And of course, he'd been right.

I'd wondered, then, if this was the reason that Michael had given Andy to me… As a means of manipulating me… But it couldn't be that, could it? Still, he'd made sense, so I'd accepted the cash… Also, I had run out of energy by then, wanting nothing more than to grab a drink—at least, I can drink now, so that's a silver lining, eh? —and crawl into some dark corner where I wouldn't have to think or do much.

Then Massimo had sprung the third surprise. He'd said there would be a car waiting for me in London and that it would take me to a flat where I could live until I found one of my own. That… I had vehemently refused. No way, was I going to stay in a place owned by my husband. Not after what he'd done to me. Asshole.

If he thinks he can still try to control my life…even when he's not in it, he has another think coming. Why would he do that anyway, though? He's the one who wanted me out of his life, so why is he now concerned about me, huh?

I had been firm on that point and Massimo had finally given up. He'd left and I had boarded the plane. I'd turned down the prosecco the stewardess had brought me, and instead, turned to vodka… It had seemed like a drink I could drown myself in. I had managed to down a couple, then taken a brief nap on the short flight to London, where I had disembarked and walked out of the airport…

And that's when the enormity of what I had done…of what lay ahead of me had hit me. I'd wondered, then, if I should have accepted that offer of a car ride and an apartment to rent, but no… I'd made the right choice. If I had ended up in an apartment that he owned, then I would have never been able to meet my own gaze in the mirror again, if I'm being honest.

Which is how I'd come to stay at the Four Seasons. I'd woken up this morning and spent the day finding a flat for myself and Andy. I could have phoned my sister and gone over and met her… Only, I'm not ready.

Damn it. At some point, I am going to have to call her... But not today. I still need some time to come to grips with everything that happened. Also, in all honesty, I can't bear to tell her that I've been married, lost a child, and separated from my husband, all in the matter of a month.

I swallow down another sip of wine, ignore the man who's still glancing at me from the corner of his eye. Maybe it had been a bad choice to come down to the bar on my own, but I couldn't stay in the room for another night on my own. Good thing I am moving out the day after Christmas though. I had managed to not only find a flat, but with the money I had accepted from Massimo, I had also paid an advance to secure the place for the next three months. At least, it gives me enough time to figure out what I want to do next, you know?

I place my half-filled drink on the bar counter, then leave. I take the elevator up to my room and use my keycard to open the door. Andy greets me with a loud purring. I sink down to my knees to pet him, and that's when my phone rings.

# 12

Karma

"Aurora?" I stare at the woman whose face appears on the screen.

"Karma!" She smiles. "How are you? Where are you?"

"I'm in London."

"London?" She frowns. "What are you doing there?"

"This is my home, you know?" I retort. "More to the point, how did you get to a phone?"

"Ah," she glances to the side, then back at me, "the phone is Christian's."

"Christian's, huh?" I tilt my head, "Are you and he—"

"No," she says, horrified, "of course, not. He, ah, came by to check how I was doing—"

"Did he now?" I smirk.

She scowls. "It's not like that. He just wants to be sure I don't escape or anything. He's responsible for me."

"Responsible for you?"

"I mean, he's taken charge of me. I mean…" She throws up her hands, "You're twisting my words all around the wrong way, and I wasn't calling about me, I was calling to find out how you are."

"I am fine," I sink down onto a chair near the window and Andy jumps onto my lap. He meows, I pat him, and he stretches up to try and peer into the phone. Funny cat. He purrs at the screen.

Aurora laughs. "Hey, Andy," she calls to him, and he blinks at the screen. "Whatcha doin', boy?" she coos.

I blink, "I thought you'd speak to him in Italian."

"Well, he's your cat," she pushes out her chin in a very Italian gesture, "so I see him as English."

Andy yawns, then leaps down onto the floor and flounces away.

"Guess he isn't impressed by our discussion," Aurora chuckles.

"At least, he travelled well. I thought he'd have trouble on the flight, but nope. We strapped his pet carrier to a seat for takeoff and landing and he was fine. He's also not had any problem adjusting to his new surroundings."

"And you?" She peruses my features, "How are you?"

"Honestly, I don't know." I rise to my feet and begin to pace. "I am still trying to adjust to everything."

"Hold on," she murmurs. "Don't say anything more until I dial in Cassandra."

"Cassandra?" I frown. "How did you—" Before I can complete my statement, Cassandra pops up in a window on the screen.

"Karma," Cassandra exclaims, "how are you?"

"Not too bad," I raise a shoulder. "Are you at the house?" *Is he there?* That's what I want to ask, but I don't.

"He's not here," she says softly.

"Who?" I arch an eyebrow.

"You know who I am talking about."

"If you mean the man who cheated on me—"

"Cheated on you?" Aurora bursts out. "No, really?"

"Yeah," I hunch my shoulders. "I walked in on him with another woman, and they were… Let's just say, they were quite intimate."

"Oh, Karma," Aurora cries, "I am so sorry."

"Yeah, well," I flick my hair over my shoulder, "what can I say? Guess I overestimated him, eh?"

"You sure he cheated on you?" Cassandra frowns. "The Capo is not the kind of man who takes his promises lightly."

"Yeah, well... In this case, he broke his vows, all right."

"Are you sure?"

"I was there, remember?" I scowl.

"Maybe you were mistaken?" Cassandra posits. "Maybe it's not what it seems?"

"You don't think I've been trying to convince myself of that? But not only was he engaged in the action of getting his dick sucked, but when I confronted him, he told me to leave."

"Oh, Karma," Cassandra bites her lips, "I am so sorry. I wish things had worked out differently."

"Yeah, me too." I roll my shoulders. "But enough about me. What are the two of you up to?" I turn to Aurora, "When are you going to tell Christian that you have a thing for him?"

"I don't have a thing for him."

"Ha, if the sparks between the two of you were any hotter, you'd set the room on fire," Cassandra laughs.

"And you, girl," I narrow my gaze on her, "you and Adrian."

"Wha—" She opens and shuts her mouth, "Me and Adrian, what?"

"There's something there." I waggle my eyebrows.

"But—"

"Don't bother denying it, missy, I've seen how he follows you with his gaze when he thinks no one is looking, and how you steal glances at him on the sly."

"I don't steal glances at him," she protests.

"Oh, yeah, you do." Aurora laughs, "I noticed it too."

"Right?" I crow, before redirecting my attention toward Aurora. "So, when are the two of you getting on and doing something about it?"

"Somehow I don't think that's a good idea, considering I am still the captive of the Mafia."

"Some captive," Cassandra says with a wicked gleam in her eyes. "From what I've seen, you are getting the royal treatment. You have Christian hovering around you. Any excuse he has to come see you, he takes it. If ever there is a need for a doctor, and given these Mafia guys are constantly involved in some scrap or the other, there is a need a lot of times... Guess who volunteers to go get you?"

"Suppose there's something to be said for having a doctor in the house huh?"

"I'm sure it's very convenient for them," Aurora huffs. "Guess it suits them to have me locked up in here."

"You don't seem to be too put out by it, you know?" I observe.

"What am I going to do, protest?" She scoffs, "Like that will do any good. At least, I know that my family is taken care of."

"How can you be sure of that?"

"It's an unspoken promise among the Cosa Nostra," Cassandra explains. "If one of us is injured or dies in the line of duty, so to speak, then the family is taken care of."

"Huh," I blink, "I didn't know that."

"The Cosa Nostra takes care of their own," Aurora says in a soft tone.

"Their influence within the city and the community is all pervasive. They are linked into the police, the judiciary, and with the heads of Fortune 500 companies." Cassandra begins to pace the room she is in. "And of course, they rule the underworld. It's why, if you have a problem with anything, you go to them."

"With anything?" I frown. "What do you mean, anything?"

"Meaning, *anything*." Cassandra raises a shoulder, "If you have a problem with your husband cheating on you, you go to the Cosa Nostra. If you have a problem with your business being in debt, you go to them. If you have a problem with the plumbing in your house, you go to them. Hell, if you have a problem with dog shit littering your street, you go to —"

"—them," I finish her statement. "Though I don't understand why. I mean, it seems so archaic. Like you guys live in some kind of feudal country."

"We do, for all intents and purposes." She laughs. "Remember, this is the country whose prime minister, at one point, owned the biggest media company in the country, effectively controlling the media itself, and who was responsible for some of the worst scandals we have seen."

"And the only organization who could stand up to him was—"

"—the Cosa Nostra?"

She nods.

"Thanks for the history lesson," I lower my chin to my chest. "Still…not sure where I fit in with all of this."

"You are one of us, Karma," Aurora states. "You are married to the Capo of the Cosa Nostra."

"The most-wanted man, internationally."

"What…what?" I gape. "I mean, I know he is not on the right side of the law…He is a…"

"Criminal?" Cassandra suggests.

"Most people would call him that, but here in this country, he is…second, only to the Don, in terms of the sway he holds over most people's lives." Aurora seems to carefully watch my reaction.

"You make him sound like God or something." I laugh nervously.

"Close." Aurora nods.

"Jeez, if I had known all this before-hand—"

"—you wouldn't have married him?"

"Not like I actually had a choice." I drag my fingers through my hair, "You girls have given me a lot to think about."

"Don't tell me you didn't realize all of this already, Karma?" Cassandra peers at me through the screen.

"I guess, I was aware subconsciously, but honestly, to hear it from the two of you… Well, it kind of makes a bigger impact on me."

"You okay?" Cassandra half smiles. "Hope we didn't scare you with the conversation. We only wanted to make sure that you were okay."

"I will be," I say with more confidence than I feel.

"Stay in touch, eh?" Aurora smiles at me, "Let us know what you plan to do next."

"I will, as soon as I figure things out myself."

We hang up and I walk over to the window and gaze down at the garden. What the hell am I doing here? Am I really going to have to spend Christmas Eve on my own? I ponder my options, then mind made up, I head out of the room.

# 13

Michael

I glance at the sea in the distance. Clouds are rolling in, which is not unusual for late December. It's the day before Christmas and I am on my own. Not for long, as my brothers are going to arrive soon, as will Nonna.

My Beauty may have left me, but the party she organized to celebrate Xander will go on. It feels only right to do so, considering she made all of the arrangements. I have to believe she'd have wanted it to go on even though she is not here with me. Hell, I want the event to take place so I can feel close to her. So I can finally try to put what happened to Xander behind me... Not that I will ever be able to make peace with it. But mulling over it is self-defeating. I need to function at peak efficiency, to focus all of my efforts at taking down the Kane Company.

Bastards are clever. Have to be careful in how I trap them and rein them in so I can have my revenge. Right after the Christmas event today.

Do criminals take time off for Christmas too? I never have before, but this time…just for her…because she'd have wanted me to if she were here… For Beauty, I'll be present. For Xander, I'll be there to celebrate his life.

I raise the glass of whiskey and sip from it. This is bullshit. Me on my own here. My wife in London. My brother dead… Not to mention, the child I never had, the one whose absence I feel more keenly than before. Is it possible to miss something that you never had? The notion of a family, of a child I'd hoped to hold in my arms. Maybe I had counted on it more than I had realized. Maybe, I had already foreseen a future for us. Maybe I had just not acknowledged it, and it took the lack of a child, the lack of *her* in my life, to bring it all to the fore. Pain shoots up my arm and I glance down. The skin over my knuckles is white and I force myself to loosen my grip. I bring the glass up to my lips, drain it and turn; just as Massimo walks onto the terrace.

"*Fratellone,*" he jerks his chin.

"How is she?" I snap.

"She?"

"You know who I am talking about."

"The last I saw of her, she was pissed at you. I don't think that has changed."

I scowl, "Not asking your opinion on her state of mind. I mean, how is she physically? Is she safe?"

"As safe as she can be in a five-star hotel."

"And there are guards posted around her, day and night?"

"There are people who have her in their line of sight, twenty-four-seven. If they move any closer, she'll trip over them."

"Good."

He stares at me steadily and I glare at him, "What?"

"Are you sure this is a good idea?"

"Like I said, not asking your opinion," I snap.

"I am going to give it to you anyway."

"Of course, you are."

"Not sure why you think it's a good idea to pretend to break up with her, but—"

"Nothing pretend about it," I insist.

He laughs. The *testa di cazzo* laughs.

"*Vaffanculo,*" I glower at him.

He raises his hands, "So you broke up with her, sent her on her way, and now you have people watching her. I fail to understand the logic in this."

"The logic in what?" Seb walks in and glances down at my whiskey. "You need a refill."

I hand the glass over to him and he stalks over to the bar. He snatches up a few more glasses, then proceeds to fill them up.

He walks over, hands a glass to Massimo and one to me. "*Salute,*" he clinks the glass with both of ours. "What were you talking about?" he asks.

"Just how the Capo is tying himself up in knots." Massimo smirks.

"He hasn't been the same since he fell in love."

"Love," Massimo shakes his head, "it's been known to gut the fiercest of people. You'd have thought *il nostro fratellone,* here, stood a chance, eh? Considering he's, on the face of it, at least, the toughest of all of us."

"You know what they say, the stronger they are…the harder they fall." Seb chuckles.

Massimo rises his glass, "I'll drink to that."

"*Che cazzo!*" I glare at the two of them, "Since when did my love life —"

"Or the lack thereof," Massimo points out.

"What-fucking-ever. Same thing —"

"Not." Seb shakes his head. He turns to Massimo, "Ever known the Capo to be this short of words."

"Never," Massimo laments.

"He'd best get used to this state of affairs, eh?"

"*Basta,*" I growl. "Shut the fuck up, you two."

"You losing your temper again?" Adrian stalks in, heads straight for the bar. He bypasses the already poured glass of whiskey, leans over and grabs a Macallan thirty-year-old. He hefts it onto the counter and proceeds to open it.

"Thanks for checking in with me." I try to infuse sarcasm into my voice and fail. *Merda.* I am growing soft, all right. Or maybe not, considering I killed a man in cold blood yesterday. I'd hesitated, though, which had been a first for me. And now, I am unable to muster enough anger at my brothers and stepbrothers as they swarm all over my expensive liquor. I drain my glass and hold it out. Massimo grabs it from me, walks over to the bar and places it on the counter. Adrian opens the bottle and tops me up, then Massimo's glass, then his own. He pours liquor into three more glasses, then pauses.

I stare at the glasses. So do Massimo and Seb.

Christian walks onto the terrace. He bumps into the back of a chair, "Oops!" he apologizes to no one in particular, then weaves over to the bar. He snatches up a glass of whiskey and sniffs it. "This is *eccezionale.*" He tosses it back, then slams the glass onto the counter. "Top me up," he commands Adrian, who hesitates.

"Come on, *brother.*" Christian hiccups, "It's Christmas after all, and you know this is Xander's favorite festival. Even though the man's grown up, you'd think he was a kid the way he looks forward to the festive season. It feeds his creativity, he says, and—" Christian's voice tapers off. "Fuck," he growls, "fuck, fuck, fuck." He grabs the bottle from Adrian, tops up his own glass. That's when he spots the two other glasses. He freezes, then spinning around, carries the bottle and glass with him to a table in the far corner. He slaps them both on the table, before pulling out a pack of cigarettes. He lights one, blows out smoke.

"When did you start smoking?" I scowl.

"Don't nag, *fratellone,*" he takes another puff of his cigarette.

That's when Luca enters the terrace. He glances between us, his gaze cautious. "I assume I have been invited to this?"

I nod my head at the same time that Christian growls, "Get the fuck out of here. You don't deserve to be here, *faccia di merda.*"

Luca doesn't respond. He marches over to the bar, snatches up the glass of whiskey. That's when he notices the last glass that's topped to the rim with the amber fluid.

He pales. "Fuck," he growls as he keeps his gaze focused on the glass.

I stalk over to stand next to him. Seb prowls over to flank me on the other side, with Massimo next to him. Adrian falls in line next to him. Christian draws in a breath. He stabs out his cigarette on the bar counter, stumbles across the terrace, and comes to a halt next to Seb. Christian sways; Seb steadies him, but Christian pulls free. He fixes his gaze on that full glass on the counter.

For a few seconds, all of us stare at the glass, then I raise mine. "To Xander." I swallow down the ball of emotion in my throat. "Rest in peace, brother."

"To Xander." Seb raises his glass, "I'll miss your easygoing nature, little brother."

"And your humor," Massimo jerks his chin, "not that I understood all of your jokes."

The rest of us chuckle.

"You were way too much of a nerd... But I'll still miss the jokes that I did not understand." Massimo's lips kick up in the semblance of a smile.

"I'll miss how you always made everyone feel like you were giving them your complete attention. You actually cared for others..." Adrian draws in a breath, "unlike the rest of us reprobates, who swear by violence; you were the good one among us."

Luca goes still. He seems like he's about to say something, then shakes his head. "I'm sorry," he squeezes his eyes shut, "I am so sorry. You had the best of us all—the most goodness, the most talent, the most warmth... It should have been me, not you, *fratellino*."

"It should have," Christian says through gritted teeth. "Why don't you fuck off and off yourself, eh? Why don't you leave and never return, you *testa di cazzo!*"

"Christian," I growl.

"Don't tell me you don't agree." The skin across his knuckles whitens as he squeezes his fingers around the glass. "This asshole, here, is responsible for your child being killed. I'm sure you've thought of that."

"Christian," I snap. "Shut the fuck up."

"I am only saying what everyone is thinking," he growls. "This asshole is responsible for everything that happened. If he hadn't helped Karma leave, she'd still be here and so would your child, and Xander would not be lying in a coffin six feet under and—" he draws in a breath and his features seem to crumple. He manages to get a hold of himself, only for a tear to run down his cheek. "F-u-c-k," he cries, "fuck, this shit." He tosses his drink back, turns to leave, but Luca grabs his shoulder.

"I am sorry, brother. I really am sorry for what I did. I swear, I had no idea it would turn out like this."

"Didn't you?" Christian tries to pull away but Luca doesn't let go.

"I really didn't. I messed things up, I know that, but I am here now, aren't I? I am going to help you guys take revenge on the Kane Company. This, I promise."

"Fuck that." Christian swings, Luca ducks, and Christian's glass crashes to the floor as Luca wraps his arms around him. "Let the fuck go of me, man."

"No," Luca says in a hard voice, "This family has been fractured enough. The rest of us need to stick together now. It's the only way we are going to survive."

"And what if I don't want to survive?" Christian glares at him, "What if I don't want to go on living? What if I—"

Luca slaps his face.

"What the—!" Christian gapes. "How dare you?" He tries to headbutt Luca, whose still-full glass hits the floor and rolls away.

Luca wraps his arms around Christian and holds him immobile. "How dare you talk about dying, you asshole? If anything, Xander's death should have taught you how lucky you are; how lucky we all are to be alive. We love you, Christian, don't you get that?"

"Yeah," Adrian, nods. He moves around, throws his arms around the both of them. "We need you with us, bro."

"Totally," Seb walks over to them and hugs the lot of them.

Massimo heaves a sigh, "Can't believe I am going to do this," He tosses back his drink, glances around for somewhere to place it. Then, still clutching the glass in his gigantic hand, he closes the distance to them, and enfolds his big arms around the group.

He glares at me over the heads of our brothers. I glance away, stalk over to the bar and place the glass on the counter. I draw in a breath, square my shoulders, then turn and prowl over to the group where I wrap my arms around all of them.

For a few seconds we stay that way, then Christian grumbles, "Enough of this emo shit."

Instantly, I step back. So does Massimo, then Adrian, Seb, and Luca.

Christian rubs the back of his neck. "I need another fucking drink."

"And I," I roll my shoulders "have something I need to do."

# 14

Karma

I stand at a distance from the penthouse, not far from Tower Bridge in London. The place belongs to Dr. Weston Kincaid, one of the Seven, as they like to call themselves. Seven billionaires who co-own 7A, one of the leading financial companies in the country. Weston is a friend of Sinclair Sterling, another of the Seven. Sinclair is married to my sister Summer. The one whose wedding I had attended before I had run into my Capo.

I had gone to Summer and Sinclair's townhouse on Primrose Hill, just as they had been leaving the house. I had grabbed a taxi and followed them here. I had jumped out of the cab and walked toward them as they had left their car and approached the entrance of the building. They had paused halfway and Sinclair had hauled my sister close to him and kissed her... Okay, he had practically devoured her face, if you want to know the truth. The heat between them had been palpable enough that my face had reddened. My toes had curled, and gah! That's wrong. This is my sister and brother-in-law, for chrissakes! Still, the way they had been going at it, in the open... It had reminded me of how it was with my Capo... My cheating Capo—*the asshole who'd decided to have his dick sucked by another woman, making sure that you'd see it, remember?*

Ahead, Sinclair had finally released Summer, who'd laughed. She'd reached up and rubbed the lipstick off of his mouth. "Your friends are going to know what we have been up to."

"Like I bloody care?" Sinclair had snorted. "Honestly, I'd rather have stayed home with you, but I couldn't pass up the opportunity to surprise the twat, Weston in his love nest."

That's when I'd realized where they were going.

"You'd have hated it if they had done the same to us." She'd giggled.

"All the more reason to spring the surprise on him." He'd smirked.

Another car had driven up, and that's when I had fallen back. I had darted away behind a parked van. Then peeked around it in time to see Saint, another of the Seven, get out of the driver's seat. He'd walked around to open the door to the passenger's side and Victoria had gotten out. Huh? I guess Victoria is with Saint now? What else have I missed in the time that I have been away?

Clearly, the entire group is converging at Weston's. Of course, they are. It's Christmas, right? They want to be together to celebrate.

I'd peeked around the side of the van again and seen Summer moving forward to greet Victoria with a kiss. Guess my sister has found her tribe. Her people. Her husband...

And me? Shit, I'd had it all...and lost it... I flatten my palm against my stomach and tears slide down my cheeks. I have to stop breaking down at the least provocation. I can't go through life always thinking of what I could have had. I need to focus on the now, on what I still have. Myself... My health... And I still have my new friends, Aurora and Cassandra...who know what I have been through. And I have Andy, of course.

I wipe away my tears, glance around the van just as another car draws up. Jace and his wife Sienna, both friends of Sinclair, step out.

Then Jace reaches into the back seat, and a few minutes later, emerges with a baby carrier.

The group exchanges greetings, the women kiss, they coo over the baby, then all of them enter the building. I take a step forward, then stop. If I go in there now, I'll have to confront all of them, and honestly, that's the last thing I want to do right now. Guess I'll just have to find another time.

I hunch my shoulders, turn away and begin walking down the road. The hair on the back of my neck rises. I glance around. What the hell caused that feeling? Am I being watched? I look up and down the road. The sensation fades and I start walking again. I reach the end of the road, glance around for a cab, but can't see any. I hear a noise behind me and stiffen. My heart begins to race; my pulse pounds at my temples. Shit, where's a taxi when you need it, eh? I increase my speed and head for the tube station that I remember passing on my way here. Footsteps sound behind me, and I break into a run. I race down the street, turn another corner and see the entrance to the tube station ahead. Thank god! My breath comes in huffs as I run toward it. I am almost there when someone grabs my shoulder.

"No," I yell as I try to pull free, "let me go. Now!"

"Beauty?"

"No, no, no," I struggle wildly, "don't fucking come near me."

"Language, Beauty."

I blink, then pause. I am turned around and find myself staring at a broad chest, clad in a plain white T-shirt that outlines the sculpted planes. A black jacket that has seen better days clings to his broad shoulders. The dark, masculine scent that could only belong to one man envelops my senses. I swallow, refuse to look up. He notches his knuckles under my chin and applies pressure. I tilt my chin up and meet his cold blue gaze.

"You?" I whisper. "What are you doing here?"

"I came to see you."

"No," I try to pull away, but his grip tightens. "You told me to leave, remember?"

"And I came after you."

"You cheated on me."

He shakes his head, "I only pretended to."

"A likely story," I snap. "I was there, buster. I saw you, remember?"

"You thought you saw her going down on me—" I wince and his jaw hardens. "The mind can play tricks on you, so you think you see what you expect to see."

"Your pants were unzipped."

"I had my boxers on."

"I saw her bob her head."

"Larissa's a good actress."

"Larissa!" I spit out. "That woman again? You let her touch you? You let her put her hands on you again?"

He frowns, "She doesn't mean anything to me."

"You wrapped her hair around your fingers and pretended you enjoyed what she was doing to you."

"I did what I thought was right."

"Well, this is me doing what I think is right, too." I try to knee him in the groin but he swerves. My knee brushes against his hard thigh instead and I stumble. His grip tightens. He pulls me toward him so I fall against his chest.

"Listen to me, Beauty," he growls.

"Don't call me that you...you asshole."

"Beauty," his voice lowers to a hush, "just give me a chance to explain."

"No."

"I had a reason for what I did."

"Nothing you say can justify what you did to me."

"I did it to save your life."

"Ha!" I scoff, "That's how men justify getting away with dipping their dicks in other vaginas."

"The only vagina I want to dip my dick in is yours."

"I don't believe you."

"How can I make you believe it?"

"You can't."

"I can, and I will." He hauls me to him and my breasts flatten against his chest. "I sent you away because I needed the word to spread that we had separated."

"Uh-huh, sure." I turn my head so I don't have to gaze into his eyes. If I do, I'll be lost. Asshole will use his charm, his ability to influence me to get me to do what he wants.

"Don't you see? After what happened, after almost losing you... And our child. After losing my brother, I couldn't...risk anything else happening to you."

My pulse rate ratchets up and my ribcage tightens. I try to draw in a breath and my throat burns. My head spins and flickers of black dot the edges of my vision. To think, I went through the car blast and the surgery without it coming to light, only for my heart to act up now. Of course, no-one in Italy had access to my medical records, and unless I had revealed it, the doctors would not have had any way to know. Still... This is so not the time for my ailment to make itself known. Sweat beads my forehead and a black hole opens up where my heart should be.

"What's wrong?" He scowls down at me, "What's happening, Beauty?"

I shake my head, try to regulate my breathing. In-out-in, I will my heartbeat to slow down, for my pulse to stop hammering in my wrists.

"Karma?" He cups my face and turns me to face him, "Talk to me, baby. Are you okay?"

"Y...yes," I cough.

His features pale. "*Cazzo*, you're definitely not okay."

I sway and he makes an angry noise at the back of his throat. He scoops me up in his arms and I slap my hand against his shoulder.

"Put me down."

"No." He turns, walks back the way we came.

"Where are you going?" I glance up the street. "Why are you going this way?"

"I am taking you to my car." He walks faster.

At least, we are not on the same street as Weston's penthouse. So, there's less of a chance of running into my sister or any of the Seven. He reaches a black Maserati—of course, it's a Maserati that he's driving, even in London—and unlocks it. He opens the passenger door, slides me onto the seat, then leans over me. He buckles my seatbelt and his big body dwarfs mine for a few seconds. The scent of him intensifies, my core clenches, and my mouth waters. Then he moves back and I sag against the seat. I wipe my damp palms on my thighs and try to fight the weakness that grips my limbs. I draw in another deep breath and my nostrils flood with the dark, edgy scent that is so very Mika. My toes curl, even as my heart refuses to let up its relentless hammering. Shit, shit, shit. Even stuck in the middle of these heart palpitations, I can't stop myself from being aroused.

Apparently, being away from him has only made the yearning I feel for him so much worse. He walks around to take his place behind the wheel. He starts the car, eases it onto the road. There's silence as he drives forward.

I close my eyes, focus on my breathing, on willing my muscles to relax, on bringing the trembling in my arms and legs under control. My body slowly responds, and by the time I feel like myself again, a good ten minutes must have passed. I finally open my eyes, take in the familiar surroundings of Park Lane. "Where are you going?" I turn to him.

"To your hotel."

"To my hotel?" I frown. "You know where I am staying?" I shake my head, "Of course, you know where I am staying."

We don't speak for a few more seconds, then I burst out, "Why did you come after me, Michael?"

"Because I had to."

"Bullshit," I wrap my arms around my waist, "you asked me to leave, then not even forty-eight hours pass, and you turn up after me." I rake my fingers though my hair, "I mean, this is just...crazy."

"What is?"

"This entire, elaborate, set-up—you breaking up with me—"

"Pretending to break up with you."

"Then putting me on your plane and getting me out of there, only to follow me."

"I hadn't intended to come," he says in a low voice, "but I couldn't help myself."

"Gee, thanks," I murmur.

"That was a compliment," a thread of humor runs through his words.

I shoot him a sideways glance, "I still don't believe that you fabricated that entire scene."

"Sure, you do."

"Eh?" I turn to him, "Care to explain yourself?"

"In your heart of hearts, you knew that I wasn't capable of cheating on you."

I scoff, "I am not a mind reader."

"You know me Beauty. You know how much I care for you."

"If you did, you would have taken me into your confidence and explained your plans. But you didn't."

He stays quiet.

"If you did actually consider me your wife—"

"Which I do."

"If you considered me your partner, you'd treat me as your equal. You'd share your plans with me...not... Pull that stupid shit like you did...where you upset me so much that I leave you."

"I needed it to look authentic."

"To whom? The only people there were you, me and..."

He nods.

"Oh," I blink rapidly. "OH! You mean Larissa... She..."

"Is enough of a gossip that, by now, all of Palermo knows that my wife has left me."

I think for a minute. "But if you were pretending, she knows that too."

"As far as she knows, I just wanted her to pretend so that you would leave. I implied there might be room for her after you were gone, but..." he shrugs.

"Hmmm. Do they know that you've come after me?"

He shoots me a glance and I raise my hands. "Hey, I'm only asking. I mean, you took the plane—"

"A private plane."

"Landed in London, and now you are driving around in this Maserati—"

"I cleared immigration through a private channel, whose agents are sworn to secrecy, and do you know how many Maseratis are in London?"

I shake my head.

"Let's just say that, while it's not my favorite city, god knows the Brits are too uptight for me, still, one advantage of being here is that it's difficult to track anyone."

"Yeah, but you with your bodyguard and your brothers... You guys draw attention wherever you go..." my voice trails off. "So, you ditched your bodyguard?"

He nods.

"Do your brothers know where you are?"

He doesn't answer.

"So, they don't know you are here, either?"

He continues to focus on the road and I turn on him, "Michael, is that wise? You here on your own, without any security?"

"You worried about me?"

I snort, "Not that you can't take care of yourself, but I am told that you are an international fugitive, so..."

He shoots me a glance, "How did you find out about that?"

When I stay quiet, he frowns, "Who have you been talking to?"

"No one."

"You're not a good liar." He scowls as he navigates the road, "Was it one of the women? Cassandra? Did she tell you?"

"You leave her out of this, okay?"

He glances at me again, "I am not going to hurt her. You know that, right?"

"I don't know much about you at all, Michael."

He smirks, and my cheeks heat. "I mean, I know you in *that* way... But as for how your mind works or what motivates you... Well, I am only slowly coming to grips with that."

"I'd rather come to grips with you."

"If you think you can simply barge back into my life and into my bed, think again."

His features soften, "I wasn't planning on that, Karma. I merely wanted to see you. It's Christmas, and I missed my wife. I wanted to be with you."

"So, you hopped a flight—"

"I flew the plane."

"Of course, you did." I resist the urge to roll my eyes. Is there anything this man can't do? "You flew the plane, and tracked me down—Shit!" I slap my forehead, "The stupid tracker. Of course, you tracked me down. You knew exactly where I was all this time."

He doesn't reply.

Damn it… Somehow, the fact that he had tagged me, so all he had to do was literally look at a screen and find me… Makes everything somewhat less than what it should be.

"What are you thinking?" he asks softly.

When I don't reply, he shoots me a sideways glance, "I know you hate the fact that I could find you so easily…"

I don't reply and his jaw tics. A pulse flares to life at his temple and he seems like he's about to slam on the brakes and tell me off, but he doesn't. Instead, he turns the corner and the hotel looms in front of us. He eases into a slot at the entrance, then shuts off the engine. He reaches behind his seat, grabs a duffel bag, then gets out. He slings the bag across his chest, then walks around, to open my door. I slide out, then brush past him and head for the hotel entrance. Behind me, I hear him speaking to the valet who agrees to park the car and deposit the key with the concierge.

We enter the elevator, and damn him, but his size dwarfs the space. "If you think you are staying the night, you have another think coming."

"Ask me to stay," he growls.

"That's never happening." I swipe my hair over my shoulder. "What's with the get up anyway?"

"Get up?"

"The jeans and jacket and boots thingy you have happening?"

He glances down at himself, then back at me. "What's wrong with it?"

"Nothing's wrong with it." It's perfect, actually. That entire mussed-up, sexy look he has going on is bloody hot. It makes me want to throw myself at him and wrap my legs around his waist. "If you think that's going to help you blend in with the crowds, you thought wrong."

"I was trying to dress down, yes," he raises a shoulder, "was trying for a casual look, I suppose."

Only, he'd never blend into a crowd. Hell, my Capo will always stand head and shoulders above anyone else. He'll always command attention, always suck up the oxygen in any room that he walks into. He'll always be a leader, and no matter how much he tries to disguise that part of himself, it won't work.

"Next time, don't try so hard," I drawl.

"Next time, don't lie."

"Ha," I snort, "I am not lying.

"You are."

I shrug, turn away, and he makes a sound deep in his throat. "Don't look away when I am talking to you," he snaps.

"A-n-d there he is." I throw up my hands, "If you think you going all macho on me is supposed to make me all hot and bothered, you are wrong."

He closes the distance between us so quickly that I yelp. He backs me up into the wall, then slaps his hand on the stop button. The elevator jolts to a halt and I gasp.

"Wh...what are you doing?" I squeak.

"You may deny that you still have feelings for me, but your body says otherwise."

"It...it... Doesn't."

"Oh?" His lips twist and my pussy spasms. He thrusts his face into mine, holds my gaze as he raises his hand and pushes away a lock of hair that has fallen over my eyebrow. I shudder and his mouth curves. The tenderness in his touch is so at odds with how intense his gaze is that moisture laces my panties. His nostrils flare, and I swear, the man knows exactly how turned on I am. He drags his finger down the side of my throat and I shiver. He reaches my breast, circles one taut nipple. The hair on my forearms rises. He continues the journey until he reaches the waistband of my jeans. A moan bleeds from me. He slides his hand between my legs and cups my pussy. "If I cram my fingers inside your pussy, will I find you wet and needy and aching for my cock, Beauty?"

Yes.

*Yes.*

"No," I shake my head.

He laughs. "Liar."

He stays there, holding my gaze, the heat from his large palm sinking through the crotch of my jeans, through my panties. My belly clenches and the flesh between my thighs throbs, yearns...for more, so much more. I jerk my pelvis forward, wanting to feel him squeeze my throbbing core, and his smile becomes a full-blown grin.

"I rest my case." He raises his hand as he pushes his face into mine, his mouth positioned just over mine, his eyelashes entangled with mine, and I pant. *Please, please, please.* I close my eyelids. The next moment, the heat of his body moves away, and the elevator jerks as it starts its journey upward. I snap my eyes open to find him leaning against the opposite wall.

"Asshole," I say in a low voice.

"That's alphahole to you, darling wife." He smirks, and goddam him, why does he have to look so goddam hot when he's being all antagonistic to me? I open my mouth to tell him off, and that's when the elevator dings. The door opens and he beckons me to exit first.

*Jerk.*

I exit the elevator and he follows me to my room. I open the door, and with a loud meow, Andy immediately brushes past me.

"Hey, cat!"

I sense him bend down to pick up Andy. By the time I drop my keys on the table and turn, he has Andy nestled against his chest. The cat purrs and snuggles in. Lucky cat. I frown as he pets the animal, then carries him inside the suite. He glances around the large space, then walks over to Andy's basket. He places the cat down and Andy settles in. Michael straightens, then stretches. The jacket pulls across his shoulders as he raises his arms above his head. His T-shirt lifts and I catch a glimpse of that flat stomach. It would be rock hard, if I touched his belly. I wouldn't be able to make out an ounce of fat. And if I touched the space between his legs, that part would be even harder. And long and thick and fat and—

"Beauty?"

"Eh?" I glance up in time to see him smirk. "What?" I scowl, "What is it?"

"Can I use your bath? I'd like a shower."

"A shower?" I ask with suspicion, "You want to take a shower?"

"I've been on the road for more than half a day; I just wanted to freshen up."

"Hmph," I purse my lips and he holds up his hand.

"Just a shower; that's all."

"No hanky-panky from you, okay?"

"Hanky-panky?" He chuckles, "You're adorable, you know that?"

"Whatever," I huff, "go take your shower, but be quick about it."

"Will you come in and check in on me if I am gone too long?"

"Of course, not." I scowl, "See? This is what I mean. No innuen-dos, no sexy smirking, no—"

"You think my smirk is sexy?" He smirks at me again and my stomach flip-flops. My pussy flutters.

Argh! What's wrong with me? So, he's my husband and I know exactly how his muscles feel under my fingers, and yeah, he's the hottest man I've ever met... But he also kidnapped me, married me against my will, tagged me, then pretended to have his dick sucked off by someone else... All so he could try to protect me... Or so he says. *And he did cross countries to see you; now, you don't have to be lonely on Christmas.* I jerk my chin toward the door of the bathroom, "Ten minutes."

# 15

Michael

Ten minutes, and five seconds later, I walk out with a towel around my waist. If she thinks she can order me around, she has another think coming. I walk over to where I'd dumped my duffel on a chair and pull out a pair of sweatpants.

"Hey," she protests, "don't get too comfortable. You're leaving, you—"

I turn around, whip my towel off and she opens and shuts her mouth and I suppress a smirk.

"Wha...what..." She lowers her gaze to my crotch, and her breathing quickens. Her chest rises and falls, and the almost imperceptible motion of her thighs signals that she's squeezing them together.

"You were saying—"

"I was—" she clears her throat, "I was..." She swallows, licks her lips. "I...ah... I mean..."

"I was going to wear my sweatpants, but if you'd rather I not—"

"I'd rather you not—" She scowls, "I mean, don't wear your sweatpants. I mean..." Color suffuses her cheeks. She raises her hand, seems like she is about to speak, then pivots and heads for the bathroom.

I chuckle. "You sure about that?" I call after her as she slams the bathroom door behind her. I turn back to survey the contents of my duffle bag. This is a temporary reprieve. And it had been an under-handed move, maybe, to drop my towel... But hey, it had been a surefire way to grab her attention. Don't judge. I pull on my pair of sweats.

By the time she returns, having scrubbed her face clean and wearing a nightshirt that I recognize as one that I bought for her, I am settled on one side of the bed. I take in the hem of the shirt, which hits somewhere above her knees, revealing a portion of her creamy thighs, her calves, her tiny feet with toenails painted — black, of course — and the blood rushes to my groin. *Santa-Maria*, those toes of hers. I'd love to suck on them, run my tongue between them and down across the sole of her foot, over the arch and down to her heel, before I retrace my steps and nip on her toes again. She digs her toes into the carpet, then clears her throat.

I glance up as she stomps over to me, then dumps my jeans and T-shirt on my chest. "You left your clothes all over the bathroom floor."

"Thanks, honey." I smirk as I pull out my secure phone — the only reason I carry it is because not even the FBI should be able to break into it, at least, in theory. Ideally, I shouldn't be carrying a phone at all. It does make me more vulnerable to being tracked, but I have to stay in touch with my brothers.

I wasn't lying when I told her I had slipped into the country without informing anyone, but at least, my brothers know how to get in touch with me. Also, the security detail I have on Karma is sure to have seen me, so it's not like I am completely unprotected.

When I check my phone, there's a message from Seb asking me to let him know when I decide to head back and that they'll be holding down the business in my absence. Goddam!

I drag my fingers through my hair. Had I been that transparent to them about where I was headed? I could have sworn I hadn't mentioned anything to them. Then again, I guess it wouldn't take a rocket scientist to figure out where I could have disappeared to. Guess my brothers know me too well.

I put my phone aside as she scoffs, "If you think acting all nice and domestic is going to make me take you back, you're wrong."

"Hey, only being myself, sweetheart."

"Argh." She throws up her hands and stomps around the bed to the other side. She slips under the covers, then turns over on her side facing away from me.

I turn off the lamp, and bend my arm behind my head. For a few seconds, there's only the sound of us breathing. Then she wriggles around, making herself comfortable.

"How are you feeling now?" I murmur. "No pain or anything?"

She draws in a breath and the silence stretches. I am almost sure she isn't going to answer me when she sighs. "I am okay. I guess, I am surprised at myself as to how fast I've recovered. I was lucky, I suppose, that I wasn't hurt more."

I curl my fingers into fists. "You shouldn't have been hurt at all," I say in a low voice. "If I could do anything to go back and prevent what happened—"

"Don't beat yourself up over what happened, Michael... It's just one of those things that we need to move on from."

"Have you moved on from it yet?"

I sense, rather than see her shake her head.

"Me neither," I murmur. "I wanted to take you out somewhere nice for dinner, but it's Christmas Eve, and everything is closed."

"It's fine." She moves around, tugs the sheets in her direction, then quietens.

"I thought you'd have spent the evening with your sister and her new husband?"

She blows out a breath, "I thought about it... Even went to their house, then I changed my mind."

"You did?"

"Yeah," she half laughs. "Don't know why I am telling you this because I don't really see you as my friend right now."

"You're right."

"I am?"

"Yeah, I am your husband, your dom, and your master... Certainly not, your friend."

"Seriously?" She switches on the lamp and sits up. "You're going to pull that line on me, now?"

"What's wrong with it?"

"You'd think you'd try to grovel, at least a little, if you wanted to get into my good graces."

I smirk, "Why should I grovel when I have something far more lethal that you'd prefer?"

She narrows her gaze on me, "Do I even want to know what that is?"

I hold up my fingers and wiggle them, "How about these?"

Her gaze falls to my fingers and her eyes widen.

"Or this?" I drag my tongue across my lips. Her breathing grows ragged.

"Or..." I slide my hand under the sheet and down my sweatpants, "this?" I grip my cock, and despite the sheet over my crotch, it's clear what I am up to.

She swallows, the sound audible in the silence.

"You have a preference, *piccolina*?"

Her gaze is fixed on the movements visible through the sheet. Her chest rises and falls, she licks her lips, and the blood drains to my groin. My dick lengthens and I swipe my fingers around my thickness and drag them up the length. A growl rumbles up my chest and she shivers.

"What are you doing?" She clears her throat, "Are you touching yourself?"

"Would you rather touch me instead?"

"I..." she draws in a breath, "I...I'd rather that we go to sleep." She tears her gaze away, turns on her side, facing away from me.

I continue to drag my fingers up my shaft, and again. A groan rumbles up my chest, and she wriggles around on her side of the bed. I throw off my cover, shove my sweatpants down, then begin to jerk myself off in earnest. Not what I had planned, damn it. I had come here simply to spend time with her. I couldn't keep away, and I hadn't really thought if it meant that I was going to fuck her... But considering everything she's been through, I wasn't going to do that… Not unless she asked me to… But just being near her is enough for my dick to swell, my balls to throb, and my groin to harden and knot until I have to relieve myself. So what, if it means I am lying next to her in bed, wanking off.

*Che cazzo! Get a grip on yourself, stronzo.* I squeeze my shaft tighter —exactly what I am doing…not what I meant…but no matter. If this is the only way of getting off…then so be it.

I increase my pace, squeeze my dick from base to crown, again and again. My shaft thickens and my balls harden as the sound of flesh hitting flesh fills the space. The tension at the base of my spine coils, the blood pounds at my temples, and a bead of sweat crawls down my spine. I throw my head back as I squeeze my cock and yank on it again and again. The pressure in my groin increases and I groan as my balls draw up. That's when she throws off the sheet and crawls over to me.

# 16

Karma

I had tried to go to sleep. I swear, I had shut my eyes and tried to forget that he was lying in bed next to me, dressed in nothing but that pair of low-hung, grey sweatpants. Argh! Why did he have to wear grey sweatpants? I mean, it's good that he wore them, rather than not wearing anything... Like when he had dropped that towel. OMG... I had seen his perfect arse followed by that full-frontal view of him, his thick cock which had stood to attention the crown leaking precum, and that vein that ran up the underside of his length, and my heart had almost stopped.

Not that I haven't seen him naked, but it has been a while since I've seen all of him, every single inch of his gloriously-sculpted form showcased in the light from the lamp on the bedstead...and... I'd almost sunk to my knees and crawled over to him, and raised myself until I was at eye level with him, and opened my mouth and taken him down my throat, and sucked him off. I had barely managed to tear my gaze off of his gorgeous cock and stagger to the bathroom to wash up. So, when he'd begun to get himself off and the wet sound of flesh hitting flesh had filled the space... My pussy had clamped down so hard, I'd had to stuff my knuckles in my mouth to stop myself from moaning aloud.

I had resisted. I swear, I had tried so hard to resist, had tried to shut out the sounds as he'd dragged his fingers up his shaft, and increased the pace with which he'd fucked his own palm. I'd tried to squeeze my eyelids closed and my thighs together, and tried to pretend that it didn't matter that he had thrown off the covers and was now beating himself off and was so close to coming... But when he'd gasped and I'd known that he was almost there, I hadn't been able to stop myself. My mouth had watered, my fingers had tingled, and in something resembling a dream or a trance... I find myself crawling over to him.

I swing my leg over his thigh, then nestle between his legs, and he glances up as I wrap my fingers over and around his. He pauses mid-motion and I hold his gaze as I lower my head to his crotch. Without breaking the connection between our eyes, I lick the head of his cock.

His jaw tics and a pulse leaps to life at his temple. The blue in his eyes deepens until it's almost black in color. I have never seen him this turned on... This...almost beside himself with desire. I close my mouth around the tip of his cock and a growl rumbles up his chest. He pulls his hand out from under mine, folds his palms behind his neck and leans back. The expanse of his chest stretches out in front of me. Acres of cut planes, of sculpted muscle and hewn flesh that ripple as he glares down at me.

"Suck me off," he growls and I swallow. The suction on his dick has the muscles under his skin jumping. His biceps twitch, his nostrils flare, and he fixes his gaze on my mouth, watches as I swirl my tongue around the head of his shaft. His chest rises and falls, his scowl deepens, and I bob my head. I open my mouth, swallow down on his length, and he groans. I pull back, until my mouth is once more fitted around the crown of his length. He thrusts his pelvis forward, chasing the suction that only I can provide, and I can't stop my lips from curling. I lick around the circumference of the head, then drag my tongue down the length of his shaft and his shoulders flex. His gaze intensifies, he sets his jaw, and a bead of sweat slides down his temple. I lower my head and take his cock in my mouth and he hisses.

"Fuck," he growls and I hold his gaze as I swallow. Color flushes his cheeks. The next moment he leans forward, wraps my hair around his fingers. "You little tease," he says in a hard voice. "Are you wet yet, Beauty? Is your pussy clamping down, imagining my fat cock is inside of you? Stretching you, thrusting into you, cramming your hole as I squeeze your ass cheeks, and driving up and into you, hitting that place deep inside of you that only I know, that only I can reach every time I fuck you... Are you empty and needy and straining for my fingers in your asshole as I tear into your swollen channel?"

The moan vibrates up my throat and his shoulders go solid. He wraps the fingers of his free hand around my neck as he begins to fuck my mouth in earnest. He pulls my head forward and I choke. Tears slide down from the corners of my eyes, saliva drools from my mouth, and his gaze intensifies. "Do you know how it is to feel my cock down your throat?" he says in a hard voice. "Do you know what it does to me to see you all messed up as you swallow around my shaft, Beauty?"

I press my tongue against the column of his thickness and his features contort. "F-u-c-k, Beauty, you are killing me." He pulls me up until the crown of his dick is poised between my lips, then thrusts me down so his cock impales my throat. I swallow and his jaw tics. He continues the movement, down-up-down, and again. His chest muscles bunch, his shoulders flex, his jaw hardens, and I know he's close again. I grip his thighs as he pulls me up, then thrusts me down so I take him down my throat again. His stomach muscles ripple and he throws his head back.

"Fuck, I am coming," he growls as his hips jerk and he shoots his load. His cum fills my mouth and I swallow, and yet, he keeps coming. Drops dribble down my chin, onto his thigh, splashing on my chest. He pulls out, and at the same time, he hauls me up and locks his mouth over mine. He thrusts his tongue in between my lips and I can taste his cum, and his lips, and that essence that is so dark and so him, and my pussy clenches. I moan deep in my throat and it's like a signal, for he flips me under him.

He settles between my thighs, then deepens the kiss as his still turgid cock stabs into my lower belly. I knot my arms around his neck as he continues to kiss me and suck on my tongue, before he licks my lower lip. He breaks the kiss, only to kiss my chin, nibble his way down my throat. He grips the bottom of my sleep shirt, pushes it up so its above my breasts. He squeezes my tits together then bites down on one nipple. I yelp, then moan when he licks the engorged flesh, then repeats the action with the other. He blows on the flesh and I shiver. He works his way down to kiss my belly button, then kisses the flesh between the waistband of my panties and my navel.

"How do you feel down there? Are you still sore?" He gazes up at me, "Are you, Beauty?"

I shake my head and he holds my gaze. He pushes aside the gusset of my panties, then lowers his chin to my center. Without taking his gaze off of mine, he licks my clit. A whine bleeds from my lips. His lips curve up and he drags his tongue between my pussy lips. I shiver, then bury my fingers in his hair as I try to coax him down to the opening of my channel. He swipes his tongue down the length of my core, then up to my clit again. A shiver runs up my spine, as he wraps his fingers around the tops of my thighs and pries them apart, his touch still gentle as he buries his nose in my core.

"Oh," I moan as he presses his lips to my throbbing clit. "Oh, my god, Mika." I lean my head back as he licks his way down my pussy, then up again and again. He doesn't thrust his tongue inside my channel though. I jerk my pelvis forward, chasing the intrusion I need—that rough tongue of his as he licks inside me, the thickness of his fingers as he stretches me, the hardness of his dick as he crams it into me... And it would hurt... Not gonna lie, but I want that hurt. I need it, I need... "You, Mika, I need you."

"Don't want to hurt you, babe," he murmurs, his breath hot against my tender flesh. "Don't want you to feel sore again."

"I won't," I insist, "I'll be fine."

He scowls up at me, "Are you sure?"

I hesitate and he tilts his head, "Doesn't mean I can't make you come."

"Oh?" I blink, "I..." I gasp as he buries his face in my pussy again and closes his mouth around the flesh. With his tongue, he strums my pussy lips, with the roughness of his whiskered jaw, he scrapes the tender flesh, with his teeth, he bites down on my clit, and I explode. The climax vibrates out from my center, gathering speed as it roars toward my extremities. My arms and legs tremble, my entire body shudders as I try to close my thighs and end up capturing his head between them. I release his head, grab hold of the headboard behind me as he thrusts his tongue inside my channel. He curves his tongue and the orgasm continues to explode deep inside of me. The moisture gushes out from between my thighs and he laps it up. He licks my pussy lips, and my clit again and again, as if he can't get enough. I sense him move up my body and open my eyes to find his face in front of mine. He presses his lips to mine, and our combined essences fills my palate.

The taste of him, the scent of him, the heat of him overwhelms me. I press myself closer to him as my eyelids flutter down.


When I awaken, the room is dark. I try to move, but a weight around my waist pins me down. I try to turn and realize that Michael is holding me close, his chest pressed to my back, his leg flung over me. The man gives off so much heat that even though the cover is thrown off, sweat beads my brow. I wriggle my butt into him so I can turn, and a thick column stabs into the valley between my arse cheeks. "Oh." I freeze. I draw in a breath, another, then push my butt back again and the thickness hardens. I bite the inside of my cheek, manage to wriggle my hand free from under his arm. I try to turn my torso and his grip tightens. He pushes his pelvis forward so every last ridge of his dick is imprinted into the curve of my hip. My pussy spasms, my nipples harden, and moisture laces my core. I gulp, wriggle my backside again, and this time, his cock seems to stab through the thin material of my underwear. I begin to move my butt against the column. Back and forth, back and forth. That's when he shoves me onto my front.

# 17

Karma

"What the," I protest, "what are you doing, Michael?"

"You started this, Beauty." He lowers his face so his cheek is pressed into mine. "Don't think I didn't notice you wriggling your little tush against my cock." He presses said cock into the curve of my hips and I can't stop the moan that wheezes out.

"Michael," I whisper. "Oh, Michael."

"Do you know how much it turns me on to hear my name from your lips?"

I swallow, "I... I didn't mean to wake you up."

"Liar," he murmurs without heat as he licks the shell of my ear. He sucks the earlobe and I feel the tug all the way to my core. My pussy clenches and I dig my fingers into the bedspread. "Mika, please," I implore. "Please, Mika."

"Tell me what you want, Beauty," He flicks his tongue inside my ear and goosebumps pop on my skin. Who'd have thought that could be so sexy, him licking, nibbling, biting down on my earlobe and every part of my being responding to that action. I wriggle under him and he slaps my butt. "Stop that."

"Wha—" I splutter, "what was that for?"

"For causing me so much distress that I had to fly across three countries to see you."

"Hey," I scowl, "I am not the one who put on that stupid show then asked me to leave."

"I'm sorry about that."

He kisses the side of my temple and I blink. "You apologized?"

"I've been known to do that," I sense him smirk, "on occasion. Just don't get used to it."

"Like I would dare?" I peer up at him from the corner of my eyes. "Are you going to use your monster dick, or what?"

He pauses, then laughs. The rich sound fills the space, and my heart stutters. It bloody stutters. Will I ever get used to this man's magnetism, his sheer charisma, his preening, the force of his personality, his allure that draws me to him constantly, until I am sure I'll never be able to live separately from him? Tears prick the backs of my eyes and I blink them away. Or I think I do, but his gaze narrows. He bends, licks up the lone tear that has escaped from the corner of my eye. "What's wrong?" he murmurs, and I shake my head.

"Nothing."

"Don't lie," he admonishes me. "Tell me what's on your mind."

"Nothing." I scowl back.

"It's something that when I am plastered to you, you are crying." He pulls away, "Is it me or—?"

"No," I protest. "No, come back."

He chuckles, "You're fucking adorable, wife."

"Yeah, yeah," I mumble, "what-bloody-ever."

"Love it when you talk dirty, babe."

"Oh, for fuck's sake," I push up and into him, only to be met by that thick hardness between his legs which, on its own, is enough to pin me down. "Let me go."

"Thought you wanted me to use my monster cock on you?"

"Well, are you?"

He sobers, "I'm still not sure if you are fully healed, baby."

My heart melts a little. Fuck, all he has to do is call me baby, and I'll throw myself at his feet panting. Hell, I'll throw myself at him anyway, as I have been doing since practically the first time I met him. I squeeze my thighs together, and scowl up at him. "I really am fine, promise."

"I am not convinced."

"The doctor said it was okay to start having sex when I felt ready."

"And do you feel ready?"

"I told you I do."

"Hmm." He pats the curve of my arse and my belly flip-flops.

"What?" I scowl.

"Given you're so horny, and since I don't feel comfortable shoving my monster shaft inside your pussy—"

"Y-e-s," I frown, "what is it you're thinking?"

"We could, of course, satisfy ourselves with sex of the non-penetrative kind—"

I shake my head, "I want to feel you inside of me, Mika."

"Hmm." His eyes gleam, "There is, of course, another way for me to be inside of you."

"Oh." I blink rapidly, "OH!" I swallow, "You mean?"

He nods.

"You mean you want to come in by the backdoor, again?"

He stares at me, then throws his head back and laughs, a full belly laugh.

"What the hell?" I grumble as I try to wriggle out from under him and he merely leans more weight on me, so I can barely move. "Let me move, you oaf."

"No."

"Why are you laughing like a hyena?"

"Because you are so fucking cute."

"Argh," I growl, "I hate it when you use that bloody 'c' word."

"What do you say, Beauty?"

"I have to admit that the thought of you putting the python between your legs in my arse again doesn't exactly fill me with joy."

"Didn't hear you complaining about it the last time." He smirks.

I redden, "That...that was different."

"Oh, yeah?" He leans in close enough for our breaths to mingle, "How was it different?"

"Umm," I blink rapidly, "I don't know, it was just different."

He stares at me and I raise my shoulders, "It was in the heat of the moment, okay? That first time, at your fake funeral, I figured I might as well do it because it would please you."

"So, it didn't please you?" He frowns.

"It...it did." I try to shift my body, but again, I'm pinned in place. "It was a bit painful, at first, but then, you know, once I got into the uh, swing of things, it actually did accentuate the pleasure," I admit. "And then, of course, there was that second time at your place..." I glance at him, then away.

"And," he prompts me, "how was that for you, Beauty?"

"It was..." I shake my head. "It was when you took me against the wall of your room," I whisper.

"And?" He nuzzles at my temple, "Do you remember what I did to you then?"

I draw in a breath, "You..." I clear my throat, "you pounded into me so hard that I felt you all the way down to the tips of my toes. You breached me with such force that I was sure that you were going to split me in two. It...it was..."

"It was?" He peers into my face. "Complete the sentence," he insists when I hesitate.

"It was intense and filthy and indecent and yet," I swallow, "there was something deeply satisfying about it. Like we were communicating on a different level. Like we were arguing without words. Like our bodies were straining to push away, and yet also, come closer. It felt like we were fighting more than fucking. It was..." I tip up my chin, "it was the most erotic experience of my life, okay?" Heat flushes my cheeks, and I am sure that I am blushing even more.

"Only," he searches my gaze, "you still have doubts about doing it again."

"I didn't say that."

"It's written all over your face."

"And when did you become so good at reading my mind?"

He tilts his head and I blow out a breath, "Yes, okay, I admit, I am still not a big fan of anal sex."

"I am sorry if you weren't completely comfortable with it earlier, which is why..." He releases me, then rolls off of me and pads over to his duffel bag. He squats and rummages around, then straightens. He turns to walk over to me and I take in the three packages he holds. One is a small square and another is rectangular in shape. Both have ribbons tied around them. The third one is not wrapped and he sets it down on the side table.

"Oh," I turn over, then sit up. "You bought gifts?"

"For you, and for that beast," he nods toward the sleeping cat. He hands the rectangular one over to me. "That's for Andy," he adds. I pull off the cover, then open the box and pull out a plush toy in the form of a mouse.

"You bought him a cat toy."

"Apparently, I did." He shakes his head.

"Aww," I coo, "sooo sweet."

He grimaces, "You make me sound like I've lost my mind."

"Or found your heart."

His features tense. "No emo shit, okay?"

"Can I kiss you to show my gratitude?"

"You can kiss my cock, instead, and I would be most grateful."

I huff, "Do you always have to equate everything with sex?"

"Is there any other way?"

I nod toward the other package, "What's that?"

"That —" he hands it over to me, "is for you."

I tear off the wrapping, then stare at the square velvet box. "Oh," I swallow, "what is it?"

"Open it."

I pull off the top, then stare at the short, ribbed column which tapers on one side, before broadening out, then narrows into a notch before it flares out into a heart shape. A tiny black stone is set into the center of the heart around which is set a circle of red stones. I stare at it, "Is that a…?" I blink rapidly, "That is a…"

"A butt plug," he supplies helpfully, then picks it up and hands it to me, "for you."

"For me?"

"It's going to make the entire experience of our fucking even more pleasurable."

"Oh." I swallow. I glance from the sparkling plug thingy to his face, then back at it. "You sure about this?"

"Very," he promises me. "I promise you that it'll make your orgasms even more intense."

"I don't know about that," I laugh, "they've been plenty intense with you already."

"This will make it even better for you, baby." He leans over and presses a kiss to my temple, then to my cheek, then to the corner of my lips, "Go on. Let me put it in."

"You really want this, eh?"

"I want to imprint myself on every part of you. Own every cell of your body. Rub my cum into every inch of your skin. Kiss every curve, every finger, every toe, every piece of your flesh, so you never forget who you belong to."

I gulp.

"I want to own every inch of you, Beauty," he peers into my eyes. "All of you." He places his lips over mine, "Only you. Just as you own me, completely."

My toes curl and my pussy clenches. I squeeze my thighs together, already wanting him inside me, in me, filling every hole in my body, goddamn! I draw in a breath, then place the velvet box on the side table. "Fine."

"Good girl." He kisses me hard and heat flushes my skin. He takes the jeweled plug from me, then presses on my shoulder and I turn over on my front.

He sweeps my hair aside and presses a kiss to the nape of my neck and I shiver. He kisses his way down my spine and I swoon. OMG, I almost swoon as he presses his lips to the hollow of my back. He peels back my panties, kisses the curve of my arse, then yanks down my underwear until it's just above my knees. He reaches over and I turn my head to find him flipping open the third box. He extracts a bottle of lube, and pours out a little of the liquid in his palm. He warms it between his hands, then leans over me again. He kisses first one arse cheek, then the other, then slides his finger inside my backhole.

# 18

Karma

Too much, too thick. His fat digit stretches my butthole. I huff, try to pull away and he flattens his palm on the small of my back. "Relax," he murmurs as I clench down on his finger. "Draw in a breath," he instructs me.

I do.

"Now hold it."

I hold the breath in my lungs.

"Now release," he exhales and so I do.

He guides me through the next few breaths and at the end of it, to my surprise, I find that my muscles have, indeed, relaxed. I exhale again and his finger slips inside. "Oh," I gasp as he allows me to adjust to the intrusion.

He leans down and presses another kiss to the nape of my neck, "Okay?"

"Y…yeah," I swallow.

"How does it feel?"

"It feels…strange… And yet, it also feels, weirdly, good."

"Good," he nips the curve of where my shoulder meets my neck and heat tugs at my lower belly. He curves his finger inside of me and tendrils of sensation crawl up my spine. I bite the inside of my cheek to keep from crying out. He pulls out his finger, slides it back in, repeats the action until it feels much more normal.

The next time he withdraws his finger, he replaces it with something cold, metallic. Oh, I clench down and he bends to place his cheek next to mine. "Trust me, *Bellezza*," he murmurs. "You do trust me, right?"

"I.." I swallow, then nod. "Yeah, I do." And I mean it. Despite everything that has happened, despite the fact that he had staged that scene which had almost shattered my heart, despite the fact that our entire relationship had started in the most unorthodox of terms… I do trust him. More than anybody else.

"Beauty?" He nuzzles the space behind my ear. "Eyes on me." He pinches my chin, turns my head toward him. I raise my gaze to his and he nips on my lower lip. I open my mouth and he swoops in. He slides the butt plug in past the tight ring of my sphincter at the same time.

"Oh," the breath whooshes out of me and he inhales it. He sucks on my tongue, kisses me with such passion, such intensity, that my head spins. I lean into him, try to flatten myself against him, but already, he is moving back. "Wha—?" I open my eyes to find him sliding off of the bed. "What are you doing?"

I turn my head in his direction as he holds out his hand, "Come on, we have to leave."

"We…do?"

He nods. "I may have risked being detected by coming to this country, but I don't take unnecessary chances."

"You don't?"

He wiggles his fingers and I automatically reach for them. He grabs my hand, tugs me up and off the bed. I stand before him, tip my chin up, "Where are we going?"

"You'll see."

. . .

Half an hour later, I stare out of the window of the plane. Below me is a void of darkness which I have been told is the sea. Michael had barely allowed me to get dressed as he'd coaxed Andy into the pet carrier. I'd packed fast, and then he'd ferried me out of the room, down a private elevator, to a side entrance where his Maserati had been waiting. He'd driven us through the almost empty streets, to a private airport in the heart of the city. The same airport at which I had arrived. To the same plane that had dropped me off, or at least it seemed like the same one. Do all luxury private aircrafts look the same? The interior had seemed the same but the crew was different.

After takeoff, I had let Andy out of the carrier. He had retreated to a corner of the cabin and hadn't been particularly happy. That was, until the steward had fussed over him. Turned out, Michael had also sprung for a comfortable cat-cave like bed for him, and Andy had been somewhat mollified when he'd discovered it.

Meanwhile, Michael had guided me to a seat near the window and taken the one next to me.

I've just dozed off when something buzzes right between my legs. I yelp, then realize the source is the butt plug which is still firmly wedged in my back entrance. I turn to find Michael watching me with a smirk.

"Wh…what are you doing?" I stutter. "More to the point, how are you doing it?"

He holds out his palm, uncurls his fingers, and I spot the little remote control. He presses down on the button on the remote and the thing in my backhole vibrates again. My thighs quiver and my pussy spasms. The vibrations seem to go on and on, and by the end of it, I am gasping. Heat flushes my cheeks and a bead of sweat slides down my spine.

He smirks, then lean in to kiss me. "Happy Christmas and Happy Birthday," he whispers as he tucks an errant strand of hair behind my ear.

"How did you know it's my birthday?"

"I know everything about you, *piccola*," He brushes his lips over mine. Then, the asshole leans back in his seat and closes his eyes. Letting me stew in my own juices… Literally. I clench my thighs together, try to block out the gnawing ache that flares between my legs, and turn to glance out of the window.

The cabin is silent, and I take in the dawn breaking over the horizon. The pinks bleed out across the skies, darkening into blues and golds as the sun rises. I glance below to see the waves stretching out before me, and in the distance, I sight land.

Next to me, he stirs. Then heat envelops me as he leans in to peer over my shoulder. "Almost there." His dark voice rumbles up his chest. My nerve-endings instantly flare to life. Goosebumps pop on my skin and I shiver. "You cold?" he nuzzles the hair at my temple and I shake my head. "Here," I turn to find him shrugging out of his leather jacket.

I slide it on, and have just finished zipping it up when the steward comes over with Andy back in his traveling case. She places Andy in the seat opposite us and secures the seatbelt over the case.

Within minutes, we have begun our descent. I glance down to find the flight circling what appears to be a small island.

"Oh," I blink as the pilot brings the flight over the water and onto a landing strip that seems to be surrounded by water. The flight comes to a halt, and Michael unsnaps his seatbelt and rises to his feet. He helps me up, then grabs Andy's traveling case. He swings his duffel bag over one shoulder, snatches up my suitcase in the other hand and heads out. I follow him down the steps and up the path that leads away from the airstrip. We have barely made it behind the trees that line the space, when the plane's engine revs up. I turn to find it taxiing up the runway, then turning around to take off.

"The plane's leaving," I remark.

When he doesn't respond, I increase my pace to catch up with him, "Is there another way off of the island?"

"I do have a motorboat in the boathouse and a jetty, in case of contingency; but yeah, outside of that, there's no other way off of the island. If anyone approaches the island, either by plane or by boat, I'll hear them."

"Oh," I open and shut my mouth. "Guess this is as safe as it gets?"

He jerks his chin and I follow him up a path that leads another half a mile upward before we reach a plateau that looks out over a beach that abuts the sea. There, in the middle of the space, is a two-story, Greek-style bungalow. The walls are white-washed, and the cube-shaped building's smooth-edged corners lend a sense of space and freedom to the structure. The sun shines down on us, bathing the entire area in a golden glow. A bead of sweat trickles down my temple and I unzip his jacket.

"Where are we, anyway?" I glance around the space, "It's much warmer than London."

"I should hope so," he laughs. "We are on an island off the coast of Malta that has its own microclimate."

"Microclimate?"

He nods, "We are about two and a half hours away from London, but as you can see, the weather here is infinitely better."

"You're not a big fan of London, huh?"

He raises his shoulder, "It has its charms."

"But you prefer Sicily?"

"For the food, absolutely. For the weather, normally, except when it gets too hot at the peak of summer. That's when I normally escape here."

"On your own?"

"Mostly; I've had my brothers over on a few occasions."

"And girlfriends?" I force the words out, "Have you brought them over as well?"

"And if I have?" I can't see his face, but hell, if I don't hear the smirk in that voice of his.

I pause and he walks forward for a few seconds before he pauses. He places my suitcase and Andy's case on the ground, then turns to glance at me over his shoulder, "What?"

"So, you have brought women here before?"

"I haven't not brought them here."

"Argh!" I plant my hands on my hips, "Michael Byron Domenico Sovrano, if you're taking me to your love nest, then I have absolutely no interest in going there."

"Are you jealous?"

"Of course, not," I sniff, "and you haven't answered the question."

"I've brought..." he walks over to me, "no other woman here before."

"Oh," I bite the inside of my cheek.

He pauses in front of me, then notches his knuckle under my chin. He peers down into my features, "You are the first woman to have set foot on this island."

"Not even Nonna has come here?"

He laughs, "Nonna hates traveling. She hasn't left Sicily in, maybe, twenty years."

"Ah," I murmur, "okay."

"Okay," his lips kick up, "now, can we go inside?"

# 19

Karma

The inside, as it turns out, is not exactly the rough-and-ready holiday getaway bungalow I had envisioned. From the exterior, the place is whitewashed, and the lines are that of a structure that had been built to blend in with the island's surroundings.

Inside... Well... I follow him through the wide doorway and take in the large space. One entire wall is made of glass, beyond which, is the beach, and then an uninterrupted view of the sea. Facing it is a large sectional in the center of which is a coffee table. A fireplace is set into one wall. Diagonally opposite is a kitchen separated from the main area by a breakfast bar. In the other corner is a dining table with four chairs. He walks past the kitchen and down the short corridor into a bedroom....which is also massive. High ceilings, one wall made of glass through which the same uninterrupted view of the sea spreads out before us. A king-sized bed is set against a wall. I assume the double doors opposite the bed lead to the ensuite. Another set of double doors must lead into a closet.

He places Andy's pet carrier down next to a large cushion in the form of a cave.

"The litter box is in the bathroom," he murmurs.

I walk over, open the door to the carrier and coax Andy out. He mewls and I carry him in my arms. I cuddle him as Michael carries the bags inside. I walk into the bathroom, place Andy down near the litter box and allow him to get acquainted with it. Then walk out and across the bedroom to the large glass wall to take in the view. I hear his footsteps approach.

The next second, he wraps an arm about my shoulders, pulls me back to rest against his chest. He tugs my head under his chin, and for a few seconds, we stand there admiring the view.

"So, this is the kind of privacy money can buy, eh?"

"Or notoriety."

"You know," I tip my chin up, "that is the first time I've heard you refer to your profession honestly."

"I am on the wrong side of the law; I was born with that knowledge. It's who I am."

The band around my chest tightens. I am not sure why, but hearing him put that out there so baldly...sends a shiver of apprehension down my spine. Not that I didn't know about his vocation... I mean, from the very first time we met, it was clear that he wasn't an ordinary, law-abiding citizen. It's just, maybe somewhere, I'd held onto the hope that he might change. *And yet... It's the darkness within him, that edginess, that cloak of danger that clings to him that you find so attractive.*

"I can hear you thinking, *Bellezza.*" His grip around me tightens, "Want to tell me what's on your mind?"

I turn to face him, "I was thinking of the cat cave."

"The cat cave?"

I jerk my chin toward the cushion shaped like a cave, which I know Andy is going to love. "You got that for Andy?"

His features smoothen out, "And if I did?"

"So, you were that sure I was going to come with you?"

"Let's just say, I can be persuasive."

"And you had enough time to have someone come in and place the cat cave here?"

"And place the litterbox in the bathroom, as well as make sure there's enough food to last us for, at least, a week."

"A week?" I blink.

"If not more."

"Guess even mob bosses take time off over Christmas and New Year, eh?"

"Not usually," he smirks. "But this year I've asked my men to spend time with their families, so yes, things will be quiet."

"How convenient for you." I brush past him and walk over to the cat cushion, just as Andy pads out of the bathroom. He prances over to the cat cave then jumps onto the cushion. He tips his head up and mewls at me. I scowl at him as Michael walks over to me.

"Not sure why you are angry, but I think the beast needs to be fed."

"You're not sure why I am angry?" I straighten, "And I am sure your minions ensured the place is stocked with cat food."

"I did tell them to make sure to do so, yes," he admits.

I turn on him, "Well, don't let me keep you from whatever it is you normally do when you come to your uppity island retreat." I stalk off in the direction of the kitchen. I know I am being unreasonable, but really, the fact that he could fit me so neatly into his schedule rankles a little bit... Okay, a lot. Also, I don't want to admit it, but the fact that he's been so thoughtful about making sure that Andy is taken care of... It paints him in a favorable light...which I am not happy about. He could try a little harder to be unlikeable, right? It doesn't help that he's decided to sweep me off to an island for some time off. An island that I am dying to explore. Gah!

I reach the kitchen, yank open the nearest shelf. Spices. This one is packed with spices. I slap it shut, pull open the next one. Dried pasta, loaves of bread, risotto rice, other packs of products with Italian names that I am not familiar with. I slam it shut, open the next one. This has pots and pans. The next one has plates and mugs. I yank open the drawer below it and find cutlery. "Argh!" I step back, survey the room. "Where the hell have you hidden it?"

He pulls open the door of the shelf closest to him, then reaches in and extracts a pack. I flounce over and grab it from him. Glancing around, I spy the bowls set out for food and water on the window ledge. "Of course, you'd even have his name engraved on the bowls, right?"

I stomp over to it, pour out the food, top up the water bowl. Before I can turn to call for Andy, the bloody cat pads over to me. He leaps onto the ledge and laps up the water. I watch him to make sure he's happy to eat the cat food, then turn, brush past Michael and back to the bedroom.

"I think it's presumptuous that you thought I'd share the bedroom with you."

"You're my wife; of course, you'll share my bed."

"And if I don't want to?"

"You will."

"But I don't."

"You do."

I throw up my arms and turn on him, "And if I refuse?"

"Then I'd—"

"What?" I snap. "What would you do? Tie me to the bed until I agree to cooperate?"

"That's not a bad idea." He tilts his head, "But I have a far simpler method."

"What?"

He slides his hand inside his pocket. The next moment, the plug between my arse cheeks vibrates.

# 20

Michael

I press down on the button of the remote control and she stiffens.

"What the—" she gapes. "You... I... Ahhhh!"

She looks about ready to strangle me and I smirk. I hadn't meant to, but...it had been the easiest way to shut her up. Not that I don't find the fact that she's having a meltdown attractive. Hell, I love every mood of hers... None more so than when she's angry enough that her green eyes dart sparks at me and color fills her cheeks. But when I slid my hand in my pocket, my fingers brushed over the button, and I couldn't resist. I simply wanted to see what her reaction would be.

And I am not disappointed when she sputters, "How...how dare you? That's so underhanded of you."

"You think?" I allow my smile to widen and she plants her hands on her hips.

"Argh, you are so damn annoying."

"Admit it. You like it, though."

"The only thing I admit is that I am going to take that goddam butt plug out right now." She pivots, marches toward the door.

I call out, "Stop, Beauty."

She holds up her middle finger as she reaches the door, and I press down on the button again. And keep it pressed. She gasps, stiffens, then clutches the frame of the doorway.

"Oh, my god," she moans. "Oh, god." She squeezes her thighs together, presses her cheek against the wooden frame.

I turn a dial to increase the intensity. Instantly, she rises up on her tiptoes, throws up her hand, and grips the door. "Jesus," she huffs, "this...this thing is—"

"Turning you on?" I reach for her, grasp her shoulder and turn her around.

Her breath comes in short gasps, her chest rises and falls, sweat beads her upper lip, and she swallows. I turn the button further to the right and she groans, thrusts out her luscious breasts.

If I move the jacket—my jacket, that she's wearing—out of the way, I am sure I'll see her pebbled nipples. The blood rushes to my groin, and fuck, if my balls don't throb.

I turn the button even more, as far as it will go, and she throws back her head. "Oh, bloody hell," she groans as she bites down on her lower lip. She throws out her hand, as if looking for support, and I grab it. I release my hold on the button and she slumps. I catch her around the waist, then throw her over my shoulder. She half protests and I slap her butt. Which must send vibrations through her aching backhole, for she moans again.

She wriggles around and I squeeze her butt. She chafes her thighs tighter, and fuck, the scent of her arousal seeps into the air. My vision tunnels. My blood begins to thud in my veins. I increase my pace until I am half jogging toward my bedroom.

I reach my bed and lower her to the mattress. She sprawls on her back, dark hair spread out about her shoulders, cheeks flushed, pupils dilated until there's only a circle of green around her pupils. I rake my gaze down her chest, her narrow waist, her generous hips and thighs, those tiny feet clad in the sneakers she'd worn when she'd left my home in Palermo. I sink down to my knees, untie her shoes and pull them off, then her socks.

"What are you doing?" she mumbles.

"Making you more comfortable." I smirk as I rise up to my feet. I tear off my own shoes and socks, then plank my body over hers. "You're fucking gorgeous, Beauty."

She swallows as she stares up into my face. I lean down, brush my lips over hers once, twice, thrice. A moan bleeds from her lips and she flutters her eyelids shut. I press kisses over each eyelid, then to her nose, to her chin. To the hollow at the base of her throat. I inhale that moonflower scent of hers, and my balls harden. An urgency grips me.

I lean back on my knees, grab her hands and haul her up. She blinks as I divest her of the jacket, then unbutton her shirt and pull it off. I glance down at her lace bra and the dark nipples that are visible through it. I lower my head and kiss her in the valley between her tits. She shudders, and the drumbeat of her heartbeat against her ribcage ratchets up. I pull back, then reach behind her to unhook her bra. It falls down her shoulders and I pull it down her arms and fling it aside. She stares at me, holds my gaze as she thrusts out her breasts proudly.

"*Minchia,*" I growl, "you're a fucking goddess."

Her cheeks heat as she glances away, then back at me. I reach for the waistband of her jeans, unhook the button and pull down the fly. I step back onto the floor, pull her up to her feet. Then roll her jeans down her thighs, along with her panties as I drop to my knees. She steps out of them and I throw them aside. Then glance up to find her gaze on me. Her lips are parted, her elbows tucked into her sides as she watches me from under hooded eyelids.

I grip the tops of her thighs, pull her close as I reach in and bury my nose in her pussy. The scent of her, sweet and sexy and fucking erotic, fills my senses. I draw her essence into my lungs, until it feels like it's invading every pore in my body. I thought I'd wanted to imprint myself on her, but the fact is, she's already stamped her impression onto every part of me. I'll never be the same, never be able to go back to being the emotionless, focused, tunnel-visioned man who'd only wanted one thing. Power.

With her, I feel vulnerable, yet alive... I felt like I can experience the highs of life...and the lows... She made me real, human... She makes me *feel*. It won't help me to do my job better. To become emotional is the beginning of the end for any made man. It has caused the downfall of too many of them to count... And yet... It feels right. Being with her feels right. It feels like the only thing worth living for. What is this life if I can't open myself to her, allow her to see what she does to me, allow her to invade my secrets, to see my weaknesses. To strip myself bare as I've stripped her.

I rise to my feet, reach for the back of my T-shirt and pull it off. She stares at my chest, drags her gaze down the planes to my waist. I lower the zipper on my jeans and step out of them. Then straighten once more. I widen my stance, hold my arms at my sides, and allow her to take in every part of my body. Naked. Open. At her mercy.

Her breathing grows ragged, her lips part, and when she raises her gaze to mine, the look in her eyes is hungry, horny, and so needy that my breath hitches. I turn around, walk over to my duffel, remove the box I've been carrying, and return to place it on the nightstand.

She glances at it, then at me, and grows a shade paler.

"Shh," I reach over and kiss her, wrap my arms around her, and hold her close so every inch of her body is plastered to mine. I massage her shoulders, rub circles over her back, and bit by bit, the tension seeps out of her. I step back, turn her around then push her onto the bed.

"On your hands and knees, baby." I place my palm flat on the small of her back. She shivers but complies as she bends over, beautifully. I take in her heart-shaped behind, arched up, showing the valley between her ass-cheeks, the glittering butt plug, and finally, the pink of her pussy, already glistening with her arousal. I move in closer and she shudders. I grip her hip, then grasp the heart-shaped head of the butt plug and work it out of her. She groans as it comes free and the sound coils somewhere deep inside of me.

The blood drains to my groin and I have to widen my stance to accommodate my cock, that twitches and throbs and insists that I get inside of her. I lean over, grab the lube, then pour it into my palm. I warm it up, then rub it over my shaft before I move in and slide a finger inside of her. A moan tumbles from her lips as I add a second finger, and curve it. Her entire body jerks and I grab her to keep her from falling. I slip a third finger inside, and she throws her head back, "Oh, my god, Mika, that feels—"

"Good?"

"It feels..." she seems to search for the right word, "it feels like you're stretching me apart...but in a good way."

I pull out my fingers, then fit the swollen crown of my cock to her back opening. "I am going to fuck you now."

# 21

Karma

I draw in a breath and before I can protest, he breaches me. A groan wells up and my knees tremble. Shit, shit, shit... This...feels...different. He feels so big, so hard, so thick as he stretches me. He pauses to allow me to accommodate his girth, and as he leans over me, he grips the back of my neck and a shiver runs down my spine. To be at his mercy like this, as he impales me and holds me captive, as he massages the curve of my arse, as his cock twitches inside of me, as he pushes forward, sinks deeper into me, as his thickness distends my backchannel so I can feel every millimeter of his throbbing cock... OMG... It's filthy and erotic and forbidden and... So bloody good.

I taste something metallic on my palate and realize that I have bitten down on my tongue. I swallow down the coppery taste, turn to glance over my shoulder and freeze.

He's gazing down, watching the place where he's entered me, watching as he thrusts forward, this time, with enough force that my body jerks. He slips inside and sheaths himself completely. He grits his teeth, and I can't stop the gasp that slips from my lips. He glances up and his blue gaze locks with mine. His jaw flexes, a look of controlled restraint on his features as his chest heaves. He holds my gaze as he pulls out, slowly, so slowly, leaving me strangely empty and craving more. He slides his hand around to play with my pussy lips gently, so gently, then lunges forward and impales me. His balls slaps against my inner thighs. A whine bleeds from my lips, he bares his teeth. He touches my clit, just a brush of his fingertips, and a trembling grips me. He rubs his fingers through my pussy lips and I moan.

"Please," I huff, "more; I want more."

He slides one finger inside my soaking pussy. I squeeze my eyes shut. "Sooo good," I moan as he pulls out his finger, then pushes it back in, and again. I clamp down on his finger, clenching around his cock, and a growl rips from him.

"You're killing me, *Bellezza*. I can barely hold back as it is."

He withdraws his dick, only to push forward inside me again, at the same time he works his finger in and out of my soaking cunt.

"Please," I mutter, "please, Mika, add another finger."

"You sure?" I sense the hesitation in his tone, and reach down between my legs. I slide my finger inside my pussy next to his and he hisses. "Fuck me," he says in a hard voice, "that's hot, Beauty."

I pull back my finger then hold it out to him. He leans over and wraps his mouth around it. He sucks on it and my pussy clenches. His cock throbs inside of me and I groan. "Mika, please…" but before I can complete the sentence, he's added a second finger inside my cunt. He moves it in and out of me as he thrusts his dick inside me again and again. Then he pulls out, and at the same time he withdraws his fingers from my pussy.

"Wha—" I protest as he flips me over on my back. He slides his arms under my knees, throws my legs over his shoulders, then holds my gaze as he notches his cock against my puckered hole. He slides in easily, filling me, stretching me again, and I sigh and he groans.

"*Cazzo!*" He swears aloud. Seriously, why does 'fuck' in Italian sound so damn erotic? He reaches between us, strums my pussy lips as he thrusts in and out of me again and again. He hits a spot deep inside me and a whine bleeds from my lips. He pushes into me, hitting that spot again as he grinds the heel of his hand into my clit, and that's when it hits me.

"Mika I'm—"

"Come," he growls, "come for me, *Beauty*."

The climax rips through me, smashes into me and I scream. I swear I see sparks behind my eyes as I collapse. I am aware of him continuing to plunge in and out of me, before he growls as he comes inside of me. Hot spurts of his cum bathe me. He drags his fingers across my clit, then holds them up to my lips. I lick them and the taste of myself, mingled with him, sinks into my blood. Lust twangs my underbelly and I stare up at him.

He lowers his head and licks my lips. "So gorgeous," he rumbles, "so damn sweet."

He pulls out and I wince.

"Does it hurt?" he murmurs and I nod.

He scowls and I smirk, "In a good way."

"Brat." He falls onto his back and gathers me onto his chest. I cuddle into him as he runs his palm across my back. "Sleep," he kisses my temple, "I've got you."


I wake up sprawled on my front. The sheets tangled around my legs. Through the undrawn curtains, the evening light pours in to bathe the bed. A touch on my lower back makes me shiver. I glance over my shoulder to find him staring at my back. He touches the letters that he carved into me, and another shiver runs down my back. I squeeze my thighs together as he bends and traces the letters with his tongue. He bites down the curve of where my back meets my arse and I moan. "Michael?"

"Hmm?"

"What are you thinking?"

"Did it hurt when I wrote this into your skin?"

I lower my cheek to the pillow. "A little...but it was also, strangely, erotic."

He pauses and I sense him staring at what he can see of my face. "Erotic?"

I swallow, "Yeah… I knew you were angry and that you needed to mark me in some form."

"You knew that, huh?"

I nod, "Well, knowing how possessive you are, and I had left with your brother."

He stiffens and I try to turn on my back but he stops me, "Go on… Complete what you were going to say."

"It's not like it wasn't a shock when I realized what you had done, but at the time, when you were marking me… It made me feel close to you. It was one way for you to show me that I couldn't do that again."

"And now?" His voice lowers to a hush, "Now, how do you feel about it?"

"Knowing that I am your whore, you mean?"

"My whore," his voice thickens, "my slut, my wife…mine to do with as I want."

I turn over and this time he lets me. He bends and kisses my belly, swirls his tongue in my belly button and my goosebumps pop. "I am sorry you lost the baby," he continues to kiss his way down to my pussy. "I am sorry you got hurt," he presses a kiss to my still swollen clit. "I am sorry you were in that car." He crawls up my body until his lips are over mine, until his nose bumps mine and his eyelashes tangle with mine. "But I am not sorry for kidnapping you."

I swallow.

"Or forcing you to marry me."

I bite the inside of my cheek.

"Or tagging you, or marking you with my knife."

He brushes his lips over mine.

I reach down between us, wrap my fingers around his cock. He hisses out a breath, but doesn't break my gaze. I notch his dick against my pussy and his gaze intensifies. "You're sure?"

I nod.

"I won't hurt you, will I?"

"I want you to hurt me, Mika. I want you to show me how it is to be yours wholly, completely, and —"

He thrusts his hips forward and impales me. I gasp, grip his biceps as he stays there, holding most of his weight off of me. I wrap my legs around his waist, tilt my hips up, and he slips in further. I moan, and he grits his teeth.

"*Cazzo!*" He growls, "So wet, so tight, Beauty." He grinds his hips against mine, breaching me further, deeper, hitting that spot deep inside of me again. A whine spills from my lips as I grind my heels into his arse. I dig my fingernails into his back, wanting to mark him as he did me. He wraps his fingers around my throat, pressing down slightly. I draw in a breath, and my lungs burn. I open my mouth and he kisses me. He plunges his tongue in between my lips, mirroring the way his cock saws in and out of me. He increases the pressure on my throat, cutting off my airflow, then raises his head to peer into my eyes. I gasp, tears squeezing out from the corners of my eyes as he pulls back, then slams into me. My entire body jerks as he begins to fuck me in earnest. I can feel every ridge, every striation of his dick as he shoves into me. At the same time, he releases his hold on my throat. "Come," he growls, "come all over my shaft."

The climax slams into me as I draw in a breath, then darkness overwhelms me.

When I wake, I am alone.

# 22

Michael

I sip from the cup of espresso as I stare out at the sea from the patio outside the living room. I'd left her asleep... Okay, I had watched her sleep before I'd slipped out and made us both dinner. I'd even fed and replenished the water for the cat, who had followed me into the kitchen. The beast had lapped up the water and finished off his food as if he hadn't just been fed a few hours ago. Hell, we had forgotten to eat but we had fed him.

To be fair, we had been otherwise occupied. I hadn't been able to keep my hands off of her, or my dick out of her. I had intended to take out the butt plug and give her time to adjust to the trip, the fact that I had whisked her away without giving her time to mentally adjust to it. But the moment I had touched her, I had lost all sense of control. I had needed to claim her all over again, possess her completely. Ensure she understood who she belongs to. That she is mine, only mine.

I hear footsteps behind me, then she wraps her arm around me, and presses those full tits up and into me.

"You smell good." She presses her nose into my bare back.

"Do I now?" I chuckle.

"You smell of the salt air, and yourself and... Something else..." She sniffs me again. "Food," she says in a surprised voice, "you've been cooking?"

"I've been making dinner, yes."

"You cooked breakfast for me." She slides around to face me. "Now dinner too?"

"I am a good Italian boy. I learned cooking from my Mama when I was very young."

"I thought Italian men were fussed over by their mamas, who made sure they didn't have to lift a finger around the house?"

"Not my mama," I laugh. "She made sure we could hold our own in the kitchen. She may have been weak when it came to standing up to our father, but she made up for it by showering us with love." Some of the heaviness fades from my chest, "She said she wanted to make sure that we would be good husbands. Unlike her own."

She places her palm against my cheek, "You loved her?"

"Very much." I turn away.

She grips my chin, "Tell me about her."

"What's to tell?"

"Everything. Do you look like her? What else did you do together?"

I peer into her eyes, "You really want to know?"

"Of course, I want to know. It's why you brought us here, right?"

I tilt my head.

"So we could get to know each other. This is a kind of delayed honeymoon, isn't it?"

"Am I that transparent?"

"No," she chuckles, "normally, you are very hard to read."

"But not right now?"

She half smiles, "Something about being here... You are so much more relaxed, and you've lowered your barriers. You're not wearing that tough Capo look anymore."

"What's my tough Capo look?"

She rises up on her tip-toes, raises her arm then frowns "Bend your head," she instructs. And because it's Beauty asking me to do it... And only because yes, I want to indulge her, I lower my head. She traces the lines between my eyebrows. "Normally, you have a groove between your eyebrows and," she touches the skin around my eyes, "lines at the edges of your eyes, and," she drags her fingers around my mouth, "the skin around your lips is stretched."

I turn my head, pretend to bite her fingers, and she yelps.

"Do I now?"

"Mmhmm." She wraps her arms about my waist. I'd pulled on my sweats before heading to the kitchen and now she slides her fingers under the waistband, "These sweatpants are something else."

I chuckle, "I take it you like them?"

She grips my ass and I raise an eyebrow, "Correction. I take it you really like them."

"They're bloody hot on you."

"You mean it's the way I wear them, isn't it?"

She rolls her eyes, "Yes, yes. It's the way they hang low on your waist, then cling to your butt and mold your powerful thighs, and of course," she slides a hand between us and traces the outline of my cock, which is already standing at attention, "highlights just how much you are packing."

"Didn't hear you complain about that when I was inside you."

She bats her eyelids, "Were you, now? I hadn't noticed."

"Excuse me." I step back from the circle of her arms, place the cup on the table, then straighten. "You were saying—"

"Was I?" She bites down on her lower lip.

"Something about not having noticed I was in you?" I take a step forward and she skitters back. I lunge for her and she screams. I move toward her again. She pivots, runs forward, jumps off of the patio, and races ahead. She turns, panting, then screams when she realizes I am right behind her. I grab for her and she ducks, then takes off running, throwing up sand in her wake. The T-shirt that she's pulled on, my T-shirt, flaps about her thighs. The fabric clings to her shapely butt that twitches as she runs. She glances over her shoulder, "What? Can't keep up, old man?"

"Who are you calling old man?" I sprint toward her and she squeals. She puts on a burst of speed and she dashes toward the water's edge. I dart toward her, closing the distance between us. I tackle her around the waist and she yells as she hits the ground. I clamber over her, flip her over, then pin her down to the sand with my hips. She flails around with her arms and I grab them and hold them above her. I wrap my fingers about her wrists and shackle them. "Do you submit?"

"No!" She spits out sand, "No way."

I begin to tickle her under her arms and she screams, then begins to shake with laugher. "Stop," she gasps, "stop, please."

"Submit to me, Beauty."

"No!"

I release her arms, only to tickle her down both sides of her body. She laughs and chokes, "Fine," she gasps between bouts of laughter that make her entire body shake, "fine, I submit."

I lean back, "Good."

I pin her arms on either side of her as I straddle her. There's sand on her cheek, on her throat, in the valley between her breasts. I lean down and bury my face there and she moans. "Oh, Mika!"

I slide down until I am positioned over her core. I shove my sweatpants down, notch my dick against her pussy, and in one thrust, impale her.

She gasps, "Oh, god, Mika!" She wraps her legs around my waist, and in that move which always drives me crazy, pushes her hips upward so I slide further inside her.

I stay there, allowing her to adjust to my size as I gaze into her green eyes. Pupils blown, color flushes her cheeks as I begin to move inside her. Once, twice, thrice, I release her arms then yank down the neckline of her T-shirt. I squeeze her nipple and she sucks in a breath. I twist it and a whine bleeds from her lips.

"The noises you make, *Bellezza*... They drive me fucking crazy." I lower my head to her breast, bite down on her nipple, and she screams. Her body bucks. I straighten, hold her gaze as I begin to fuck her in earnest. Once, twice, thrice, I slam into her with such force that my balls slap against the insides of her thighs. Her entire body goes rigid, her eyes roll back in her head, then she wheezes, "Oh, my god, I am going to —"

"Come, Beauty," I growl, and her features twist as she cries out. Moisture bathes my cock as her body spasms. I plunge in and out of her, in and out. My balls draw up and I empty myself inside of her.

Twenty minutes later, I glance up from the tub I've run for her. "What?" I murmur as she watches me with a strange look in her eyes.

I'd carried her inside and run a bath for her while she'd discarded the now sodden shirt that she'd been wearing. I'd divested myself of my sweats as well and poured in the bath salts I'd specially ordered for her.

The scent of moonflowers fills the air and she starts. "That... that's my favorite fragrance."

"I know," I murmur as I rise to my feet. She runs her gaze down my chest to my crotch, where she takes in my already semi-aroused state.

"Again?" she murmurs "You're already hard?"

"Seems to be my constant state around you." I walk over to her and push a strand of hair out of her eyes. "What was that earlier look for, hmm?"

"I am still getting used to seeing you so relaxed, is all."

"It helps that we are on an island, and no one can get on it without my noticing."

A purring sound reaches me and I glance down to find the cat brushing up against my leg.

"I think he's beginning to grow on you."

"Feed the beast a couple of times and he thinks he owns you."

"And this beast?" She grips my cock and squeezes, "Do I own him, now that I've fed him a few times?"

"Why, Beauty, where have you been hiding this filthy mind of yours?"

She chuckles, "It's one of the things you like about me; admit it."

"I like everything about you. Haven't you realized that?"

"Oh, my god!" She pretends to be shocked, "Who are you and what have you done to my alphahole Capo?"

I grin as I smack her butt, "Into the water, before it gets cold."

## 23

Karma

Five days. We've been here five glorious days, where we've fucked. A. Lot. And everywhere. Against the kitchen counter, on the kitchen floor, in the tub, in the shower, on the beach—many times. And of course, in the bed. Tonight, being New Year's Eve, Michael wants us to dine out on the patio.

I've decided to dress up a little. Well, a little more than the last few days when I've walked around almost naked. It had seemed ridiculous to be putting on clothes when all Michael would do was to pull them off. He, himself, had taken to wearing a pair of shorts that he'd pulled out from the clothes that had been there in the closet.

While he is off setting the table, I take in the dress I've chosen. He's refused to let me cook in all the time that we've been here. Which is good, considering my cooking skills are nowhere close to the level of expertise he's showed. The man is not only good in the bedroom, but also in the kitchen... How the hell have I gotten so lucky, eh?

This dress is one of the few I had packed when I left his home—
an alternative version of my wedding dress that I had stitched
before I'd left. It's in the form of a sheath with the skirt cut high
over one thigh and low at the breast line. The dress is sleeveless with
halter neck that I've tied around my neck, leaving most of my back
bare.

It's the kind of dress that could be worn for a formal occasion but
would look as good on a beach. There had been so much material I
hadn't used for my wedding dress that I had managed to cut a
second dress from it. I consider my light make-up—just eyeliner and
lipstick; it hadn't felt like I needed anything more for this evening—
then turn and head out to the patio.

In the kitchen, I find Andy already eating his food. The cat seems
to have taken to Michael a lot more than when we had been in his
house. Guess he really does know who is responsible for the food he
is getting here.

I walk toward the patio, then pause when I see the table laid for
two. There are plates, silverware, even starched white napkins, and a
bottle of prosecco chilling in a bucket. Beyond that, the sea forms the
perfect background.

"Wow," I breathe as heat envelops me. I lean back and into his
hard chest, and Michael wraps his arm around my waist.

"Like it?"

"I love it," I say simply, then turn to face him. "I love you."

He glances down at me and his lips kick up in a real smile. "I..."
he hesitates, "I know." He leans down to brush his lips over mine.
The kiss is soft, tender... So different from the Capo I knew when
we were in Italy.

Was he going to say 'I love you'? Why had he stopped himself? I
open my mouth to ask, and he thrusts his tongue inside. He deepens
the kiss, and all thoughts drain from my mind. I press into him, revel
in the hardness of his sculpted chest, the thickness between his
thighs that reveals how much he wants me.

He must love me. All of his actions say so. So what, if he hasn't
said those three words to me yet?

He seems to tear his mouth away with reluctance, his breathing heavy, color flushing his cheeks. "*Cazzo,*" he growls, "I can't get enough of you."

"Then don't," I lean up on my tiptoes, wanting to kiss him.

He evades me. "First food," he counters.

"First sex," I insist.

"I've created a sex maniac!" He chuckles, "I can't have you wasting away. Besides, you need your energy for when I am going to have my wicked way with you." He slaps my butt, then steps back, "Come on, sit down."

Once I am seated, he makes sure that my chair is pushed in properly. Then he opens the prosecco and pours out a glass for me and one for himself. He sits down and I raise my glass, "To us."

"To you," he clinks his glass with mine, "my sexy, smart wife whose darkness matches mine."

I laugh, "Only you'd compliment me on that."

He takes a sip of his prosecco, then glances at me, "It's what attracted me to you. I saw you…and I knew there was something inside of you calling out to me. That you would be as depraved as me. That I could bare my soul to you and you wouldn't be afraid."

"But I was," I take a sip from my glass, then peer up at him from under my eyelashes. "I was afraid that once I fell for you, I'd never be able to leave you."

"And that's bad?"

I tilt my head, "I am still making up my mind about that."

"Now that, I hadn't anticipated… That you'd turn out to be this bratty. Clearly, I haven't been punishing you enough."

"Please, Daddy," I flutter my eyelashes, "will you spank me?"

His nostrils flare and his shoulders flex. He places his glass on the table, then rises to his feet. He walks around to tower over me. He holds my gaze as he lowers his head to mine, "Only if you ask me nicely."

Heat flushes my skin and my belly trembles. A gust of wind blows my hair across my cheek and he pushes it aside. His touch sends a pang of need shooting through my veins. I part my lips. He drops his gaze to my mouth, "And only after we've eaten."

He straightens and stalks away.

"Asshole," I yell after him and he laughs.

"Jerk," I murmur to myself, then snatch up my flute of prosecco and toss it back. I grab the bottle and am about to top up my glass, then change my mind. He wants me? He can come get me.

Walking out to the patio, I shut the door...to make sure Andy can't get out, then walk out onto the beach, then away from the house toward the jetty I'd seen earlier.

The setting rays of the sun bathe me in their warmth. The heat from the cooling water seems to rise in the air. I stand at the edge of the jetty, raise the bottle to my mouth, and drink the sparkling prosecco. It slides down my throat and cools me enough that goosebumps pop on my skin. The waves lap at the edge of the jetty as I tilt the bottle to my mouth and take another sip.

The hair on the back of my neck rises. I turn to find Michael is silhouetted against the window of the kitchen. I raise my hand and wave at him and he waves back. This man... He's the best thing that has ever happened to me. To think, I'd thought the opposite when I had met him. Guess love can come in so many different ways, eh? And he does love me. So what, if he hasn't told me so?

It's there in his every gesture, in how he takes care of me and of Andy. He's so gentle with my pet... Always taking care of his needs first. If he can be so tender with that kitten... Surely, he'd be a wonderful father, too. And I am not on birth control, so maybe I'll leave this island pregnant. I slide down to sit at the edge of the jetty, with my legs hanging over. I take another sip of the prosecco and set it aside. Then stretch my arms above my head.

I circle my head once, then glance down to find waves rippling out from a spot in the water. Huh? I lower my arms, glance at it, not sure what I am looking at. A black shadow appears under the water, and before I can pull up my legs, it swoops up, grabs my leg and tugs. I yell, but I am already falling.

# 24

Michael

She is going to love this dish. I slide the roast back into the oven, then straighten and turn my attention to the salad that I am assembling. Andy prowls into the kitchen and brushes against my leg. I smirk as he glances up at me, then at the dish I am cooking.

"No food for you yet, boy." I chuckle. "Your mother's gonna be pissed if I feed you between meals. But if you are a good, little kitten, I might sneak you a little snack to keep you going."

The beast blinks at me, then with a huff, turns and walks away. I swear, that cat can understand me. And here I am, talking to it. I shake my head.

That's the kind of magic she has woven over me, my Beauty. My *piccola*. Mine.

I glance through the window and find she's not at the jetty. Huh? I peer through the pane, take in the surroundings. There is no sign of her. What the hell?

Maybe she just went for a walk. Yea, that's all it is. She just

walked out of sight of the house. I glance down at the salad, then
back at the now empty jetty. The hair on the back of my neck rises. I
place the knife on the counter, turn and head for the doors that lead
to the patio. I throw open the door, rush out...then pause.

"*Cazzo!*" That cat needs to stay inside. If he wandered out and
something happened to him, she be beyond pissed-off about it. I
retrace my steps, close the door behind me, then take off again.
Around the house, across the sand that surrounds the house, toward
the jetty. I reach it, and there's still no sign of her. I glance around at
the water and freeze. A figure dressed all in black, tows another
figure that is prone and on her back. Ahead of them is a motorboat,
manned by a second man.

*Che diavolo!* Who'd dare come to my island and try to take my
wife from right in front of me? My heart pounds in my chest and
adrenaline laces my blood. I dive into the water and swim toward
them. Every time I surface for air, the distance between us seems to
have shrunk, but it's not fast enough. Once they reach the boat, I'll
lose them and not be able to find out their identity.

Oh, I'll be able to track her down, thanks to the tagging device,
but damn, if I am going to let them get their hands on her. I increase
my pace, propel my body, and cut through the waves. I kick and
move forward bit by bit.

When I surface again, it's in time to see the diver handing the
prone figure to the man on the boat. *How dare he touch her! How dare
they take her from me? I am not going to lose you, Bellezza; not this time.* I
thrust forward through the waves, just as the sound of the motor
starting reaches me.

Fuck, fuck, fuck! I push forward and reach the boat just as it
takes off. I lunge up, grab at the boat. My fingers graze the side of
the boat but it leaps forward. Bloody fuck! I fall into the water, then
begin to swim in the wake of the boat. I kick and propel forward,
almost reach the boat again, only it pulls forward.

I watch helplessly as the distance between me and the boat
grows. Motherfucker! This can't be happening. My heart pounds so
hard in my chest that I am sure it's going to leap out of my rib cage.

I had gotten swayed by my Beauty. So immersed in her that I

had gotten sloppy again. I hadn't been able to protect her. It's my fault that they got to her. I should have stayed in Sicily and focused on tracking down the men responsible for rigging the car that caused my brother's death. Instead, I had given in to my need to see her and I had put her in danger. Again. But this time, I am going to find them and put an end to this. Never again, will they be able to harm me or what's mine. I am going to reveal the true wrath of what it means to cross the Capo of the Cosa Nastro. And when I am done... No one will ever defy me. Ever again.

Turning, I begin to swim toward the island.

Fifteen minutes later, I pull up the app on my phone that allows me to track her. *There.* I see the blue dot moving across what appears to be the expanse of the sea. They are heading toward England... What the hell? It has to be the Kane Company who took her. Fuck.

I had known who it was, and yet, I hadn't moved in on them. If I had, they wouldn't have been able to take her. *Stop that.* I shake my head. *Focus, I need to focus. I need to get to her.* I strip out of my wet clothes, pull on jeans securing them with a belt, then a T-shirt, and the jacket that I had loaned her earlier. I reach for my knife and slip it into the sheath at my waist. If only I had brought my guns. I drag my fingers through my hair. The, one time in my life I had lowered my guard and she had been taken from me. It's dangerous to go in without my weapons but fuck that, my knife will have to do.

I turn off the oven, top up the food and water in the cat's bowls, then race for the door. Andy darts out from under the settee and I sidestep him. He races for the door, plants himself squarely in front of it and stares up at me.

"Out of the way, cat. I need to get to her."

He blinks, and I swear, he is aware that something has happened to her. I bend down, grasp him gently by the nape of his neck and move him to the side. He tries to dart past me, and I manage to hold him in, then shut the door before he can leave the house. I hear the angry hisses as he scratches at the door. I dial Seb's number as I race toward the boathouse where I have the motorboat stored.

*"Fratellone?"* Seb answers on the second ring. "Where are you?"

"Enroute to her." I slow down a little so he can hear me speak "They took her again; motherfuckers snuck up on me on the island and took off with her."

"I don't understand," his voice is puzzled, "how did they reach you without your noticing their arrival?"

"They swam underwater, got to her when she was on the jetty." I growl, *"Maledizioni!"* I raise the phone, ready to bring it down and smash it, then draw in a breath. Another. Force my muscles to relax as I lower the phone to my ear.

"Get the plane, then get to the island and arrange to have her cat taken to safety," I order.

"A plane? Just for the cat?"

"It's *her* cat," I growl. "Just do it, Seb."

"Got it, Capo, and what about you?"

"I am going after her."

"Alone?" His voice grows concerned, "Wait for us, Mika. We'll be there soon with back up."

"Fuck that. If you think I am going to wait around here not doing anything while my wife is in the hands of my rivals, then you are mistaken."

"So, you are going to barge in, knowing that this is what they want? That they want you to lose your composure enough to walk into a trap?"

"Fuck that!" I bark. "Of course, it's a trap. Likely, I'll be overpowered the moment I get there, but at least, I'll be there with her. At least, she'll know that she is not alone."

"Mika, you're making a mistake. You're the Capo; you—"

"You'll be able to see her location on the app; get there as soon as you can."

I cut the call, then squeeze my eyes shut. *Fuck, fuck, fuck.* I pull up the app, focus on the dot again. *Wait for me, Beauty. I am coming after you as soon as I can.*

# 25

Karma

I cough, sputter, then sit up with a gasp. I glance around the room I am in…which is empty, save for the bed I am on… Well, calling it a bed is giving it too much credit. It's some kind of bunk built into a wall. Starlight slants in through the only window, which is high up in the wall. *Shit, where the hell am I?* One second, I had been sitting on the jetty, sipping my prosecco and planning my future with my Capo. The next, something… No, someone had swooped up from out of the water, grabbed my leg and pulled. I had screamed… Or tried to scream, but I had hit the water and swallowed a few mouthfuls before remembering to hold my breath.

The guy had started towing me away. I had resisted and he had cuffed me on the side of the head. He'd stunned me enough that I didn't resist as he towed me along the surface, then hauled me onto the boat. Then, I had pretended to lose consciousness while they fired up the engine and set off.

I'd stayed still, in the hopes that I'd hear the men speak and give me some clues of who they were and where they were headed. But they had, annoyingly, spoken very little to each other.

When they cut the engine, I peeked through half-closed eyelids to find that they were docking the boat. One of the men reached for me and I lost it then. I struggled, tried to evade him, and he hit me on the back of the head. And then I found myself here.

A headache builds behind my eyes. I touch the back of my head and wince at the bump there. Damn it, I am tired of being kidnapped and used as a pawn in this stupid game that the Mafia seems to want to play with their rival gang. It has to be a rival gang holding me, right? The same one who had kidnapped me the last time. The same one who had planted the bomb in my car. The one that killed Xander and my unborn child. I squeeze my fingers at my sides. This time, I am going to have my revenge. No way am I going to let them get away with this a third time.

The door to the room opens and light streams in. I throw my hand over my eyes to protect them from the glare, when footsteps sound. The light bulb overhead is switched on and I wince.

"Come on," a woman's voice says in precise English, "he is waiting for you."

I lower my hand, stare at the middle-aged woman wearing a black dress that comes to her knees. Her hair is black and pulled back in a bun. She wears minimal makeup and has the kind of looks that would help her blend into the background anywhere. It's almost as if she's trying not to draw any attention to herself, and succeeding quite nicely, by the looks of it—no pun intended.

I snort to myself as I rise to my feet. My knees threaten to give way and I have to dig my feet into the ground for purchase. I tip my chin up, walk to the door. She steps out of the room and I follow her. She leads me to an elevator...and I blink. Of course, there is an elevator. Not sure why, but I imagined this was a room in a place where such modern trappings would be nonexistent. I watch her profile, but she gives nothing away.

The car ascends two floors, then jolts to a halt. She heads out and I follow her up the corridor and into a room. She beckons me to enter. I walk in, turn to find her standing at the entrance to the room.

"You are to get dressed and come down to the dining room for dinner in an hour."

"An hour?"

She nods.

"And how do I tell the time?"

She points to a small antique alarm clock on the dresser.

She turns to leave and I yell out, "Hey, you do realize that I have been kidnapped right?"

She closes the door in my face.

I walk toward it, and open it, to find she's striding away. "One hour; you don't want to keep him waiting," she calls over her shoulder.

I take a step forward, then hesitate. Guess it's not going to help if I follow her now. She'll probably just call one of those two idiots who grabbed me earlier to come get me. Also, I want to take something for this headache that has been growing in intensity.

By the way, I am taking all this rather calmly, aren't I? I mean, I am tagged, so he is going to come after me. Bet he's already on his way. All I have to do is sit tight, and make sure I don't get myself killed in the meantime.

Half an hour later, I step out of the shower. The hot water has taken the edge off of my headache and made me feel almost human. I walk into the bedroom and find a simple black dress, underwear made of white cotton, still in its packaging, and a pair of sneakers laid out for me. Did the same woman place it here? Probably.

I pull them on and they fit. So, whoever took me had anticipated that I'd need clothes, but he or she isn't going to keep me here for too much longer? And given the utilitarian feel of the clothes, he or she doesn't have a romantic interest in me… At least, I don't think so.

I dress quickly, then dry my hair with the hairdryer provided. I head for the door when it opens. I pause as the same woman from earlier beckons me. I follow her. This time, down two flights of stairs. So, we are back on the same floor as the room where I had been kept earlier.

I follow her down a long corridor with closed doors leading to other rooms. Each of the doors are ornate. There are paintings on the walls depicting scenes from the English country side. "Are we in England?"

"Yes," she confirms.

"In the countryside?"

She doesn't say anything, but I am sure we are.

"Whose clothes are these?"

"They were purchased for you."

O-k-a-y. Not what I was expecting.

She reaches the door at the end of the corridor, and pushes it open. I walk in to find a long table with places set for two at the head of the table, facing each other. I walk toward it, when the door on the opposite side of the room opens.

A man prowls in. He is tall, broad shouldered, dressed in a black suit that clings to his shoulders. His features are hard, his gaze intelligent as he takes me in. Gray threads the hair on his temples, hinting that he is in his early forties, maybe? It's difficult to say, because with his trim build and the obvious muscles that stretch his jacket, he could be anywhere from late thirties to early fifties.

"Finally, we meet, Signora." His voice is very cultured, very British.

"You?" I frown, "I know you."

"We haven't been formally introduced though, have we?" He prowls over to me. "JJ Kane, at your service."

I glance down at his hand and hesitate. The man looks like Daniel Craig toward the end of his career as James Bond—cynical, hardened, and I hate to admit it, but he radiates raw sex appeal that fills the space between us. He's not as sexy as my Capo, but this man... He's as dangerous.

"Why did you kidnap me?" I demand.

Amusement lurks in his gaze. He doesn't seem to be offended by my obvious snub. "Not my style, but something I couldn't avoid."

"Were you also behind the rigging of my car that killed Xander?"

"I heard about that." He tilts his head, "Sad affair. But no, also not my style. Too messy."

I glower at him, "What's your game anyway?"

"No game," he holds up his hand, his gaze steady, and his tone reeks of sincerity. All the more reason I don't believe him.

"I am simply inviting you to lunch."

"Oh, so that's why you took me from my husband's island, because you wanted to have lunch with me."

"Indeed," he gestures to the table, "and because I wanted him to realize that he shouldn't underestimate me."

"You couldn't have told this to him directly? Honestly, this entire 'being a pawn in the games that you made men play' is proving to be a little tiresome."

He laughs, "You don't mince words do you?"

"Please," I hold up my hand, "enough with the false praise; I can do without it."

I walk over to the chair at the head of the table and drop into it.

His features go solid. A pulse flares to life at his temple, then he throws back his head and laughs. It's a full-bodied laugh that comes from the pit of his belly and makes him seem younger than his years. He stalks over to the chair on my left and slides into it. "You have balls, *signora*."

I sniff, "Lady balls, don't you mean?"

"Precisely," he glances at me closely as if noticing me for the first time, "so this is why Michael is so taken with you."

"Aren't you his arch rival or something?"

"Rival?" He frowns, "I wouldn't use such a common word. More like we are two players who are competing for the same thing."

"And what is that?"

"Power."

"Of course, it is." I roll my eyes and notice a man walking through the door. He's followed by a second man holding a tray on which there are two steaming bowls of soup. Both men are dressed in uniforms, clearly indicating that they are staff.

They retreat and JJ gestures to the food, "Please, eat."

"Don't mind if I do." I reach for the soup spoon then hesitate. "This doesn't have any seafood in it does it?"

He shakes his head and I scoop up some of the broth.

The scent of coriander and ginger fills my senses. And the taste? Whoa, creamy and light at once, spicy and nourishing, and yet, there are traces of some ingredient that I can't identify but which adds such depth that the taste lingers in my mouth long after I've swallowed it. "Wow," I stare at the food, then back at him, "that is good."

"Indeed, it is." He chuckles, "Gordon is the best chef right now on the entire continent."

"And he's cooking this meal for you?"

"A favor." He inclines his head, "It's not every day that I have such a distinguished guest."

I stare at him. Should I believe him? Why would I? The way he had me brought here shows that he has something up his sleeve. But what?

I turn my attention back to the soup and don't stop until I've swallowed down most of it. I lean back with a sigh and find JJ watching me with a pleased expression.

"And she also doesn't stint when it comes to eating well. You are, indeed, a catch, signora."

"*Grazie*," I murmur as I pat my mouth with my napkin.

The next course is a fragrant rice dish with vegetables and pieces of chicken that have been marinated so well, they melt in my mouth. And the dessert… Chocolate mousse, with a vanilla ice-cream that is so fresh I can taste the vanilla pods.

"I'm stuffed," I admit when the last dish has been cleared.

JJ pushes back his chair and stands up. He comes around and holds out his arm, "May I escort you into the library for an aperitif?"

"Why not?" I rise to my feet and allow him to guide me out of the room, down the corridor, and to a room whose door is now open. I walk in and take in the floor-to-ceiling books that fill the wall opposite the fireplace. In between is a bank of windows that looks out over the grounds, and above the fireplace, is a portrait of a family.

He catches me staring at it. "My family," he says simply as I take in the likeness of a younger JJ, a woman who is seated, and next to her, a teenaged boy who resembles both JJ and his wife.

"That's your son."

He nods.

"I saw him at Xander's funeral."

"Indeed."

"Is he here?"

A shadow crosses JJ's features. "He's back in LA. He seems to prefer the US to our country."

"Oh." I sense something else he's not telling me, but I am not going to ask him to explain that.

He guides me to a chair in front of the fire. "What will you drink? Coffee? A brandy maybe?"

"A brandy sounds good."

He moves to the bar, pours out two snifters of brandy and walks over to hand one to me. He seats himself then holds up his glass, "To you, *Signora*."

I raise my glass and take a sip. The taste is exquisite. "To what do I owe this wining and dining?" I fix my gaze on him.

He laughs, then contemplates his drink, "My father, rest his soul, was not a very empathetic man. Well, that's putting it mildly. He was a complete villain."

"Coming from you, I'd better believe it."

He chuckles. "There was only one piece of advice he gave me which I adore, to this day."

"Which is?"

"He told me to always keep one step ahead of the enemy. To never show him your cards, and to surprise him when he least expects it."

"So that's why you decided to take me from the island; so you could show my husband that you're better than him?"

"Not just better, but faster, more lethal, more dangerous, more unpredictable, more everything…"

"Never."

"Excuse me?" He frowns. "Would you mind repeating yourself?"

So polite. Fuck, this guy's a joke. "I said that you couldn't hold a candle to him."

"Is that right?" He stares at me, then breaks into a laugh that sends shivers down my spine. This guy…he's certifiable. He straightens, and just like, that all mirth is wiped from his face. He leans forward, his movements careful, precise, as he places his glass on the table in front of us.

"But then, you are biased." He strokes his chin, "You would be; you are his wife."

"Why have you brought me here?"

"You are a clever girl; haven't you figured it out by now?"

"To hold me as ransom?"

He clicks his tongue, "How pleb would that be? No, nothing like that... I am simply going to use you as a negotiating tool to get what I need from him."

"Like I said, a ransom."

"A simple give and take. He has what I want, and I have something that is very precious to him. All he has to do is give me what I want, and in return, he can take what's his."

"Michael will never forgive you for this."

"Not doing this to win friends."

"He is going to kill you."

"Love a challenge."

"So, if you didn't rig the car, then who did?"

"That's something he'll need to figure out himself, won't he?"

"So, while we wait for him, we are simply going to sit here and shoot the breeze?"

"Probably, but to be fair, I don't think we need to wait that long either."

"You're that sure that he'll come for me?"

"Surely, he must be able to keep track of you wherever you are?"

I frown, "How would you know that?"

"You are important to him—probably more than anything else he owns at the moment. Of course, he'd find a way to track you even when you are not in his line of sight."

I shake my head, "You Mafia guys."

"Not Mafia. I'm simply the leader of an organized crime group."

"Gosh, is that a posh way of saying you are a crook, or what?"

"Never claimed to be on the straight and narrow."

"No one would ever mistake you for that." I take another sip from my glass. "So, how long do you think I have to make conversation with you?"

"Surely, it's not that much of a chore."

I glance at him, then away, "If you want me to be honest—"

"Always."

"I'd much rather be back on the island. But considering you took me from there, I doubt I'll ever be going there again," I say glumly.

He chuckles, "Now, young lady, never say never again. If there's one word of advice, I can give you it's that…"

"That?"

He leans forward and touches my arm, "That you never know what's going to happen next."

That's when the door to the library is pushed open with such force that it slams against the wall. "You *testa di cazzo*!" a familiar dark voice growls, "I am going to kill you."

# 26

Michael

I lunge inside the room, spot the man seated opposite my wife. My wife... who seems to be in good shape overall, and he has his hand on her. He has his hand on her. JJ. Has. His. HAND. On. Her. Fuck. Anger thrums at my temples. My vision tunnels. I pull out my knife and throw it at him. The asshole ducks. She screams. The sound slices through the noise in my head. I jerk my head in her direction, in time to see her features pale. She jumps to her feet, takes a step in my direction, but JJ grabs her. The next moment he has a gun in his hand that he's pressed into her temple.

I freeze. Glare at the traitor, who smiles. He gestures toward the chair he's just vacated. I growl, deep in my throat, take a step in his direction. That's when three men burst into the room.

Two of them grab me by my shoulders, the third pushes the butt of a gun into the back of my head. Anger suffuses me, pours thorough my blood. My stomach ties itself in knots as I take in the fear in her gaze.

FUCK! I had sworn to myself that I'd never allow her to be afraid. Never need for anything else. And I had broken my promise in a matter of days. Why am I unable to hold myself back when it comes to her? Will nothing I do ever be enough to protect her?

I had made it here as fast as I could, following the tracking device. Then had searched the house until I had found them.

The men push me toward the chair. She follows me with her gaze as they apply pressure on my shoulder so I sink down into it.

The man behind me removes his gun. He proceeds to pat me down, then when he finds me clean — not that I didn't want to carry weapons, but if I had any chance of getting close to her, I knew that I had to be clean — he pulls out a length of rope. He proceeds to run it around my arms and chest and tie me to the chair. He also knots it around my ankles. I flex my muscles, hoping to get some slack as he does so. I don't take my gaze off of her. She swallows, and I shake my head. *Don't be afraid, my love. I won't let anything happen to you.*

Almost as if she can read my mind, she jerks her chin in a downward direction. If I hadn't been paying such close attention to her, I'd have missed it.

Their job complete, the men holding me back away. They leave the room and the door snicks shut.

"Sit down, *Signora,*" JJ murmurs. He slides the gun back into the waistband at the small of his back. Karma doesn't move and he touches her shoulder.

I growl, lunge forward again and the chair shifts. The scrape of wood against wood sends a screech through the space.

JJ glances at me. "Impressive," he tilts his head, "but unnecessary. I have no wish to hurt her."

"That's why you took her." The blood pounds at my temple, my pulse rate ratchets her. "How dare you touch her?"

"Calm down." JJ arches an eyebrow, then turns to Karma, "You'd better get your husband in hand, *Signora,* else I won't be responsible for my actions."

Karma swallows.

"Do it," he snaps, and her lips tighten.

A growl rips from me as she moves forward. She closes the distance between us, then sinks to her knees in front of me.

"Capo," she whispers, "my Capo." She places her palm against my cheek and every pore in my body seems to pop. I stare into her green eyes, take in the golden sparks that flash there. I hold her gaze as she leans up and presses her lips to mine. "I love you," she murmurs, "only you, Capo." The sound of my title from her lips... Fuck, but right now, I'd tear the world apart, just to hear her say it again.

She peers into my face and an expression of hope, of anticipation laces her features. I hold her gaze...knowing what she wants to hear. Wanting to say it. Wanting her to feel it. I try to form the words, but my tongue doesn't seem to work. I don't glance away, allowing her to read my expression, the raw need I feel right then, the helplessness. Do I have any right to love her, if I can't even protect her?

She moves back and I spring forward. I smash my lips to hers and kiss her and kiss her. I lick her lips, thrust my tongue inside her mouth and absorb her. I kiss her until someone taps me on my shoulder, "That's enough, ol' chap."

JJ's voice cuts through the haze in my head. I tear my mouth from hers and survey her flushed features. She licks her lips as if absorbing my taste within her before she rises to her feet.

JJ walks around and pats the chair opposite me. "Please, *Signora*," he says in a casual tone, "do take a seat."

With a last glance at me, she heads over and sits down.

JJ picks up the snifter of brandy on the table between us. He takes a sip as he glances first at her, then at me, "Now where were we?"

"What the fuck do you want?" I snap.

He smiles. "You know what I want."

"The cybercrime syndicate," I say in a low voice. "That's what this is about?"

"Right on one." His smile broadens. "Now that I have your attention on it, what say you?"

"What do you want with it?"

"I don't want you to hand it over to me."

"You don't?"

He shakes his head, "That would mean getting in the trenches and monitoring the day to day, which wouldn't work for me."

"You simply want to share in the profits," I surmise.

"Right again," he says in a pleased tone. "Look at that, *Signora*. Your husband is being exceptionally cooperative. Makes me think that I should have tried this tactic earlier."

"You rigged her car with an ignition bomb, you *pezzo di merda*!"

"Now, now, that wasn't me."

"You think I am going to believe you?"

"That's not my style. If I wanted to kill your brother, I'd have done it to his face. And yours."

Anger sears my blood. I attempt to jump to my feet, only to be restrained by the ropes. I growl as the bonds cut into my arms and my ankles.

"Don't talk about my brother, you bastard."

"I had nothing to do with his death," he insists. "Whether you believe it or not, that's not my problem."

"By bringing her here, you've brought an entire shitload of problems to your doorstep, you *carogna!*"

"Nothing I can't face," he drawls.

"You sure about that?"

The door flies open, and he jerks his head toward it.

Sebastian prowls forward, his gun trained on JJ. Luca follows, then Massimo and Antonio. All three of them have their guns drawn. Christian brings up the rear; he drags the man by his collar—the one who'd restrained me—and throws him on the floor. Then levels his gun at the temple of the guy and fires.

Karma shudders, glances away as the man's body jerks. He slumps to the floor and Christian slams the door shut behind him. He takes his position in front of it.

JJ takes a sip from his brandy. The man's one cool customer; I'll give him that. Seb keeps his gun trained on JJ as he jerks his chin in Luca's direction. Luca stalks over to where the knife is embedded in the wall next to the fireplace. He grunts as he works it out, then pivots and walks back to me. In two strokes, he's cut through the ropes. I rise to my feet and he hands the knife back to me, handle first. I snatch it from him, stalk over to where JJ is seated. He raises his tumbler to his lips and I press the knife to his throat. "I am going to kill you," I growl.

That's when the windows explode.

# 27

Karma

The panes of glass explode and the pattering of what sounds like hail stones fills the space. My throat hurts, and that's when I realize, I am screaming. The sound of my own voice echoes in my ears. The next second, I am pushed to the ground; a big body covers me. The scent of leather with a hint of woodsmoke. Fresh snow fallen on the earth… His scent envelops me. The heat from his body pours over me, cocoons me. I push up and into him, trying to get as close to him possible; to touch as much of my body to his as I can. Even though we are in the middle of what sounds like a gunfight, I can't help but exult in the fact that he's near me, on me, around me. I turn my head and push my cheek into his T-shirt covered chest. I draw in deep lungfuls of Michael, and my head spins. His chest heaves, the hard planes digging into my breasts as he gathers me even closer.

His arm moves and I realize that he's holding the knife out and over me. Guarding me, protecting me. My own personal bodyguard.

My champion. My knight... Stop... Clearly, I am in shock. That is the only reasonable explanation for why my thoughts are in such free fall.

I draw in a breath and my lungs burn. My stomach twists, my arms and legs tremble, and I squeeze my eyes shut. Shit, shit, shit. Not the time to be going into shock.

The silence lengthens, I sense him move, then he grips my chin. I feel his gaze peruse my features, and crack my eyelids open. His blue gaze burns into me. In their depths, there's so much fire, so much concern... So much everything. I open my mouth, but my brain seems unable to put the words together. I draw in another breath, feel a tear run down my cheek.

Stop that. Why am I acting like such a weakling? I can get through this. I've survived this far; hell, I've faced the biggest trans-formation possible and come through the other side. I lost my child, almost died, lost a man who I had grown to love like a brother in such a short time, and I am still here, aren't I?

So why is my heart racing, my pulse pounding, my arms and legs trembling like I am in shock...? *Um, it's because you are in shock?* Because I may be married to a Mafia Capo but I am still not used to being shot at. Hell, I may never be used to being shot at, truth be told. Because as much as there is darkness at my core... I am also a creature who craves the life I once had?

A home, a career, a focus on creating art through my designs. Producing clothes that will bring my visions to life, and getting them out in the world. Where does all of that fit in with this life that I have been thrust into? Where do I fit in with this world that is Michael's life? This is where he came from and this is where he will always be. And if I want to live with him, I'll have to fit in. Do I want to fit in with this life that he has chosen for me? Do I want to walk away from everything I have spent my life working toward...to be with him?

So far, he has led and I have followed. Since I met him, it's been a roller coaster ride, and I've been happy to go along for the ride. But now... It's as if I am waking up from a long sleep and realizing that I have a choice.

I hear the sound of someone moving and glance around to find JJ belly-crawling forward toward the doorway. He reaches it, straightens, keeping as close as he can to the wall, and hits the light switch.

Gloom descends on the room. The rays from the sun slant into the room, but I guess switching off the lights makes us less of a target? Maybe? JJ's eyes glitter as he glances toward Michael, who nods. Something silent passes between the men. That's when another burst of shots rings out, and JJ drops to the floor again.

"*Merda!*" Michael swears as he throws his body over mine again. This time, the shots seem to go on and on. Things hit the floor around me. People? Or pieces of the furniture that the bullets have ripped out? Or bits of the wall that the bullets have loosened and which are now hitting the floor? A moan wells up and I swallow it down. My entire body trembles.

Michael seems to sense my anxiety, for he presses me into the floor. Thump-thump-thump; his heartbeat pounds against my back. Strong, steady...grounding me. I focus on it, on him. Strange, even though I know that our time together is, surely, drawing to a close, I still can't stop myself from leaning on him. Another tear runs down my cheek and I try to swallow the ball of emotion that clogs my throat.

Silence descends and I realize the shooting has finally stopped. No one moves, then something else crashes to the floor.

I turn to find Seb and Massimo have upturned the table so it's another barrier between us and the windows. While Luca keeps his gun trained on JJ, Seb and Massimo use the edge of the table to balance their guns and return fire. The sound of gunshots fills the room again. It's so loud, so close... Too close.

A tremor runs up my spine. I am not a weak person, but my daily life and my fashion designing business seem so far away right now. One wrongly– or rightly-directed bullet, and I'll be dead. Gone. A soft moan leaves my lips before I can stop it.

"Shh," Michael presses his lips to my temple, "you're safe, *Bellezza*. I promise, I won't let anything happen to you."

*And you? Who will ensure that nothing happens to you? Will we spend our lives always worried about the next bullet that's going to kill one of us, or our loved ones?*

I bite the inside of my cheek, knowing there are no answers to these questions. He'd never leave the Mafia... He wouldn't want to, and even if he did, they'd never leave him. Besides, what would he do? Work in an office behind a desk? Ha! As if he'd ever be able to fit into an ordinary lifestyle.

Michael is too big. Too vital. Too real... Too much everything. Maybe he's always been too much for me, but I haven't wanted to see it. I've been too consumed by his larger-than-life image, his sexiness, his over-the-top attractiveness, his dominance which consumes me, overpowers me completely.

I had lost myself in him... And now, I am finding myself again... And I am not sure whether I want to be this woman I've become being with him.

The firing ceases.

The room plunges into silence again.

"*Fratellone,* we need to get out of here," I hear Luca murmur. I peer from the corner of my eye to find he still has his gaze on JJ. Guess they weren't taking any chances with the boss of the Kane Company.

"I am not sure that's a good idea," Seb's voice protests. "We leave here, and whoever is shooting at us will kill us."

"We stay here and we are sitting ducks," Luca hisses back.

"I vote we fight back," Christian interjects.

"With what?" Massimo growls, "We'll be out of ammo very soon."

"I have guns in the basement," JJ speaks up.

Silence, and I imagine all of them are glaring at JJ. I push at Michael's chest and he rises to his feet.

"Stay down." He bends low and I follow suit.

He guides me toward the back of the room. I step over pieces of wood, pieces of paper that have been torn out of the books that the bullets hit. I try to avoid stepping on them but there's too much of it. That, combined with the bits of plaster from the ceiling that have fallen to the floor, have turned the once beautiful room into a war zone.

Michael urges me behind the settee. He pushes down on my shoulder so I have no choice but to sink to my knees behind the sofa. It's some kind of protection, in case the shooting starts again, I suppose. I stare up at him and for a second, it's so erotic, so hot to have him looming over me, the breadth of his shoulders shutting out the sight of everything else, his gaze on me as he reaches down and cups my cheek. "You okay?" he asks in a soft voice.

I swallow, not trusting myself to speak, then nod.

He holds my gaze a second longer before glancing toward JJ. "Weapons," he snaps, "how many guns do you have?"

"You're going to take his help?" Christian glowers, "You're going to take the help of the man who murdered our brother."

"I didn't kill him," JJ retorts and Christian lunges for him. He brings the butt of his gun down on JJ, who ducks, but not fast enough. The butt smashes into the side of his temple and blood spurts from the wound. JJ grabs Christian's arm and twists it. His gun falls to the floor. Both leap for it, only someone fires a shot in the air. It hits the ceiling and chunks of rubble pour down in the center of the room. Neither JJ nor Christian move.

Massimo stalks forward. He grabs JJ by his collar, hauls him to his feet, then presses a gun to his temple. Christian picks up his gun and straightens. He brushes off the dust that has settled on his jacket. "Thanks, bro," he jerks his chin at Massimo.

"You have something to say, Christian?" Michael demands.

Christian stares at him, then at JJ. "I understand why you think we need to take his help," Christian growls, "but as far as I am concerned, he is guilty of our brother's murder until proven otherwise."

"And this…is why the Mafia is struggling to hold onto their position as the most notorious of all the organized crime bodies in the world." JJ smirks, "You guys are too emotional."

"No one asked you for your opinion, *stronzo.*" Christian's shoulders tense and anger vibrates off of him. His jaw is clenched so tightly, I wonder if he's going to pop a blood vessel any second.

"He's right, though," Michael says slowly, and Christian turns on him.

Michael raises a hand, "I understand how much you miss Xander. We all do. And if he is, indeed, the person responsible for his death, then trust me, I'll ensure that he dies in the most painful way possible. But right now, we need to find a way out of here."

"And quickly," Luca adds. "They've stopped shooting, but this is only a temporary reprieve. They must be reloading their weapons and planning their next move."

"Agreed," Seb nods his assent.

Michael glances between them, then at Christian, who glowers back. "How about we kill the *bastardo* first, then head down to get his weapons?"

"Won't work, ol' chap," JJ drawls. "You need my retinal scan to get through."

"We could always cut off his head and take that to unlock the door," Massimo offers.

Luca chuckles, "Now that's something I have been looking forward to."

"Cutting off his head?" Seb asks.

"Specifically, the heads of our rivals and parading them around the streets of the city to teach our enemies that they can't fuck with us," Luca retorts.

Seb scowls at him, "This is not an episode of *Game of Thrones*, you ass!"

"More's the pity; I always did prefer a sword to a gun." Luca raises a shoulder.

"You always did like to overcompensate," Seb chuckles.

Luca's frown deepens. He points his gun toward Seb, then blows out a breath, "Pity, I can't shoot you for that."

"I'd like to see you try," Seb waves his own gun in the air.

"Gotta say, your brothers make for a fascinating comedy act." JJ trains his gaze on Michael, "And these are the jokers you count on to have your back in a sticky situation?"

"Asshole," Luca trains his gun in JJ's direction, "one more word and I won't hesitate to shoot."

JJ firms his lips. The bastard still doesn't seem to be put out by the fact that he's surrounded by men who would not hesitate to kill him if he breathed too hard. Jesus, the man has nerve, all right.

He trains his gaze on Michael, who jerks his chin, "Let's go get those guns."

# 28

Michael

Am I a fool to trust JJ—the man who stole her from my island, under my watch, and brought her here? Am I totally *stupido* to follow him as he walks us down another flight of stairs to the basement?

He reaches a closed door, presses a code into the keypad, in the space next to the doorframe. He places his eye in front of the retinal scanner which glows green, and the door buzzes open. I shoulder open the door, Karma at my side.

Luca, who's taken great pleasure in holding a gun to JJ's head during the entire trip, brings up the rear. He pushes JJ through the now open door, then follows him in, along with Seb and Christian.

Massimo stands guard outside the door.

I take in the row of guns on the opposite wall.

Sebastian whistles, "He wasn't kidding when he called it an armory." He grabs a gun, then the ammunition next to it. He checks the gun, loads it, slides it into his waistband at the small of his back.

Christian glares at JJ before arming himself. I reach for a gun, slide it into the empty holster at my ankle, then under my bicep, a third in my waistband at the small of my back.

Karma slips away to stand at the side. She folds her arms about her waist, a haunted look on her features. I glance at her, then snatching up one more gun which I slide into the front of my waistband, I walk toward her and she glances away.

"What's wrong?" I murmur and she bites down on her lower lip. I glance at the glistening flesh and my cock twitches. Fuck, this is not the time to be turned on…but with Beauty, just being close to her makes me want to throw her down and bury myself inside her again.

"Tell me, Karma," I insist.

She tips up her chin, "It's nothing."

"It's something." I bend my knees, peer into her face. "What is it?"

"I was wondering…"

I tilt my head.

"Is that a gun or are you happy to see me, Capo?" She shoves her hand down my pants and pulls out the gun.

"Know how to use that?"

"Aim and shoot?" she ventures.

I smirk, "First thing I am gonna do when we get out of here is teach you how to use a gun."

Her forehead crumples.

"What?" I search her features, "What is it?"

"Nothing."

"Don't lie," I growl, "tell me what's bothering you, Beauty. If not—"

"You two love birds ready to leave before whoever is shooting at us starts up again?" Seb's voice cuts through the space, and she glances past me.

"We have to leave," she murmurs and I know she is hiding something. "This is not over, Beauty," I warn her as I cock the gun and hand it to her. "Take care with that," I murmur.

"Always," She stares into my features, then reaches up and

presses a quick kiss to my lips. My heart begins to thud against my ribcage. What is she hiding from me? What is she not telling me? *What are you up to, Beauty?* I deepen the kiss, thrust my tongue in between her lips, and kiss her with everything I feel for her.

"Michael," Seb's urgent voice reaches me, "we need to go, *fratellone*."

I straighten, then step back from her, "Stay close."

I pivot and head for the door, Karma right behind me.

"What about him?" Luca jerks his chin toward JJ, "What do we do with him?"

"Give me a gun and let me fight with you."

I hold his gaze.

"Not the time to think with your heart, Capo." JJ tilts his head, "You need men on your side. You need *me* on your side to fight your way out of this one."

Fuck this, but he's right. If I let my ego get in the way and don't give him a gun, and if whoever is attacking us manages to hurt us... I'll never be able to forgive myself about it.

I close the distance between us and bury my fist in his face. JJ rears back. Blood streams from his nose and spills onto his shirt.

He shakes his head, then curls his fingers into fists. "The fuck was that for?" He scowls.

"That," I growl, "was for taking my wife to get my attention."

He rolls his shoulders, then uncurls his fists, finger by finger. "Fair enough," he rumbles.

"Don't fucking touch what's mine again, you hear me?"

"And you keep your hands off of what's mine," he growls.

We glare at each other, then I jerk my chin toward the array of weapons, "Now, you may grab a gun."

"No fucking way!" Christian explodes. "You're going to give him a gun?"

I turn to him, "Not the time to debate this, *fratellino*."

"You can't give him a gun, Capo," he insists.

"That's my final decision," I say in a hard voice. Christian holds my gaze, then turns away. He marches toward the door and I watch him go with mixed feelings. "Fuck," I growl, "fuck, fuck, fuck."

"You're doing the right thing, if it's any consolation," JJ pulls out a pristine white handkerchief and dabs at his face. "And to prove it to you, I'm going to take you to a place from which we can return fire in relative safety."

"And you are telling us this now?" I arch an eyebrow.

"Had to make sure that I could trust you, first."

"Don't trust him, Capo," Luca growls. He grabs a few more firearms for Massimo, then turns and marches off after Christian.

JJ grabs the guns and arms himself, then turns to me, "Follow me."

I hold his gaze, trying to read the expression on his face. Next to me, Beauty shifts her feet, while Seb glares at JJ, before turning to me. "You going to trust this motherfucker, boss?"

I scowl at JJ, then nod, "Lead the way."


Five minutes later, we are in the room next to the library, and surprise—we used a hidden door from the armory that had a staircase that led directly up to this room.

"The walls are made of reinforced cement, and the windows," he jerks his chin toward the panes "are made of reinforced glass."

"You have a regular Fort Knox here," I say mildly.

"Never can be too prepared in our line of business." He shoves his gun in the opening between the panes.

Seb follows suit, and so do I.

Karma hunkers down behind me, that same distant look on her face. The one that makes my gut churn every time I glance at her. I want to talk to her, to reassure her that everything will be okay. That I will not let anything happen to her. I reach for her, and that's when the first shots ring out.

Seb returns fire, as does JJ.

The shots die away. In the silence that follows, my phone buzzes. I put it on speaker, "Massimo?"

"There's an entire group of them." He speaks rapidly from his perch up on the top floor of the house. Along with Christian and Antonio, he'd headed there to take stock of how many people we're up against. Additionally, they were going to try to take down as many as they could from their vantage point. "I count at least fifteen men surrounding the house and closing in on the grounds," he adds.

"Fuck," Luca swears from the other side of Karma. I had asked her to stay in the corridor, out of the line of fire, but is the woman having any of that? Of course, not. In this, she was as adamant as ever. She'd insisted that she'd be here with me. When I had protested, she'd said that she felt safer with me. And how could I argue with her after that?

JJ stiffens on the other side of me. "This would be a good time to have more of my men," he mutters.

I growl.

He raises a shoulder, "Not putting the blame on you for offing them. It's merely a fact that we need more men on our side."

In their zeal to get through to us, Seb had gunned down JJ's men. The only people who remain are the household staff, and JJ had instructed them to stay in the kitchen and not come out. They had been more than happy to oblige us. Not that I blame them. It's going to get a lot uglier here before it gets better.

"You sure you don't want to join the rest of the household staff?" I ask Karma.

She shoots me a scathing glance, "And leave you here on your own?"

"I am quite good at surviving tricky situations."

"This time, I am going to be with you every step of the way."

I glance into her green eyes that are dilated...with fear? With the adrenaline of the fight. Her lips part and my cock thickens.

"I don't want to sully your hands with blood," I murmur. "You don't have to do this, Beauty."

"But I do." She stares back, "I want to see what it is about fighting with a gun that gives you such a hard-on, Capo."

"Nothing and no one gives me a hard-on as much as you, Beauty."

Seb groans next to me, "Can you guys keep it down? Some of us here are trying to focus on not getting killed."

Karma flushes, then rises to her feet to peek through the windows.

A shot rings out again and Seb instantly returns fire as well.

I pull her down. "What the hell do you think you are doing?" I hiss.

"N…nothing," she blinks rapidly, "uh, just wanted to see what was happening out there."

"What's happening is that, unless we do something fast, they are going to start shooting and there are more of them."

"We have more ammunition," Seb reminds us.

"Five of us—" JJ begins and Karma interrupts him.

"Six of us."

He inclines his head, "Six of us, and fifteen of them."

"The odds are not good," Seb blows out a breath.

"But not impossible, either." I am not going to let whoever they are get the better of us. I am going to bring them down and find out who's at the bottom of this attack…and likely, the attack on Karma's car, as well.

"It's time we go on the offensive," I crack my neck.

Seb scowls, "That would not be advisable—"

"I agree with the Capo," JJ interrupts him. "Let's take this situation by the horns and surprise them."

I exchange glances with JJ, who jerks his chin. Apparently, the two of us think more alike than I'd have expected. And somehow, I am not sure if that's a good thing. It means he's more astute than I'd given him credit for. It also means that I have underestimated him all this time.

Holding the gun with one hand, JJ slides the other inside his pocket.

Seb swoops down to grab his arm. "What do you think you are doing?" he growls.

"Relax," JJ drawls, "I'm only going to call for additional men."

Seb glances at me. I nod; he releases JJ's arm.

JJ pulls out his phone, his fingers fly over the keys as he shoots off a message. Then he pockets his phone again, "They should be here in the next half an hour. Think we can hold them off until then?"

Seb scowls, seems about to say something, then thinks the better of it. "What do you think, Capo?"

"I think," I bare my teeth, "that we don't have a choice."

# 29

Karma

Is this me or is it a dream? Am I really standing here next to my gangster husband holding a gun? A weapon I have never held before, and which I have no idea how to use...but which already feels familiar in my hands. The metal seems to draw warmth from my skin as I clutch it.

I should be more scared of the power I hold in my hands. The ability to play God, to fire this gun and snatch someone else's life... It's both worrisome, but also, strangely, empowering. That dark core of me is thrilled at the force I hold in my hands. With this, I could make others obey me. I could control people. I could get my way. I could—

"Beauty?" His soft whisper cuts through the noise in my head, "Are you okay?"

"What?" I blink at him, "Did you say something?"

"I asked if you were okay."

"Yes, of course." My palms sweat and I tighten my grip on the gun.

He stares at me a little longer and I tip up my chin, "I am fine, honestly."

"Good." He rakes his gaze across my features, "You sure you don't want to go inside, and get out of the line of fire?"

"And miss all the fun?" I allow my lips to curl in a poor attempt at mirroring his smirk.

He chuckles, then kisses my forehead, "I knew I was obsessed with you for a reason."

He's obsessed with me. He's. OBSESSED with me. OMG, did he just say that? I peer up at him from under my eyelashes, but he doesn't seem to be aware of the ramifications of what he just said.

He reaches for his phone and dials a number. When Massimo answers it, he glances first at JJ, then Seb, before fixing his gaze on me. "Open fire," he commands.

Instantly, shots are fired from above, and returned. Each time a bullet hits the glass, it's deflected, but the sound of the bullet bouncing off makes me wince.

The splattering sound of the bullets rebounding off of the glass increases in intensity. It feels like we are in the middle a hailstorm, only deadlier.

All through it, Michael, JJ and Seb continue to return fire, adding another layer of noise to the sound of bullets being deflected.

I thought I was prepared. I thought I could face this barrage of gunfire, but I had mistaken just how intense it was to be in the line of fire. The shooting seems to rise to a crescendo. The shots come so thick and fast that it's like the popping of corn, at the height of when you are zapping it in the microwave, only much bigger, much larger than life, much more in your face... Much more lethal.

I know I am not in direct danger, yet I can't stop myself from flinching. I hunch my shoulders and wish I could cover my ears to lessen the intensity of the sound. I sense Michael glancing at me. He puts his arm around me, pulls me closer. I huddle into him, still holding the gun in my hands. My fingers tremble to pull the trigger, to answer back, to do something... Anything, except sit here with only a wall of glass separating us from the bullets that never seem to stop coming.

The shots go on and on. My heart beat ratchets up, my pulse rate accelerates, sweat pools under my arms, and black spots flicker at the corners of my vision. My heart seems to palpitate with such intensity that I can hear the blood thud in my ears. "Bloody hell," I gasp as my knees seem to buckle.

I lean heavily into Michael, who grips my shoulders. "You okay?" he yells, close to my ear so I can hear him above that never-ending barrage of bullets. A bullet rain. I am stuck in a monsoon of ballistic proportions with my very own avenging devil. A shiver runs down my spine. My heartbeat seems to grow louder, bigger, expanding until it fills my entire chest.

Over us, the hail of bullets reaches a crescendo, then stops. The sound ricochets through the corners of my mind, then fades away. I draw in a breath, another, then gasp when he hauls me to him, "You okay, baby?" he asks in a harsh voice.

"I am fine." My voice quivers and I clear my throat. Goddammit, I am not going to act like a wimp. Not now.

He searches my face and swears, "You're pale."

"It's the light." I attempt a weak smile. "I'm fine; honest."

He nods, then turns back to the window and shoots. JJ, Luca and Seb follow suit.

I'm fairly certain Christian, Massimo, and Antonio open fire from above, for once more, the air is thick with the sound of bullets being shot. The vibrations from the recoil slam into my chest, echo through my mind, press down on my stomach, my womb. My knees give way and I sink down to the floor.

I sense Michael glance down at me but he doesn't stop shooting. I coil into myself, still holding onto the gun, as pain slices through my chest. Sweat pours down my temples, drips down my chin. Shit, shit, shit. This is it. It's my heart… It's finally giving out. How poetic that it had to be when I am holding a gun, and next to my gangster husband, in the middle of a gun fight. Am I going to die, not struck by a bullet, but because my heart finally chose this moment to show that I don't belong with a Mafia guy, after all? Something I had already realized but which the events of the past few seconds have brought home even more firmly?

I shudder and curl into myself as the firing continues on and on. The spent cases from the used bullets hit the floor in front of me, a constant stream of metal clinking...

Like the coins in my pocket when I had walked home from school and stopped to buy my favorite candy at the corner shop. It had been during the time we had been with one particular foster family who had been so good to us. We—Summer and I—had fit in so well with them, we'd thought we had found our forever family. They'd give us pocket money we could use to buy candy, a huge treat. Something we had never been able to do before. One day, we'd reached the shop, and I'd chosen my candy and brought it to the till to pay. Then I had reached for the coins, which had slipped from my hands and hit the floor and rolled away. I'd managed to gather them back. At least, I'd thought I had, but when I had handed them over, some had been missing. I hadn't had enough to pay for the candy. Summer had stepped in and bought me the candy. She had skipped her treat that day and shared mine, and I had been so happy. The jingling of coins would always be associated with that particular memory and now with this...

The constant barrage of bullets that my husband and his brothers fire at those who are trying to kill us. A chill grips me and my teeth chatter. I grasp the gun, drawing on some of the residual warmth from the metal. *I am not weak. I will not give in to the frailty that envelops me. I am not going to just sit here and allow the men to fight while I play the role of a woman who needs to be protected all the time.* I push myself up to my feet, place my gun on the barrier and fire.

# 30

Michael

One minute, she's trembling on the ground; the next, she is on her feet and firing off the gun as if she's done it her entire life. She holds her finger down on the trigger and fires. Her body shudders with the recoil. She pauses, changes her stance, then grips the gun tighter and fires again, and again.

Each time she fires, her body shakes with the recoil. Each time the gun spits out a bullet, she winces, but she doesn't stop. She keeps her finger glued to the trigger, long after the rest of us have stopped.

Her features are contorted, her cheeks flushed; her chest rises and falls as she widens her stance to better support herself and the weight of the gun she holds. At some point, I realize the rest of the men have stopped shooting and are watching her. But she still doesn't stop.

The skin across her knuckles stretches white, but she keeps the trigger depressed, keeps shooting, until the empty clacking of the chambers fills the space. Tears run down her cheeks, drip from her chin. She sways, her legs seem to give way from under her, and I catch her as she crumples.

The gun slips from her fingers, and Seb snatches it up. I lower her to the floor, take in the sheen of sweat on her forehead, the trickle of sweat that runs down her temples, and my heart stutters.

"*Bellezza!*" I haul her close as I peer into her features, "You are not feeling well."

"I am fine," she insists, and her voice cracks.

"You are not fine."

"I..." she swallows, and more color leaches from her features, "I am fine, really, I am."

Seb drops down to one knee next to us, "What's wrong? How is she?"

"We need to get out of here." I glance up at him, "I need to take her to a doctor."

"No!" She rears up, "No doctor."

"You need to see someone to find out what's wrong with you."

"I... I know what's wrong with me."

I blink, "You do?"

She nods.

"Are you going to tell me?"

"I..." she glances away, "it's nothing, really."

"It's something if it has you jumping to your feet to fire off your gun, only to collapse in the next instant."

"Michael..." she opens and shuts her mouth, "it'll pass."

"What is it?"

"Honestly, it's nothing that you need to concern yourself with."

"Everything that concerns you concerns me."

"Argh!" She makes that sound deep in her throat that she does when she is frustrated, and fuck, if my cock doesn't instantly twitch. Everything about this woman is designed to drive me mad, surely?

She glowers at me, "You're impossible!"

"And you are beautiful."

Her lips tremble, "Don't say that." She glances away from me.

"Why not?" A cold sensation coils in the pit of my stomach. "I'll say it as many times as I want to you. You're my wife, after all."

"Am I?" she muses in a low voice, but I catch it.

"What the hell is that supposed to mean?"

She doesn't reply and that knot in my stomach pulls tighter. "Karma, what's going on in that head of yours?"

"If we don't do something about those men shooting at us, nothing is going to go on, because we'll all be dead," JJ interjects.

I jerk my chin up in his direction. "Don't you dare interrupt when —"

"He's right," Seb says in a hard voice. "We're stuck in the middle of a gunfight."

"You don't say?"

"What do you want to do, Capo?"

I glance down at Karma, then at Seb, "We need to —"

"We're going to stay and fight it out," Karma retorts.

I glare at her, "Now, you're going to make my decisions for me?"

"She's right," JJ cuts in. "Try to leave here and you will be gunned down."

Seb nods, "Our only hope is to stay and fight and take down those shooting at us."

"We have the weapons needed to outlast them," JJ reminds me.

Karma grimaces. If possible, she turns even more pale. Sweat dots the front of her dress, which clings to her chest. Her chest rises and falls and her lips twist. She's in pain. She's not admitting to it, but she's in pain.

"No," I say in a cold voice.

"What?" Seb stares. "What do you mean, no?"

"I mean, no." I glance down at Karma, "I am going to find a way to get her out of here and to a doctor."

"Fuck," Luca swears from above us, "that's suicide."

"We'll survive. I'll make sure we survive."

"*Cazzo!*" Seb growls, "*Fratellone,* that is not a good idea."

"I'm going to do it anyway."

"Think of her, if not yourself; you don't want to put her life in danger."

"I am thinking of her," I say in a low voice. "If I don't get her out of here, her life will be in danger."

"But—"

"Let him go," JJ murmurs. "You can take her to my doctor; I'll text you the address. I'll call him and let him know to expect you."

"*Grazie*," I jerk my chin at him.

"You're welcome." JJ pulls out his phone and walks away to make a call.

Just then, footsteps sound outside. The door flies open and Christian, Massimo, and Antonio burst through the door.

"What's wrong?" Christian sinks down to his knees next to Seb, "What's happening?"

"Karma is not feeling well, and the Capo has decided he is going to make a run for it to get her to a doctor."

"You are both going to die," Christian says flatly. "There are still, at least, ten people out there, and probably more on the way."

"I am not going to let my wife suffer. I am going to get her to a doctor."

"And how are you going to do that?" Christian growls, "I assume you parked your car a distance from the house so you could approach without being discovered?"

"*Cazzo!*" I swear aloud, "It's not going to be easy to get to it without being spotted."

"You can use my car," JJ pockets his phone as he prowls over to us. "It's in the garage and it's bullet-proof."

"No vehicle is completely bullet-proof." Christian snaps. He turns on me, "I speak the truth and you know it. Try to take her out of here and you endanger both of your lives."

I hesitate. Do I want to be more beholden to one of my enemies...more than I already am.

Making my decision for me, Beauty gasps. She grips my hand and I glance down to find her eyes closed. Her chest rises and falls; her breathing is shallow. Fuck this. "Fine," I snap, "I'll take the car."

"What the—!" Christian explodes, "How can you willingly put yourself in danger, and after what happened to Xander—"

"It's because of what happened to Xander that I can't allow anything to happen to her." I scowl up at him.

He holds my gaze and whatever he sees on my face must

convince him, for he blows out a breath. "Fuck," he growls. "Fuck, fuck, fuck." He rises to his feet, then stares down at us, "I am coming with you."

"No, you're not," I snap.

"If you are putting yourself in danger—"

"Nothing is going to happen to us."

"Then let me come with you."

"No," I say in a low voice.

He opens his mouth to protest and I slice the air with my palm, "This is not open to debate."

"*Cazzo!*" He sets his jaw. "We'll cover you. We'll fire at the motherfuckers and make sure they are so occupied that they won't be able to stop you."

"Good plan," JJ remarks.

Christian glares at him. "We're out of ammo."

"You know where to find it," JJ replies.

"Don't we need your iris scan to unlock the door?"

"Do you?" JJ smirks.

Christian's face suffuses with color.

He jumps up to his feet, swoops out and jams his gun into the side of JJ's temple. Everyone freezes as the two glare at each other. JJ doesn't flinch, doesn't lower his gaze. The staring match goes on and on, then Christian nods. He slowly lowers the gun, pivots and walks out.

"I'll come with you." Antonio follows him.

A bead of sweat slides down JJ's temple. "The boy has balls," he concedes, "and he's hurting."

"We all are." It's not lost on me that in the space of a few hours I've gone from wanting to kill the motherfucker to trusting him… albeit grudgingly. Perhaps it's because of the life and death situation in which we currently find ourselves. It's what happens when you are under pressure. You need to make snap decisions, and trust your instincts. And right now, my gut says JJ is on our side. Temporarily. Until we find out who the hell is after us.

"You'll need this," JJ holds out his phone, "I've deactivated the lock and the doctor's address is already keyed into the GPS."

I slide the phone into my pocket.

"Garage is at the back of the house, through the kitchen," he adds, as he hands over the key fob. I take it, then rise to my feet and scoop Karma into my arms. She protests and I scowl at her. "Don't even think about it."

"But—"

"I am not going to let you walk."

"I was going to ask for my gun back."

I scowl at her, she tips up her chin. "My gun, Michael."

I nod at Seb, who reloads her gun, then holds it out. She accepts it, and cradles it close to her chest.

"Don't shoot me with that thing."

"Don't insult me." She purses her lips. "I may not be used to holding a gun, but I can hold my own with it."

"That you can," Seb concedes.

I glance around, take in the faces of my brothers, then turn to JJ. "Thanks," I say grudgingly. "This doesn't mean that I trust you."

"Same." He jerks his chin.

Seb picks up my gun from where I had placed it on the floor. He loads it, then slides it into my waistband at the small of my back.

I head for the door and he follows me.

"Where are you going?" I frown at him over my shoulder.

"Going to get you guns so you can defend yourself."

"I'll stay here," Massimo rumbles. He glares at JJ and it's clear he doesn't trust the other man to leave him on his own. Good call.

I head down to the ground floor, then out of the back door, and into the garage. The lights flicker on, revealing six parked cars. I press the keyfob and the Mercedes in the corner lights up. As I head toward it, Seb pulls out his phone, calls Christian and asks him to come to the garage with the ammo. We reach the car and Seb opens the passenger door; I place Karma inside. Then walk around to the driver's side.

Christian and Antonio join Seb, and together, they pile guns and boxes of ammo on the floor in the back of the car.

"You realize, if any one sees this, they are going to report you to the police immediately, right?" Karma grumbles.

"Will they?" I take in the pile of weapons.

"Maybe not in Sicily, but not too many people know you here," Karma insists.

"I'll make sure not to draw attention to the car."

"And the doctor?" She frowns. "Won't he get suspicious about it?"

"It's JJ's doctor; I assume he's used to seeing guns," I retort.

"Guns are not as common in England as in Sicily."

"More's the pity." I shake my head, "Never understood the appeal of a stiff upper lip, when you could simply leave a stiff behind that wouldn't talk."

"Is that a joke?" She scowls, "That *is* a joke. OMG, Capo, you made a joke?"

"Your English sense of humor must be rubbing off on me." I smirk.

"Here," says Christian as he lays a dark blanket over the guns. "Done."

The guys slam the back doors shut.

"Wait for the diversion, then drive," Christian orders.

"Don't worry about us. Don't stop for anything; you just keep going," Seb adds.

"I wish you'd let me, at least, come with you." Antonio scowls, "I am your bodyguard. It's my responsibility to make sure that nothing happens to you."

"And I want you to stay with my brothers and fight back."

With a last glance at the men, I slide into the car.

*"Arrivederci,"* Christian calls out. *Until we meet again.*

They turn to leave, and I snap my seatbelt into place at the same time as she does.

"Now what?" Beauty lays the gun across her lap, then looks at me expectantly.

I reach over, wrap my fingers around her neck and bring her close. I kiss her, then thrust my forehead into hers. "Now we wait."

"And what do you suggest we do while we wait?"

"What do you have in mind?"

"What do you think?"

"You're not well." I scowl and she raises an eyebrow.

"Let me be the judge of that."

She reaches over and grips my crotch and my cock instantly hardens.

"Karma," I scold, "now is not the time."

"Now is exactly the time." Her eyes twinkle. Color seeps back into her face and she doesn't seem to be sweating anymore.

"You're feeling better, I take it?"

She massages my crotch, "I am now." She winces again and I glare at her.

"You lying to me again?"

"I..." She scowls, then pulls her hand back. "Fine, fine," she glances to the side, "have it your way."

I blow out a breath, "Baby, I know you want me, but your health is more important."

She scoffs, "What would make me feel better is if you eat me out."

"And get you overexcited again?" I shake my head, "not that I don't want to, but I am worried about you Karma, and I'd rather play it safe until we have you examined by a doctor."

That's when shots ring out.

# 31

Karma

"Fuck," he swears under his breath, "it's beginning." He rakes his gaze across my features, "You ready for this?"

*No.*

*No.*

"Yes," I jerk my chin.

He holds my gaze a second longer, then turns and puts the car in gear. He eases the car toward the garage door which rolls up, revealing the driveway. He revs the engine, peers through the glass as he waits…waits…

I search the driveway and what I can see of the grounds up ahead. "Shouldn't all the shooting have attracted cops by now?"

"It would have if we'd been in London."

"We aren't?"

"We are on the outskirts, and the grounds are so big that there are no neighbors around for miles."

"So, he lives close to one of the most expensive cities in the world and his estate is so big that he could literally commit murder and go undetected?"

He shoots me a glance and I raise my hands. "Just saying. I guess crime does pay, eh?"

"Does that bother you?"

"It's your world."

"And yours," he points out.

"Not yet."

"That's the second time you've come up with a cryptic remark in the past twenty minutes." He scowls.

Ahead, there's a muffled boom, then a section of the trees catches fire. Instantly, he puts the car in gear and roars forward. A creaking sound reaches me. I peer through the windshield, then gasp. "Mika!" I point to where the tree on the side of the driveway in front of us begins to topple over. He accelerates with such speed that I am pushed back into the seat. The Mercedes leaps forward, and the tree misses the tail of the car and hits the ground. The crash seems to resound through the space. The dust from the impact flows over the car.

Mika slaps on the wipers and their rhythmic *whoosh-whoosh* fills the car. He keeps his foot pressed on the accelerator as he races up the driveway, past the trees that surround the house on either side.

More shots ring out, bullets pepper the sides of the car, slam into the windshield. I scream and throw up my arms, only to realize that the bullets are bouncing off the car. Each bullet embeds into the windshield, and on the glass of my door, leaving a star shaped crack on impact. More shots ring out and I flinch with each impact. I glance sideways to find Mika focused on the road ahead.

The shooting seems to go on and on, there's a yell, then all noises fade. Except for the *whoosh* of the wipers, which he switches off as the car hurtles forward. Silence fills the car, for a beat, another. We continue up the driveway, and the gates to the estate loom in the distance.

"The gates are open? Was it JJ who...?" I shoot him a sideways glance in time to see him nod.

His jaw is hard and a nerve pops at his temple. His muscles seem to have turned to stone as he keeps his gaze focused forward.

Less than a mile now to the gates, three-fourths of a mile, half a mile… He leans forward as if urging the car forward with his entire being.

I draw in a breath, hold it. Twist my fingers together in front as I part my legs, push my heels into the floor of the car and brace myself. Adrenaline pours through my veins, and the blood pumps at my temples, thrums at my wrists. My heart beat ratchets up again, and this time, I don't care. I feel the flush that stains my cheeks, that sensation of the pulse flaring to life in my stomach, between my legs, as I stare through the windshield and the scenery zips by. I am excited and turned on. I shouldn't be, but I am.

Speed… Goddamn, I love speed, even though I've never had the chance to indulge in it. Not unless you count the video games I'd managed to play with one of my foster siblings. It had been only for a few months, but it had been long enough to give me a taste of what it would be like to take on an opponent, to race forward, eyes on the prize, as you mowed down anyone who dared to come in your way. As I hope Mika will do too. I shoot him another sideways glance and find his gaze completely focused on the road forward.

He presses down on the accelerator and the car seems to fly forward. Less than fifty feet to the gates...forty…now, thirty… That's when a car shoots out from the undergrowth and onto the center of the driveway in front of the gates. Then a second car from the other side. They park nose to nose in the center.

"*Cazzo!*" Mika growls, and for a second, I am sure that he is going to crash into the cars, but he slams on the brakes with such speed that I am slammed against the restraint then back against the seat. A scream boils up, even as a part of me relishes the adrenaline rush that builds within me.

Even as I turn to him Michael is already out of the car. He pulls out his gun as he fires at the man getting out of first car. Blood gushes from his chest and he drops to the ground. Michael continues to fire at the second man who's come around from the car, then at the driver from the second car, who's stepped out, and the other men who pour out from the second car.

He runs out of bullets, flings the gun aside, grabs another from the holster under his arm, and continues firing in such a smooth move that I blink. The men fire at him, he drops to the ground, rolls, comes up firing. It's like a dance, a much-practiced, smooth motion which he's rehearsed so many times, it's a part of him. *Of course, it's a part of him.* He was born into this world. The sound of bullets echoes in his cells, the scent of ammunition is steeped in his veins, this... weaving, ducking the shots that come his way, as he returns fire, taking out man after man who dares to threaten him... This is Michael at his rawest, truest, stripped-to-the-bone naked. This is Michael unadorned. Just how I like him. How I like the darkness that clings to his core. This...feeling of danger that surrounds him is what I crave, and what I worry may consume me until I can't differentiate right from wrong.

It's why I know I can't be with him.

It's also why I will not be a woman who cowers in the background while her man is fighting a war.

I snap my seat belt open, grab the gun from the floor, push open the door and step out, still holding the gun. I raise my gun, depress the trigger, and it doesn't fire. What the hell? I apply pressure on the trigger, again and again. Still, nothing happens. What the—! The breath whooshes out of me. Michael switched on the safety. That's why I am not able to fire. I reach for the safety, when the barrel of a gun is pushed into the back of my head.

# 32

Michael

"Stop or I'll shoot her."

A familiar voice rings out. I keep my finger pressed down on the trigger, take the last man out, then pivot, gun pointed toward the man who has his weapon trained on her.

"*Cazzo!*" I growl as my gaze collides with a pair of blue eyes so similar to mine.

"Don," I growl, "What the hell are you up to?"

"Sorry it had to come to this, Capo," he says without any change in expression, "but I have to protect what's mine."

"You wanted me to become the Don."

"Correction," he looks me up and down, "I wanted you to think that I wanted you to become the Don."

"Why," I shake my head trying to understand what his intentions are, "Why would you do this?"

"Why would I hold a gun to your wife's head?" His lips curve,

"You know why. You let it become personal, Capo. You allowed her to get to you. You went against everything I taught you."

"Everything you taught me?" I explode, "You didn't teach me shit, you bastard."

"Technically, I am not a bastard. Neither are you, for that matter." He shakes his head, "American insults; they're so predictable, don't you think?"

"There's enough American in me to use the insult when it fits the occasion."

"That was my first mistake. Agreeing to let you go to the US to study. You came back, not just with an American accent, but with their sensibilities as well, which don't fit in with our way of life."

"What doesn't fit in with our way of life is you."

"And you?" His lips kick up, "You are going to modernize the ways of the Mafia, eh? Bring us into the digital age with your virtual businesses? The very nature of which has resulted in this mess."

"It did," I agree. "The virtual businesses which you mock are so profitable that it led to my partners trying to betray me to get a hold of it, but thanks to you," I allow my own lips to curve in a smile, "I've not only sorted that out, but at the same time, I've made allies of our closest rivals."

"You'd engage in a partnership with our enemies?" My father's features harden. "That is a recipe for disaster."

"What is a recipe for disaster is that you still have your gun trained on my wife."

"What are you going to do about it?"

I curl my fingers around the trigger and the Don shakes his head, "Don't do it; not unless you want to see your wife's brains all over the ground."

Karma pales and her fingers holding the gun tremble. He leans around, grabs the gun from her. I stiffen, take a step forward, but he wiggles his gun in my direction. I pause, take in Karma's features. Her chin wobbles, but her gaze never wavers. Magnificent woman. She squares her shoulders and firms her lips. She's scared, but she's trying her best not to show it. I hold her gaze for a second longer, then turn my attention to my father. "What do you want?"

"You. Dead," he points her gun at me, then releases the safety. The sound is loud in the silence, broken only by the sound of the hot metal of the cars contracting as they release some of their heat into the air.

She winces, but doesn't give any other sign of the fear I am sure grips her right now.

"I thought you wanted your legacy to continue."

"It's why I have five sons."

"Four," I say in a low voice, "you have four sons left."

"Too bad about Alessandro," he raises a shoulder, "but the way he was going… He wasn't worth the Mafia name."

"You?" Anger clouds my brain and my pulse rate ratchets. Something hot stabs at my chest. "You?" I manage to form the word with my tongue. "You were behind the rigging of the car? You killed him?"

"An accident." For a second, he seems almost contrite, then his features smooth out again. "I hadn't meant for the bomb to kill him."

My gut clenches and my vision tunnels. He killed him? My father killed my brother? He killed Xander? I clench my fingers around the trigger of my gun. I am going to kill the bastard myself. But I don't yet have a clear shot. *Merda!* I glare down the barrel of my gun at him, force my muscles to relax, "But you did intend to kill her?"

"Something to distract you from your path to taking over as Don."

"I don't understand." I shake my head. "You encouraged me to become Don; you are my father."

"So?" He raises a shoulder, "Doesn't mean I ever have to step down. I intend to stay at the helm of the Mafiosa for a long, long time…but you, were becoming too great a threat."

"You'd kill me, rather than see me succeed?"

"And then I'd still have three sons." He raises a shoulder, "Enough to continue my lineage, when the time comes."

"You've lost it," I growl.

"You're the one who's lost the fight." He narrow his gaze on me, "Lower the gun, son."

Son? He dares call me son after everything he's done to our family? Bile bubbles up my throat and I swallow it down. I glance from him to her, then back at his face.

"Do it," he warns. "If you want her to survive this, you'll lower the gun."

"If you let her walk away, I'll hand myself over."

"No, Michael," Karma bursts out, and he must push the gun into her head, for she winces again.

Anger coils in my belly, my vision narrows, adrenaline laces my blood, and I force myself to uncurl my fingers from where they have pressed down on the trigger. "Let her walk away, now," I insist, "and I won't fight this."

"Lower your gun first," he says in a cold voice. "Don't forget, I am the one who taught you the game that you now insist on playing."

I glare at him and he doesn't blink. My father's features are set in lines that I find familiar. He means it. He won't hesitate to shoot her. The only way out is to show him that I am willing to comply, for the moment. I lower my gun, and he jerks his chin. "Place it on the ground."

I follow his instructions, then straighten.

"Now kick it toward me."

I do so, and he nods.

"Now let her go."

"No," he drawls, "I am going to shoot her, then you."

"Wait," I burst out, "the man I interrogated and who said that it was the Kane company who'd put him up to rigging the car, was that your doing?"

His lips twist, "What do you think?"

"I don't know..." I draw in a breath. *Delay him, delay him.* Just until I've gathered myself together. Just until I find a way to get him to release Karma. "If it was, then that was sheer genius. It derailed us from going after the real culprit."

"Me," he bites out the word with satisfaction writ into his features.

· · ·

He holds my gaze and I can read the intent. I know he's going to do it. He's going to pull the trigger on her, on my Beauty, my soul, my wife. My everything. All of my muscles tense and I lean forward on the balls of my feet, ready to throw myself at him, when the screech of brakes sounds from behind me.

He glances past me and I yell, "Hit the ground, Karma."

I lunge toward my gun, but before I can reach it, a shot rings out.

There's a hoarse cry. I grab the gun, raise it to find Karma is on the ground, her arms over her head and smoke rising from a hole in the center of my father's chest. It's smoking, but there's no blood. Motherfucker. He's wearing a protective vest. Of course, he is. There's only one way to kill this guy.

He raises his gun, fires, and something slams into my left shoulder. Pain slices through me, burns a path down my arm. I raise the gun with my other arm, pull the trigger, and again.

Blood blooms from a hole in the center of his forehead, and a second from the hole in his throat. He seems almost surprised. Then his body begins to tumble forward. I race toward Karma, grab her under my arm, swing her up and to the side. My father's body crashes to the ground where she was.

A trembling grips her and I pull her close as I stare at the man who was my father.

He betrayed me… Hell, he had been betraying me my entire life. At each turn, I had forgiven him, because he was my blood. Was he right? Was it because I am too emotional that I couldn't see what he really was? Is that why I couldn't stop him before he killed my brother?

A coldness grips my chest. I stare at the fallen body of my father and a buzzing sound fills my senses.

"Mika, are you okay?"

Specks of black infiltrate the corners of my vision as I gaze down at her.

"Karma?"

She glances at my features, then down to my left shoulder.

"Oh my god, Mika," she gasps, "you are hurt."

"Just a scratch," I smirk... Then cough, and blood drips from the corner of my mouth.

Her gaze widens, "It's not just a scratch. The bullet... It hit you; you are bleeding out." She presses her hand to where the blood pulses from the wound, trying to stem the flow, and pain shoots up my neck. It explodes behind my eyes, and I grunt as my legs seem to fold in on themselves. I try to straighten myself, waver on my feet, and Karma tries to support me. "Help," she screams as footsteps sound behind me, "help me."

Strong arms grip me, then lower me to the dirt. I glance up into Nikolai's face.

"Sorry, I got here a little late." He grimaces. His face fades in and out of view.

"You were...not late," I force out the words. A coldness grips me and I shudder.

More footsteps sound, then suddenly, Christian is there. He takes one look at me and his features go solid. He pulls off his jacket, sinks to his knees, and hands it to Karma. "Use this to apply pressure," he growls.

Sirens sound in the distance, and I frown.

"Ambulance," JJ's voice seems to come from far away, "I called an ambulance."

I grasp Karma's hand in mine. "Don't leave me," I whisper. "Don't leave me, Karma."

"Don't talk," she swallows, "save your energy."

Darkness pulls me under, but I fight it off.

"Promise me that you'll be there when I wake up."

She moves her mouth but I can't hear her.

"Andy," I murmur.

"You're dying," she bursts out, "and you're worried about my cat?"

"I am not dying," I insist, "and you love your cat, so of course, I am worried about him."

"Please, don't exert yourself," she pleads. "Please, Mika, just focus on staying alive."

"I am not going anywhere," I smile. "Not as long as I have you by my side."

She glances away and a sick sensation twists my stomach.

"Karma, don't do it," I plead with her, or at least, I think I try to do that. Then everything goes dark.

# 33

Karma

"You've put yourself under a lot of pressure, Mrs. Sovrano," the doctor murmurs. "You are lucky you didn't come out of this in worse shape."

"I think you meant to say that to my husband, not me." I firm my lips, "He's the one who was shot."

The doctor shoots me a knowing glance, "I am talking about you, ma'am, not your husband."

After Michael lost consciousness, holding onto my hand, the ambulance had arrived. True to his word, it had been an ambulance to a private hospital that JJ owns in London.

He had briefly regained consciousness as they were strapping him onto the stretcher and insisted that they check me out.

I had told the paramedics I was fine, but Michael had refused to cooperate with them until they had finally given in and one of them had begun to examine me.

I had kept insisting that I was fine, but the paramedic had said

that my blood pressure and my heart rate were both elevated—
which I already knew, of course, but had feigned surprise when he'd
said that.

They'd asked me to ride in the same ambulance as Michael to the
hospital so they could check me out thoroughly. I'd wanted to leave
right then. I should have left right then. But how could I until I knew
that Michael was really okay? So, I had agreed.

Michael had flitted in and out of consciousness, and each time he
was lucid, he'd ask for me. He'd gripped my hand and not let go even
when he'd lost consciousness. It was only when we arrived at the
hospital and they had had to wheel him to the operating theatre that
I had managed to disentangle my fingers from his.

Seb and Christian had arrived then, along with Massimo and
Antonio. Christian had insisted that I have myself checked out. I had
refused, wanting to stay and wait for news of Michael, but my
protest fell on deaf ears.

Within minutes, I was being ushered into an examination room.
Just as I had changed out of my bloodied clothes and into a
hospital gown, a doctor had arrived. He'd already accessed my
records via the National Health Service system that the hospital
had access to, so of course, there had been no escape. He'd known
about my heart condition, and that's what had prompted this
conversation.

I set my jaw as I scowl at him. "My condition is stable," I insist.

"Only if you completed your course of medication, and only if
you manage your condition properly."

"That's exactly what I did."

"Hmm," he purses his lips, "your records indicate that you started
the course of medication prescribed by your specialist, but you
missed your last appointment, and you also did not complete the
course."

*Shit.* My cheeks flush.

"Also, judging by your current condition," he glances at my blood
splattered clothes, "I assume the latter is not something that you are
adhering to either."

Gah! Why do I feel like a student who is pulled up in front of the class for something I've done wrong? I fold my arms around my waist.

"Well, Mrs. Sovrano," the doctor murmurs, "I take it from your silence that I am right on both counts."

"Yeah, yeah," I sniff, "so what do you propose I do now?"

"I propose that I complete your check up, then restart you on your medication."

"Okay."

"Also, I am going to have to insist that you come in for your next check-up, in two weeks."

I nod.

"And," he murmurs, "you need to try not to excite yourself too much. At least, until your blood pressure and heart rate are back to normal."

I open my mouth to speak, and he arches an eyebrow, "And even after that, you need to ensure that you don't overexert yourself physically."

I snort.

"This is not a joke, Mrs. Sovrano." He frowns, "We are talking about your heart here."

"My heart is lying in the other room getting operated on," I burst out.

His features soften, "The doctors are doing everything possible for your husband."

I startle. "What do you mean by that."

He holds up his hands, "Just that he is in safe hands. The best surgeons in the country are taking care of him right now."

I swallow.

"He'd probably rest better if he knew that you are taking care of yourself too," the doctor offers.

I lower my chin to my chest and blow out a breath. "Look, I have no wish to die young, okay?" I swallow, then glance away, "It's just, sometimes I want to live a normal life. I don't want my condition to be a constant worry. I want to experience all of the highs and lows of being alive. Hell, I am barely in my twenties and I want to have first-hand knowledge of everything life can offer, you know?"

"And you will," he gives me a small smile, "provided you take your medication and your vitals return to normal. And even after that, you need to take care of yourself."

"Which I am very good at, I assure you."

He peers into my face, then nods. "You're a clever woman, Mrs. Sovrano. I am sure you understand the risks of not following professional medical advice."

"I do," I nod, "and I'll complete the course of medication this time."

"Good, the nurse will come by with your medication." He rises to his feet, "I'd also recommend that you stay in the hospital for overnight observation, and ideally, take it easy for the next few days."

"But it's not something you can force me to do, can you?"

"You're a grown woman, Mrs. Sovrano. You can make your own decisions."

He turns to leave and I call out, "Doctor, I have one more question."

He turns to me.

"Am I correct that I can still get pregnant without causing my condition to be exacerbated as a result?"

He fixes me with a shrewd glance, "There are those with your condition who get pregnant and carry their children to term, and there are those whose condition deteriorates as a result. As your physician, I should warn you that it's safer if you don't get pregnant. But the choice is yours, of course."

*Right.*

I bite the inside of my cheek. I knew it already. It's what my doctors had previously indicated to me. Only, I hadn't paid any attention to it. Hell, becoming pregnant had been the last thing on my mind then. But after losing my baby... Well, it's something that's so in my face right now that I couldn't help but ask the question.

The doctor turns to leave and I call out after him, "This...conversation is covered under doctor-patient confidentiality, right?"

He pauses then turns to me. "It is," he nods.

"So, I'd prefer it if you didn't say anything to my husband, or to any of his brothers out there."

He frowns then nods, "As you wish." And he leaves.

I glance around the space, then because my clothes are all bloodied, I change out of my hospital gown and into the scrubs he'd left behind for me.

After meeting with the nurse and getting my medication, I pad out of the examination room to find Antonio waiting for me.

"Are you guarding me now?" I scowl.

"It's what he'd have wanted." The big Sicilian doesn't seem put off by my irritation. He merely steps aside.

He trails me as I head toward the waiting room—which is a spacious area, with big windows through which light floods in. It's a far cry from the rooms I have seen in the government-run hospitals I've been to previously. I step on the carpeted floor and take in the scene. Christian is sprawled out in a chair in one corner. He glowers at Luca, who glowers back at him from the opposite corner. Massimo is by the window, and he turns as I approach.

"Karma," he comes forward and when he opens his arms, I walk into them. Of all the remaining Sovrano brothers, Massimo is, by far, the least threatening. Despite his height and the fact that he is the biggest of all of them... He is also the quietest and the gentlest.

"You okay?"

I nod into his chest and he leans back. "He's going to be fine," Massimo murmurs.

"Have they said anything?"

He shakes his head, "He's still in surgery."

"How much," I clear my throat, "how much longer do they think he'll be?"

"They don't know yet," Christian says. I turn to find him standing next to me. I glance at the blood on his shirt and my stomach churns. That's Michael's blood. Oh, my god, it's his blood. A sob wells up and I push my knuckles into my mouth. Christian glances down at his blood-splattered shirt and pales. "I'm sorry, Karma," he draws in a breath, "I didn't realize... I..."

"It's okay," I swallow down the ball of emotion that clogs my throat.

Luca rises from his seat and walks over to join us, and I survey their faces.

"I… I have something to tell you… I…" *I am going to leave him. I am going to walk away while your brother is still in surgery. I…*

"What is it, Karma?" Massimo says in a soft voice. "You can tell us," he glances around the assembled faces and they nod, "we're your family."

The rest of them murmur their assent, and tears prick the backs of my eyes.

"I…" I shake my head, "I am tired."

"Are you okay?" Massimo frowns, "The doctor examined you. Did he say—"

"I'm fine."

"Are you sure?" He brushes past me, "I should ask him myself, maybe?"

"Massimo," I call out and he stops. "Leave it."

He hesitates and I draw myself up to my full height. "I am okay, and anyway, I am not the one who you should be worried about. It's your brother who needs our complete attention, at the moment."

He seems like he's about to hesitate and I square my shoulders. "I am the wife of your future Don, and I order you to stay here so we can be together while we wait for news about him."

A frisson runs through the space. The guys glance at each other, as if just realizing the ramifications of the events that have taken place. Michael is going to be the new Don. And I am still his wife… which means my word carries weight yet, right?

"Where's Seb?" I ask, suddenly realizing that he's missing.

"He stayed back with JJ and Niko to ensure disposal of the evidence before the cops get wind of it."

Evidence. Oh, he means the body of their father. The man who killed Xander, who put Michael and his brothers through so much, who almost killed me. I shiver and that seems to galvanize Massimo into action. He shrugs off his jacket and walks over, places it around my shoulders. "Thanks," I murmur, "and Adrian?"

"Here I am," a voice calls out from the doorway.

I turn to find Adrian walking into the waiting room. He stalks over to me, then holds out the pet carrier.

"Is that?" I blink. *It can't be. Is it —* An angry meow sounds from the carrier as I drop to my knees. I peer into the carrier and Andy's indignant face looks back at me.

"Andy," I whisper. "OMG," I tip my chin up to stare at Adrian, "how did he get here?"

"The Capo was clear we had to take care of him. So, I waited on the island until the private jet had deposited these guys in London, then flew back to pick me up and bring me here."

"Oh," I blink rapidly, "so a private plane trip, just so you could get Andy to me?"

"Two trips, actually," he smiles, "but the Capo ordered it."

*And what the Capo wants, the Capo gets.* Andy peers at me through gaps in the wall of the carrier.

"How did you bring him into a hospital?" I frown. "Aren't pets not allowed in here?"

"It's a private hospital." He shrugs. "It's funded by the Mafia, so —"

So, no rules apply, I guess. I rise to my feet, grab the carrier from him. "Thank you," I say.

I bend down, take Andy out of the pet carrier, then sit down with him in my arms.

The rest of the guys disperse to different corners of the room. Antonio continues to stand by the door on the outside of the room.

Christian pulls out his phone and begins to message someone. I walk over to sit next to him and he pockets his phone again.

"Was that Aurora?" I scowl.

"What do you mean?" He asks in an a voice that sounds all too innocent.

"You were texting with Aurora, weren't you?" I accuse.

"And if I was?"

"Have you told her that you like her?"

"Like?" He smirks, "That's not the world I'd use."

"You going to marry her, or what?"

"Marry?" He looks at me in alarm, "Whatever gave you that idea?"

"Isn't that what good Italian men do when they've been struck by the 'thunderbolt'?"

"You mean *colpo di fulmine?*" He leans over and scratches Andy behind his ear. The cat purrs, then stretches his neck, inviting him to continue his actions.

"Exactly," I peer into Christian's face, "so?" I arch an eyebrow, "You going to do something about it?"

"She betrayed the Capo."

"To help me."

"Still," he hesitates, "it's not something that can be forgiven without some kind of punishment."

"But if you marry her, she becomes part of the *famiglia* right?"

He stiffens, "Marriage? Who's talking about marriage?"

"And once she is your wife, she is safe from any punishment, correct?"

He holds my gaze, "You and she have become good friends, eh?"

"She is a wonderful person, Christian," I soften my voice, "and it's clear there's something between the two of you."

"There's something, all right," he snorts, "but it's not what you are thinking."

"Oh, please, the sparks between the two of you could light up a room."

"So?"

"So, what are you going to do about it?"

He stares at me.

"What?" I frown. "Don't tell me you are going to ignore it?"

"Trust me," he says in a soft voice, "the last thing I am going to do is ignore it."

"So, you are going to talk to her?"

"Maybe more than talk." He smirks.

O-k-a-y, that doesn't sound very promising at all.

"Christian, I—"

He holds up his hand, "What's between Aurora and me is our concern and no one else's."

"But—"

"Leave it, Karma."

He glances away and I blow out a sigh.

"Fine," I murmur, "I won't push it, but you'd better not hurt her, okay?"

He simply pulls out his phone and begins to play with it again. I rise to my feet, holding Andy close to my chest with one arm. I grab the pet carrier with my free hand and walk over to a chair in an unoccupied corner.

Sitting down, I coax Andy back into the carrier. For once Andy doesn't protest, he prowls in, curls around and closes his eyes. I straighten, then take my seat. I lean my head back against the wall, and close my eyes. A touch on my shoulder jolts me awake. I open my eyes to see Massimo standing in front of me.

"What's wrong?"

He jerks his chin toward the door. I follow his glance to find a doctor standing there in scrubs. His mask is around his neck and he glances around the room before his gaze alights on me.

"Mrs. Sovrano?" he says in a neutral voice. "Please come with me."

## 34

Karma

"What…what's wrong?" I try to stand up, but my legs don't seem capable of supporting me. I push my feet into the floor then straighten in my seat. "How…" I croak, "how is he?"

"The surgery went well; we removed the bullet."

A frisson of relief rushes through me, "Is he, is he going to be okay?" I rasp.

"The bullet missed his vital organs. He is a very lucky man."

Tension drains from my limbs, and I sink against the back of the chair, exhaling loudly.

"Is he…is he awake?"

"He's not conscious, yet," the doctor replies, "but you can see him for a few minutes, if you'd like."

I nod, then rise to my feet. Christian rises with me, but I wave him off. "I'll be fine," I tell him as I walk over to the doctor. I follow the doctor as he strides down the corridor.

He leads me to a room. "He's inside." The doctor steps aside and I

push the door open and step in. The beeps of the machines monitoring his vitals fill the space. He's covered in a sheet that's tucked
around his waist. The bandage that is wrapped around his chest is
stark against the tan of his skin. His eyes are shut, those gorgeous
eyelashes fanning in an arch against his high cheekbones. His cheeks
are pale, the hollows under his eyes more pronounced than normal. I
walk over to him, reach over and take his hand in mine. My fingers
look tiny against his. I hold his big palm between both of mine, then
bring it to my face and press it against my cheek. His skin is warm,
and that dark, edgy scent of his is tempered by the scent of antiseptic. It's still him, though. My Capo. Mine.

Only, he'll never leave this life. I couldn't ask him to leave it.
Which means he'll always be in danger. Maybe a part of me has
always known that. It's why I had been attracted to him, after all...
But now, with the evidence of how it could hurt him in front of me, I
am not sure I can live with it. I lower his arm, place his hand on the
bed next to him. Then I lean in and kiss his cheek. I push away the
strand of hair that has fallen across his forehead, take in the whiskers
that have grown across his jaw, the rise and fall of his chest, the
sculpted planes still visible, despite the bandage that swathes him.

This man... Even unconscious, he's lethal. Even with his charisma
dimmed, he's potent. I lean down and brush my lips over his. Soft
lips, that could kiss so hard I could feel it all the way to my toes. I
share his breath, revel in that unique maleness of his that is a combi-
nation of everything he is.

*I am sorry, my Capo, but I am leaving. Sorry that I can't stay with you
and tell you so in person. If I did, you'd stop me and I'd never be able to refuse
you. I'd give in to your dominance and stay... And then I'd never know if it was
because I really wanted to stay, or if it was because I couldn't turn you down.
That's why I am leaving now. Do you understand?*

I turn to go and something tugs at my hand. I look down to find
his fingers are wrapped around my wrist. I glance up at his face but
his eyes are shut. Peer down at where he still holds onto me. I reach
for his fingers and peel them off, one by one.

Tears prick the backs of my eyes. *Don't cry, damn it. This is the right thing to do.* If I have any hope of living life in a way that is true to myself, then I need to do this. It's the right thing for both of us.

Just as I'd never ask him to leave the Mafia, he too should never force me to do something that I don't want. And that was how our relationship started. With him taking me against my wishes.

Lots has changed since then, though. We know each other so much better. He knows what I am all about, what I like, and don't like. Surely, he'll understand?

I turn to leave, and this time, nothing stops me. I pause at the door, turn to look at him one last time. Then I head back to the waiting room. "Does anyone have a pen and paper?"

The guys look at each other, then Massimo reaches inside his jacket. He pulls out a small diary and a pen, before walking over to hand it to me.

I glance at it, then up at him, "Molesekine?"

He flushes, "I, uh, doodle a bit when I have time."

I open the book filled with pages of his surprisingly neat handwriting, until I find a clean page. I start to write and he turns his back to me. "Use me as a table," he tells me.

I balance the diary against his back, and start writing. When I am done, I tear out the page. As he straightens and turns to me, I slip off my ring, wrap it in the page and hand it over to him. "Give it to him when he wakes up," I tell him.

"Karma" he whispers, "what are you doing?"

"What is right for both of us."

"He took a bullet for you," Christian walks toward me, "and you are leaving him?"

"Just give him the letter, Massimo," I plead, "please."

Massimo hesitates.

Christian glares at me.

Seb and Luca walk over to surround me.

I firm my lips, "Your new Don will not be happy that you refused to help his wife."

"Our new Don will be even less happy if we let his wife leave," Christian points out.

I turn on him, "What's between my husband and me is our concern and no one else's."

He winces, "Karma, don't do this."

I turn back to Massimo. "Take it." I jut out my chin, "It would be a lot worse if I left without his having this letter. He needs to read this, Massimo."

He draws in a breath, then reaches over and takes the letter and the ring from me.

I move back a few steps, take in their faces. These men whom I have come to regard as family. I glance at Luca, who jerks his chin in my direction. Even Luca, who helped me escape...then helped me return to my husband...Yeah, they are each impressive in their own right. And together like this...it brings home just how strong they are as a unit. The strongest, most impressive of them all is my husband—the one who I am going to leave.

A hot sensation stabs at my chest...and it's nothing to do with my heart condition. Damn it, I am going to miss them. Guess I didn't realize how much I've come to regard myself as one of them, and now, I am going to have to leave them. Tears prick the backs of my eyes and I turn away.

"What about Andy?" Adrian calls out after me.

I pause, "Tell Michael to take care of him."

Turning, I walk out of the room. Out of the hospital. Out of his life.

# 35

## Michael

"You let her what?" I try to sit up but pain lances through my wounded side. I gasp, lay back. Sweat beads my temples, and my muscles protest. *Cazzo!* I am as weak as a newborn. I draw in a breath, then another, wait until the pain subsides somewhat.

"You could take painkillers," Christian points out.

"And allow myself to be knocked out again?" I snap, "No, thanks." Besides, it's better this way. The pain keeps me from slipping back into the tiredness that threatens my limbs. I glare at the faces of my brothers. "Not one of you thought of stopping her?"

"Of course, we did," Seb retorts. "Not that she was going to listen to us."

"Besides, as she took great pains in pointing out, she is the wife of a Mafia Don, who wouldn't take kindly to us using coercion to have held her back," Massimo adds.

"So, you let her walk?"

"We didn't have a choice, *fratellone*," Luca murmurs.

"*Cazzo!*" I glare at the lot of them. "Five grown men, and she found a way to outwit the lot of you?"

"She also left this," Massimo pulls out something wrapped in a piece of paper and hands it over.

I take the paper, unwrap it and find her ring. "*Che cazzo!*" I stare at the ring, then notice the writing on the paper. I straighten it out, and begin to read.

*Capo (or should I call you Don?),*

*I know you are going to be angry when you read this, but please, can you give me a chance to explain? I am leaving you, not because I don't love you. Not even because you haven't yet told me that you love me, which you do (and which I know, by the way, even though you've been adamant not to admit it to me so far). I am not leaving you because our relationship started out in the most unorthodox way, or because you'll never leave the Mafia. Okay, that last thing… Maybe that has somewhat to do with it.*

*But, Capo, when that bullet hit you… It also hit me. It hurt me when it sliced through your flesh. I bled when you did.*

*I feel everything you do, Capo, just as I know you do too. I'd never ask you to give up your way of life… It's what makes you who you are. It is a part of you. It's even one of the things that attracts me to you, to be honest. But… I also can't stand the thought of you being hurt again.*

*The thought that one day there'll be a knock on the door and someone will tell me that you are gone… Like Xander… Like how I almost died… It would be much, much worse if it were to happen to you, Capo. I don't think I could survive it, actually.*

*And…I know, being a Don's wife means I need to be prepared for the worst. A bit like being a soldier's wife, you know? You just have to always be ready to have the rug pulled out of from underneath you. And maybe I will be… Maybe I won't… But I need to arrive at that conclusion for myself.*

*As long as I am with you, I can't think. When you touch me, I lose sight of everything else except wanting to throw myself at your feet and allow you to have your way with me… There you have it —the 'naked' truth. Pun intended.*

*So, I ask you to give me this time away, so I can think for myself. So I can figure out if this is how I want to spend the rest of my days...as the wife of a Don...or...or... I can't even contemplate the other scenario...but it's something I need to be open to, at least, considering.*

*If you love me at all, and I know that you do, I ask that you not track me. Do not come in search of me. Please, give me this space to figure out what I truly want for myself.*

*Yours,*

*Beauty aka Bellezza aka Karma*

*P.S. How is it that you have so many nicknames for me and I haven't even thought of one for you?*

*P.P.S. I am leaving Andy to keep you company.*

I glance up as Adrian walks in holding the pet carrier. He holds it up and Andy's baleful gaze greets me. He glares at me, then retreats to the side of the cage. Fuck, the cat is moping, all right. Probably misses her.

If she thinks that she can flounce out of my life like that, she has another think coming. I sit up, ignore the pain that grips my side. I grab the IV and yank it out of my arm, wincing as the tape used to hold it in place tears off some of my skin, Blood drips down my arm and onto the floor. I swing my legs over the side of the bed and rise to my feet, only to fall back against the bed frame.

"*Cazzo!*" I growl, try to straighten again and my head spins.

"What the fuck are you doing?" Christian growls.

I straighten again, manage to take a couple of steps before my knees threaten to give way. Massimo grabs my unhurt shoulder and I shake him off, "I am going after her."

"And I assume she specifically asked you not to?" he retorts.

I turn on him, "Did you read my note, asshole? If you did—"

"You really think I'd read the note that your wife entrusted to me before she left?"

I glare at him, then shake my head. "Forgive me," I mumble. "I'm, clearly, losing perspective."

"And she needs to gain perspective." Massimo lowers his chin, "Clearly, that's why she left. I assume she also asked you to give her space?"

When I glare at him, he raises a shoulder, "You need to respect that."

"And you are an expert on relationships now?"

"No," Seb interrupts, "none of us are, but we've seen the two of you engaged in this push-pull of a relationship, and even to jerk-faces like us— and I say that in the most loving way possible—it's clear that both of you need to sort your own shit out first."

"And that's exactly what she's doing," Luca adds.

"How? First, by taking your help to run away from me, and now, by leaving me?" I scowl.

"You know that old adage about letting someone you love go and if they love you, they'll come back?" Christian drawls and I turn on him.

"If you dare tell me that's what I have to do... Then I'm going to deck you, right now."

"You're too weak to deck me." His lips tilt up slightly, "And no, that's not what I was going to tell you...but," he raises a shoulder, "I have to admit, that statement seems to carry a modicum of truth right now."

I glare at him, then at the note in my hand. *Fuck. Fuck, fuck, fuck.* I sit down heavily on the bed, stare at her ring. Where are you, Beauty? Did you think that I'd actually allow you to leave and not track you? Did you think that the better part of me would prevail and that I'd actually let you go? I crumple the piece of paper in my palm, close the fingers of my other hand around the ring.

# 36

One month later

Karma

"How much is this dress?"

I glance up from arranging the outfits in my stall in Camden Market. When I'd walked out of the hospital, I'd headed to the flat that I'd arranged to rent before I'd left for the island with Michael. Then, I'd focused on getting my little fashion designing business up and running. I'd managed to wrangle back my place in the market and had gone to work creating outfits in the style I love. I'd poured all of my efforts into it, in an attempt to drown out thoughts of Michael and the life I had decided to leave. I'd been diligent in taking the medicines that had been prescribed to me by the specialist at the hospital and have already been back for a follow-up.

I had insisted on paying for my treatment with the money in my bank account. Technically, it was still Michael's money... Except, well, in a way, I had earned it for the time I had been his wife. I shouldn't have used the money at all, actually...but I didn't have any other means to live on. And I didn't want to take a loan from Summer... To do so, would have meant I'd have to tell her every-thing I'd been through, and honestly, I am still not ready for that. To be honest, I am not ready for any kind of company. Which is why I'd simply stuck to the flat, set up my studio in the spare bedroom and worked my ass off to get enough outfits ready for market day—which is today.

It also means I've gone an entire month without communicating with anyone. Except for the visits to the shops to choose my fabrics and to order what I needed to set up my studio, that is. I haven't spoken to any of my friends since moving to the flat.

I'd also messaged Summer to let her know that I was doing fine, but that I needed more time to figure out the status of my relation-ship with my 'guy.'

I know it's selfish of me, not speaking with Summer for so long, or meeting her now that I am in London. But I really do need to figure out where my head's at regarding the status of my marriage.

Besides, she is busy with her husband and the circle of friends she's built, thanks to being married to one of the Seven. So, although it hurts that we've gone this long without communicating... It's also a relief that I am not answerable to anyone else. Not my sister, not my husband... Not even, to my cat. I miss Andy almost as much as I miss him...

Okay, I miss *him* a lot more...when I allow myself to think of him. Which is...most nights. In those moments before I fall asleep, and those early morning moments before I wake up, when my guard is down and I am at my most vulnerable, that's when thoughts of him crowd in on me. Is he still tracking me on a screen somewhere? A blue dot that he can't reach out to but which indicates to him exactly where I am? Does he miss me as much as I miss him? The feel of me. The touch of me. The scent of me. Does he miss being inside of me as much as I miss the girth of him thrusting into me, stretching me, filling me. My toes curl. Heat flushes my skin.

I glance up to find the woman who'd been interested in buying the dress I'd created staring at me strangely.

"Are you okay?" She frowns, "You look flushed."

Which is saying something, considering it's freezing right now, at this outdoor stall where I am.

"I'm fine." I jerk my chin toward the dress she's holding, "There's only one of those in existence, you know?"

She glances at the dress, then back at me, "Really?"

I nod, "It's a Karma original. A unique dress handcrafted just for you."

She runs her fingers over the purple collar, "It has a certain *je ne sais quoi* feel about it, for sure." She rubs her palm across the embroidered vest that constitutes the top half of the dress. "And these colors... They are gorgeous."

"They are," I agree, "inspired by the colors of Sicily."

"Sicily?" Her eyes gleam. "Now the red and black mixed with the ochre yellow makes sense."

"It does, right?" I take in the dress with pride. "I tried to bring to life all of the smells and tastes and textures I found when I was there."

"Oh, did you live there?"

"Yes," I murmur, "I've only been back a month."

"Were you there on work?"

"Eh?" I frown. "No, not really, I was..." *married* is what I am going to say, then change my mind. "Uh, I was there on unfinished business."

"And did you complete it?"

I frown. "Complete what?"

"The business that took you there?"

"No," I lower my chin to my chest, "not yet."

"So, are you going back then?"

A hot sensation coils in my chest. I glance away, then back at her, "Not sure yet."

"Pity, for the place, clearly, inspires you." She digs into her purse, then hands me her credit card.

"I haven't even told you how much it costs."

"It doesn't matter." She smiles. "I'll pay whatever price you ask."

"Wow," I blink, "really?"

"You bet," she massages the fabric of the dress like it's already hers, "this is perfect for a wedding I am going to attend."

"A wedding?"

"Not mine," she laughs, "but a friend's. This will suit the occasion very well. It's unique, but it won't take attention away from the bride. It's perfect, really."

I charge her credit card, then hand over the machine for her to key in her pin. She taps in her pin without protest. One-thousand pounds. Hell, I charged her one-thousand pounds and she was happy to pay that for a Karma original. Wow!

I wrap the dress up for her, place it carefully in a cloth bag that has my brand proudly displayed on it. She thanks me with a big smile, then slings it over her shoulder and leaves. That is the single, biggest sale that I have ever made. It's a new record. It means I am good. That people will pay what I ask for my creations. That I can finally charge what I am really worth. I make ten more sales, all in the three-figure range, and by the time I close for the day, it's a record day of sales for me.

I pack up the remaining dresses, then haul the merchandise into the van that I have rented for the day. I drive home, lug the clothes back into my flat, then walk back down and return the van. I take the tube back home, and by eight pm, I am parked in front of the TV with a glass of wine.

I finish my dinner, have an early night, and I'm up by five am. By six, I have drunk my coffee and paced the floor of the living room end to end, at least twenty times. I really need to get started on creating more outfits, but don't feel like it.

I change into my yoga pants, a tank top, and throw a sweatshirt on top. I lace up my running shoes. Then, picking up my phone, my keys and my earphones, I set out to run. I keep my pace leisurely, just a little above a fast walk. I run through my neighborhood, across the road that leads to the next block. The one where I used to share a flat with Summer when I lived with her.

I am almost not surprised when I run up the road that takes me to Waterlow Park. Maybe I've known I was heading here. Maybe I've been biding my time since I walked out of the hospital. Maybe I am still finding myself… Maybe I am done searching for what makes sense. Ten minutes of half-walking, half-jogging up the incline, and I reach the park. I slow to a walk, continue up the familiar path. I pick up speed again, as I jog around the perimeter of the space, then up the hillside. I reach the top, and turn to face the vista that stretches out in front of me. The rays from the rising sun bathe the trees and the city in dappled gold. The breeze lifts the hair from my forehead and a bird calls out nearby. Another returns its call. Its mate probably. Does nature really want us to be in pairs? Is this why we are so hung up on finding our soul mates? Had I found my mate and decided to leave him behind?

To Michael's credit, he hasn't called me, or touched base with me, or tried to reach me in any way since I left. It's nerve-wracking, really, because I don't entirely trust the man. No way, could he have stayed away all this time. And yet, since I left, I've never had the sensation of being watched. Or of being in any danger.

Likely, his alliance with JJ and Nikolai means neither of those clans are out to harm me in any way. I sink down on the grass, draw up my knees to my chest.

Has he taken over as Don? How is he finding it? He's gotten what he wanted, so he must be happy, I suppose. Does he miss me, though? My scent, my touch… *Stop.* I lean my chin on my knees and stare forward.

Something brushes against my leg and I find myself staring down at a cat… A Savannah with gleaming spots, pointed ears, a delicate face, and golden eyes that glare at me.

"Andy?" I cry. "Oh, my god, Andy. Where did you come from?"

I gather the cat close and he meows, rubs up against me again. I lower my knees and place him in my lap. I rub his head and he blinks, soaking up every second of the attention.

"I missed you boy, you know that?" I tickle him under his jaw and he yawns. He wriggles in my grasp and I allow him to jump down. He prowls away, to the side, to where a man is standing.

A tall man, with wide shoulders that shut out the scenery behind him. A man with cold, blue eyes fringed by the most beautiful eyelashes I have ever seen. His features are harsh, his nose hooked; his square jaw might as well be hewn from the rocks that are set into the side of the lawn I am seated on.

His chest is so wide that his suit jacket stretches across the front; a lean waist, trim hips that lead down to powerful thighs, clad in pants that are, surely, tailor-made for him. On his feet, he wears Italian loafers that have been polished to within an inch of their life.

The cat brushes up against him and he bends and picks up the animal. He cuddles it against his gorgeously cut jacket as he approaches me. Closer, closer. When he reaches me, he sinks down to sit next to me. He's careful enough to not touch me, keeping enough space for the breeze to fan the gap between us.

He places the cat down, and Andy pads over to lay down on the grass in front of us.

We sit there, quietly watching the sun come up over the city. Andy yawns and stretches. I reach out to pat him at the same time as the man next to me. Our fingers brush and goosebumps pop on my skin. The hair on the nape of my neck rises. I keep my hand where it is, and so does he. Neither of us moves. Then he curls his little finger around my thumb. The width of his digit is wider than mine. A shiver runs up my spine.

He waits, as if expecting me to move away. As if giving me time to retreat, but I don't. I stare at the contrast between the tan color of his skin and my much paler one.

He whispers his finger over to the center of the back of my hand, and my toes curl. He wraps his fingers around mine and my entire body seems to shudder. My stomach flip-flops, and every cell in my body seems to stretch and come alive as if they've been exposed to a jolt of electricity. He brings our joined hands up to his face. I follow the length of my arm to where he kisses the tips of my fingers, then raise my gaze to meet those searing, blue eyes.

"Karma," he whispers, "I love you."

# 37

Michael

Her features crumple and tears run down her cheeks. My heart stutters and the pulse pounds at my temples. I reach for her at the same time that she throws herself at me. I pull her into my lap, wrap my arms around her, yank her into my chest, as I surround her with every part of me I can.

"*Bellezza*," I murmur, "my Beauty, I missed you, my love."

She only cries harder and my heart feels like it's about to crack open.

"Please, Karma, don't cry," I plead. "I can't stand to see you like this, *piccola*."

She turns her face into my shirt, grabs handfuls, and holds on as if she can't bear to be parted again. I rock her and run my fingers across her hair, say words to soothe her that make no sense, but it doesn't seem to help.

I tuck her head under my chin, glance out at the now awakening city. "*She walks in beauty, like the night,*"

. . .

I begin to recite.

*"Of cloudless climes and starry skies;*
*And all that's best of dark and bright."*

Her sobs quieten.

*"Meet in her aspect and her eyes;*
*Thus mellowed to that tender light*
*Which heaven to gaudy day denies."*

She hiccups, then seems to compose herself.

*"One shade the more, one ray the less,*
*Had half impaired the nameless grace*
*Which waves in every raven tress,*
*Or softly lightens o'er her face;"*

I glance down to see her eyes closed as she listens.

*"Where thoughts serenely sweet express,*
*How pure, how dear their dwelling-place."*

I continue.

. . .

*"And on that cheek, and o'er that brow,*
  *So soft, so calm, yet eloquent,*
  *The smiles that win, the tints that glow,*
  *But tell of days in goodness spent,*
  *A mind at peace with all below,*
  *A heart whose love is innocent!"*

She draws in a breath, then rubs her cheek against my shirt. We sit there in silence as the sun rises overhead. Finally, she stirs and looks up at me. Her eyes are swollen, her nose reddened by her crying jag. Her beautiful lips are pink and moist. I catch myself leaning in toward her and pull back. I tuck a strand of hair behind her ear and she shivers.

"Are you cold? I can give you my coat—"

"No," she shakes her head, "the heat of your body is all I need to keep warm. The scent of your skin is all I need to turn me on. The fire in your eyes…" she swallows, " is all I need to consume me. To take me. To mark me as your own. The darkness inside of you," she pushes her palm into my chest, "is my own. I know that now."

I tip her chin up, "When did you get so poetic?"

"Says the man who quotes Byron," her lips tremble in a ghost of a smile. "Why are you named after him?"

"It's a family tradition." I peer into her features, "Every first-born takes it as one of the given names."

"That whole four name thing... It's daunting." She blows out a breath, "Imagine giving birth to a baby and saddling him with a name that long."

"Would you have minded if I had done that with our child?"

She blinks rapidly and a lone tear slides down her cheek.

"*Cazzo!*" I didn't mean to bring that up.

"No, it's good," she swallows, "we should talk about it. It's healthy to talk about it, rather than hiding it away and pretending it didn't happen."

"I miss him" I murmur. "I miss our baby, and I never even knew him or her."

"Me too," she glances away, "sometimes I wake up from my sleep and am sure that I can hear the patter of a child's footsteps outside my bedroom door."

I draw in a breath. "Beauty," I cup her cheek, "I am so sorry for what happened."

"It's not your fault," she tips up her chin, "it is one of the reasons I felt like I had to leave, though."

My heart begins to race. Subconsciously, I had been aware that she may well blame me for the loss of our child, but hearing her say it aloud, makes my stomach knot.

"What were the other reasons?"

"Seeing you almost killed in front of me."

I open my mouth and she shakes her head, "I know, that's rich coming from someone who almost killed you." She raises a shoulder, "But things change. I stopped trying to get at you, but I forgot that there's an entire world out there who is out to get you."

"He's gone," I say in a low voice. "My father, who was the culprit behind everything that happened, is dead."

"The rival gangs—"

"I have made my peace with JJ and Nikolai. The Kane Company and the Bratva have proved themselves as my allies."

"There will be other gangs," she murmurs. "There will always be someone who'll want to get to you, who'll try to use me to get to you."

"That's the price I pay for my past." I square my shoulders, "It's where I come from, but..."

"But?"

"But it needn't be the future that we bring our children into."

"What are you saying?" she whispers. "Do you mean that—"

"With my father no longer involved in the Cosa Nostra, I have the chance to change the course of what is to come. I plan to legalize our businesses, something I have been working on for a while now."

"You have?"

I nod, "I have created a framework that I can use to capitalize both the real-world operations and the virtual businesses."

"But won't that counter the ground you have gained with the

rival gangs? Surely, they are not going to be on board with that plan?"

I narrow my gaze on her. Beautiful and clever. This woman is more than capable of holding her own against my brothers, of going toe-to-toe with me, of partnering with me in the truest sense.

"Not if I show them that the legal businesses can be as lucrative as our illicit ones."

"Oh," she swallows, "you'd do that for me?"

"It won't be easy. And it will take some time to unravel the intricacies of our businesses, and a hell of a ton of paperwork to figure out the best way to legitimize them. But yeah," I nod, "I'd do it for us, for our children, for my brothers, so they have a chance to live life to the fullest. Without having to constantly protect themselves and their loved ones from the threat of danger."

"Mika," she whispers, "please don't think that I am forcing you to do this. I know I left you, but I never meant for it to act as some kind of coercion to make you give up your way of life."

"I am merely changing lanes." I rub my thumb across her cheek. "I am smart enough to know when I need to adapt and change with the times. It's something my father wasn't good at, and look where that got him."

"I am sorry you had to…" she swallows, "that you had to…"

"Kill him?" I blow out a breath, "Me too. I am probably going to hell for it, but... I am going to hell anyway, so..." I raise a shoulder.

"It's something you are going to have to come to terms with. He may have been responsible for so much evil, but he was still your flesh and blood."

"So was Xander." I firm my lips. "It's because of my father that my mother died so early. He is the one who kidnapped the Seven when they were boys."

"That... I suspected."

"You did?"

She nods. "When Summer told me that I needed a bodyguard because the Mafia may be after me...? Well, initially, I thought it was because my father had betrayed you guys, but then I realized, there was more to it than that." She tips up her chin, "Then, I met your

father and realized just how evil he was. That he was capable of
doing things that were so morally wrong... The kinds of things you
and your brothers wouldn't be involved in. I guessed, then, that
there had to be more of a connection between the Mafia and the
Seven. That, possibly, the Mafia was behind their kidnapping when
they were children. I couldn't reconcile you doing that. But your
father? Now, he could be capable of anything."

"Including emotionally and physically abusing me and my brothers." I roll my shoulders, "It's because of him that we are so fucked
up inside."

"You're not...fucked up." She bites the inside of her cheek, "Well,
not completely, anyway."

I chuckle, "Is that a compliment?"

"Would it be terrible if I admitted that your twisted-upness is
what attracted me to you in the first place?"

"Is that right?" I can't stop the smirk that curls my lips.

She glances away, "This doesn't mean I have forgiven you for
everything you did, or that I am returning to you."

"You are, though."

"I am?" She frowns.

"You bet." I slide my hand inside my pocket and withdraw her
wedding ring. I slide it onto her left ring finger and we both stare at
it. "Admit that you missed the weight of it on your finger, that you—"
I lower her onto the grass, on her back, and push my body between
her legs, "miss the weight of me between your thighs?"

Her pupils dilate as I push the evidence of my arousal—which
has been stretching my crotch since I sat down next to her—into her
center.

I grind into her and she moans. I begin to dry hump her and she
shudders. I press my thumb in between her lips and thrust it inside
her mouth in an action that mirrors what I want to do to her when I
am finally inside her. Her entire body shudders. She sucks on my
thumb and the blood rushes to my groin.

"Fuck," I growl. "F-u-c-k, *Bellezza*, what you do to me with your
little cries, your moans, the way you wriggle your body against mine,
in a sign that you are aroused."

"I am not aroused," she protests.

"Is that right?" I slide my finger down her waistband, inside her panties and thrust my finger inside her.

She gasps. "Oh, hell," she warbles, "oh, bloody hell."

"Indeed." I pull out my finger, glistening with the evidence of her arousal, and bring it to my mouth. I suck on it and a whine bleeds from her.

"What do you want, Beauty?" I lower my voice to a hush, "Tell me."

"You," she swallows, "I want you."

That's when Andy prowls over to us.

# 38

Karma

Andy crawls onto my chest. He coils between my breasts and tips his head up. He must glare at Michael, who glowers back at him. "You and I need to have a talk, buddy. You don't interrupt when your parents are in the middle of an important discussion."

"Is that what this was?"

He scowls at me over Andy's head, "It was a very important discussion;" His gaze intensifies, "Come home with me, baby."

I swallow.

"I've been lonely without you. Andy has been lonely without you."

"Andy seems fine to me." I arch my eyebrow at him. "You, however," I tilt my hips forward so I push into the bulge between his legs.

Color smears his cheeks. "You still punishing me? Even after everything I said I'd do for you?"

"Not what I expected to hear from you, Don." I rake my gaze across his features, "You are the Don now, aren't you?"

"Only if I can have you by my side. I need your sass, your shrewdness, your ability to think fast on your feet so you pick up anything that I may have missed. I need you, Beauty, only you."

He holds my gaze and in his blue eyes I see…love, lust…and sincerity. An honesty that had been missing before, a vulnerability which I'd never thought that I'd glimpse in my Don's gaze.

"Okay," I blow out a breath, "okay."

Two days later, I rub Andy's forehead as I glance out at the sea that stretches out in front of me. Michael had taken me from the park, straight to his private jet. He'd flown me to Palermo, and to a new home that he'd purchased on the island on the opposite side from where his home used to be.

A fresh start, he'd said. A new chapter in our lives. He'd also arranged for a doctor to come and remove the tracker from behind my ear. I had protested and told him that, in retrospect, it actually made me feel safe to know that no matter what happened he'd always be able to find me.

He'd told me that he'd feel better if he had it removed, especially since he wanted us to try for a child right away, and he didn't want anything to interfere with that.

So I had agreed.

Truth is, I want to try to get pregnant straight away, too. Guess this is when I should have come clean to him about the doctor's warning that it could be dangerous for me to get pregnant. On the other hand, the doc had also said that many women carried their babies to term without any problems, despite having a hole in the heart. And I know if I mention it to him, he won't want to take the risk. And honestly, I feel it in my guts that everything will be fine. That things will work out. So, I haven't said anything to him.

Yes, I know, I should be honest with him... But if I were...he'd never agree to my having a baby. He'd never allow me to get pregnant. He'd be willing to go without an heir, and that's something I will not allow.

Besides, I can do this. I can get pregnant and carry the baby to term and nothing will happen to me. I am confident of that.

Meanwhile, he's already set up a full-fledged studio for me in the house, where I can start working on my masterpieces. All, in less than forty-eight hours. The man is relentless when it comes to making sure that all of my needs are taken care of.

And when I had suggested we have the long overdue Christmas party, combined with a New Year's Eve one — he had agreed to it.

I'd also messaged Summer to let her know that I was fine, but that I needed a little more time to figure things out. Summer was initially upset about it. She'd insisted that I return to London or she'd be on the next flight to Sicily and drag me home.

I'd told her not to do that. Begged her to give me a little more time. I'd told her that I am in love with this guy. I'd wanted to tell her that I'd already married the man. Honestly, it had been on the tip of my tongue to tell her, but then I had chickened out. Because I know that she'll be upset to find out that I got married without telling her. And then she'll want to know everything and ...

I'm still not ready to share with her all that has happened. No, I want to tell her everything in person. And yes... I am also a little worried about her reaction. She's never going to forgive me for embarking on this adventure on my own, and without keeping her completely in the loop... And I know, the more I put it off, the worse it's going to get...so... Yeah, for the moment, at least, I am okay with her. But at some point, I am going to have to tell her everything. Soon. Just not today.

Footsteps sound behind me. The scent of fresh snow, of darkness, of edgy testosterone, washes over me a second before his arms come around my waist. Andy wriggles in my arms, then digs his claws into my shirt as he attempts to climb up my chest. He peers over my shoulder, growls at my husband. Michael growls right back. Andy stiffens, then hisses at him. He turns his head away, wriggles in my arms, then proceeds to jump out and onto the wall of the terrace.

"That cat is the most fickle creature I have ever met." His dark voice coils in my ear.

I shiver, then turn in the circle of his arms, "He's my cat; of course, his loyalties lie with me. Speaking of," I frown, "did you just growl back at him?"

"He needs to learn that he can't monopolize my wife's attention."

"Are you jealous of a cat, Michael Byron Domenico Sovrano?"

"Uh, oh," he smirks, "do you know how much of a turn on it is when you say my complete name?"

I slide my hand between us and cup the bulge at his crotch, "I am beginning to guess."

He pushes into me and my hips touch the wall behind me. He tilts his hips so I can feel every single ridge of his length against my palm. Heat coils in my belly and moisture laces my panties.

"You're so damn sexy, you know that?"

"I am, aren't I?" He smirks.

I laugh, "And not modest at all."

"Can't afford to be, in my line of work, baby."

My smile promptly vanishes. "How are the talks going with JJ and Nikolai? Are they agreeable to legitimizing the businesses?"

"Not completely," he raises a shoulder, "but I am sure I'll win them over."

"Like I said, not modest at all."

"They'll come around. They'll have to, when they see that the figures make sense. This is an opportunity for them to carve out a future that is safer for their families too, after all."

"You think they'll agree to that?"

"They will, once we've figured out the practicalities of how to manage the transition."

"Meanwhile," he lowers his head so his eyelashes entangle against mine, "where were we?"

He drags his palms up my hips and his fingertips brush against the bandage across my lower back.

I freeze; so does he.

"What's this?" He scowls, "Did you hurt yourself?"

"N...no," I tip up my chin, "I, ah, wanted to add something to what you marked on my back earlier.

"Can I see?"

I nod, then turn my back on him. He raises my shirt, stares down at the strip of clear plastic which covers my lower back.

His breath catches. "Beauty, you..." his voice cracks. "you wrote my name on your body?"

"I wanted to..." I glance at him over my shoulder again, "I wanted to find a way to ink your name into my skin and this seemed fitting.

"Mika's whore," he reads out aloud. "You shouldn't have hurt yourself further, this way."

"It's a hurt that I gladly bear," I say softly. "I needed to show you that I meant it, that this time, I am not leaving you. That you are stuck with me, Don."

He swivels me around in the circle of his arms. "My whore," he kisses my forehead, "my slut," he kisses me on one eyelid, "my pussy," then the other. "My Beauty," he kisses me on the tip of my nose. "Mine." He presses his lips to mine. "Only mine."

I share his breath, drag his scent into my lungs, and my entire core clenches. I lean in to deepen the kiss when.

"Get a room, you guys!"

Seb's voice sounds behind us.

Michael groans. "Ignore him," he murmurs as he presses his lips to mine. I open my mouth and his tongue sweeps in. He deepens the kiss and my belly trembles. He hauls me up against him, and I pull my hand out from between us and wind it about his shoulders. He pushes his hips forward and the thickness between his legs stabs into my core.

A whine bleeds from my lips and he swallows it down. He grabs my arse, squeezes, and heat jolts up my spine. I press myself into him and my breasts flatten against his chest. He nibbles on my lips and I can't stop the moan the spills from my lips.

"Michael," I gasp, "we need to stop. Your brothers... Your family will be here soon."

"The fuck I care?"

"Michelangelo!" Nonna calls out, and both of us freeze.

Michael steps back, peers into my face. "To be continued," he smirks.

Then, as if he can't stop himself, he leans down and presses a hard kiss to my lips. He slides around to stand behind me, then places his hands on my shoulders. I glance toward the entrance where Nonna stands, a knowing look on her face. Seb and Massimo flank her. Seb smirks. Massimo looks like he's about to say something, then seems to change his mind.

Nonna walks toward us and I stiffen. Not that I am afraid of her, but I am definitely wary of her. Despite the fact that the last time we met, she seemed almost friendly. And of course, I am the Don's wife now... But she's the Don's grandmother, so in that sense, she still has influence over my husband. Still, I know Michael's too smart to let his grandmother manipulate him into anything, but Nonna's w-a-a-y too astute. It's why I am not sure what to make of her yet.

Michael wraps an arm around my waist, still keeping the lower part of his body hidden behind mine.

"What are you doing?" I hiss. "Why don't you walk forward and meet her?"

"Because if I did that, everyone would know just how aroused I still am from kissing my wife."

"Oh." Heat flushes my cheeks.

"Exactly," he chuckles and the sound pulls at my nerve endings. My toes curl and I have to glance away. Damn it, I am turned on and his Nonna is watching us with a curious gaze as she approaches us.

She pauses in front of us, then takes my hand in hers, "Thank you for organizing this delayed Christmas get together." Her lips tilt in a smile that is—dare I say, quite genuine?

"Thank you for coming, Nonna." I step forward. Michael removes his hand from around me and I kiss Nonna's cheek. Her skin is papery thin, and she seems more fragile than when I last saw her.

Guess burying a son can do that to you? Michael had decided to bury his father with full honors. I hadn't been in Sicily to attend it, but I'd heard that the funeral itself had been attended by all the clan leaders. Cassandra had mentioned to me that Nonna had been pale-faced and ashen throughout the funeral, but she had managed to stay dry-eyed until the end. Maybe she had shed her tears in private. She seems genuinely pleased to be here though, so that's something.

"You don't think that this was too soon after what happened with Xander do you?"

She pauses, a considering look on her face, "Perhaps for a more traditional person it might seem that way," she murmurs. "And it's not that I don't mourn him," she swallows, "but I also know that Xander would not have wanted us to dwell on the past. He was an artist, a dreamer, a visionary, even. He would have wanted us to celebrate his life and look to the future."

I peer into her features, take in the intent expression on her face, "You mean it, don't you?"

"I never say anything I don't mean, Karma." She smiles. "In fact, I am going to follow your example." Her eyes gleam with that devilish glint that is so familiar. Something I have seen in Michael's eyes, too.

"You are?" I frown.

"Absolutely." She glances between us, "This family has been through so much, we need a fresh start. A chance to know each other all over again."

*Oh, hell, do I even want to know where this is going?*

"What are you thinking of, Nonna?" Michael asks.

"A Christmas getaway."

"Christmas is over," Michael points out, "and we're already having this delayed Christmas get together to make up for not being able to celebrate Christmas."

"It's not enough." Her lips firm. "It will take more than a few hours to mend the fractures left behind by your father. It's time we came together and found a way to heal, don't you think?"

Michael blows out a breath, "Are you sure about this?"

"Are you questioning me, Michael?" she asks in a deceptively soft tone that mirrors the one Michael often uses to get his way.

Michael stiffens, then a reluctant chuckle rumbles up his chest. "You are one hell of a woman, Nonna." He reaches around me to take her hand, "If it will make you happy..."

"It will." The older woman nods her head as a smile forms on her face. "Now that you are married," she glances between us, "it's time for me to focus on getting the rest of your brothers hitched, too."

Michael groans, "I'm glad I am no longer in the line of fire."

"You were smart enough to snap up your soulmate when you met her. Now, I need to make sure your brothers follow your lead. Also," that same wicked gleam reappears in her eyes, "I'm hoping that spending a few days in each other's company will help us strengthen our familial ties... If we don't kill each other first, that is."

I chuckle, Michael laughs, and Nonna's face lights up with a proper smile. "Now, where's my drink?"

As if summoned, Cassandra walks toward us with a tray of prosecco flutes. I take a glass and hand it to Nonna. She accepts it, sniffs it, then raises her eyebrows at me. "Is this —?"

I nod, "It's your favorite."

I take a glass for myself, then smile my thanks at Cassandra. She turns, then stops when Adrian walks onto the terrace. She seems to steel herself, then walks past him. He turns and his gaze tracks her until she disappears from sight. He turns, catches me staring and a small smile tugs at his lips. He walks over to the bar just as Luca steps onto the terrace. He glances around and his gaze collides with Michael's. The tension in the air ratchets up. I glance over my shoulder to find Michael scowling.

"Be nice, Don," I murmur.

He blows out a breath. "It's going to take some getting used to, but family is family after all, eh?" He walks past me and meets Luca half-way on the terrace. The two men murmur in low voices, then Michael jerks his chin. "Get us some Macallan," he calls out to Massimo, who's behind the bar. Massimo raises his thumb in a 'will do' gesture, then goes back to pouring.

"Good to see Michael making an effort," I remark.

Nonna turns to me, "You're good for him."

"Oh?" I meet her gaze, "Are you being sarcastic?"

"Do I look like I am being sarcastic?" She tilts her head. Her faded blue eyes twinkle, and again, I see so much of Michael in her that I can't stop the smile that curves my lips.

"No," I chuckle, "that sounds like a real compliment."

"It is." Nonna raises her glass, and so do I. We clink, and I take a sip. Notes of cherry and vanilla pop on my palate as the crisp taste of the Prosecco slides down my throat.

"Mmm," I lick my lips, "that's so good."

"My husband used to get me a bottle for every celebration." She stares at her flute with a soft look in her eyes. "Roberto was a typical Mafioso, as macho as they come, but he always remembered what I liked."

"He loved you?"

"He did," she raises her glass to her lips, "in his own way." She glances past me and frowns. "Who is that with Christian?"

I turn to find Christian walking into the family gathering, Aurora's arm tucked into his, his hand on hers. Either in a soothing gesture...or in one meant to control her, maybe?

He pauses a little way inside of the entrance. When Cassandra walks over with a full tray of Prosecco, he picks up a flute and hands it to Aurora, who accepts it. She's also wearing a beautiful silk dress that clings to her curves and flows to below her knees. On her feet are six-inch heels which are very different from the sensible wedges I normally see her in. She seems...different... Like a mafioso's woman. She glances at me, then away.

*Huh? What's happening here?*

Aurora downs the prosecco in one go. She places the glass back on Cassandra's tray, reaches for another, but Christian wraps his fingers around her wrist and stops her. He leans in, whispers something in her ear as Cassandra walks away.

Aurora shoots him a glance full of hatred; Christian chuckles.

*What the hell? What's happening between these two?*

Christian straightens, then he turns and walks toward us.

"Christian Roberto Domenico Sovrano," Nonna narrows her gaze on him, "just the person I am looking for."

Christian frowns, "I am?" He comes to a stop in front of us, Aurora in tow.

Nonna's eyes gleam, "I am an old woman, Christian, I don't know how long I have left on this earth."

"Nonna, please," Christian holds up his hand, "you are going to outlive us all and you know it. So why don't you come to the point, hmm? What's on your mind?"

"What's on my mind is that I am worried about you Christian."

"You are?"

She nods, "It's high time you got married and settled down."

"Michael just got married," Christian points out.

"And now I can't wait for you to settle down."

"What about Massimo?" Christian scowls, "he's older than me. Shouldn't he get married before I do."

"Massimo didn't lose his twin, you did."

Christian pales, "Nonna, what are you trying to say?"

Nonna narrows her gaze on him, "Since before you were born you had Xander by your side. Now he's gone and you are on your own."

Christian's jaw tics, "your point being?" He finally says through gritted teeth.

"I don't want you to be alone. In fact I have someone who would make you the perfect wife, I—"

Christian holds up his hand, "Let me stop you right there, Nonna."

Nonna scowls, "Let me complete what I am going to say."

"I know what you are going to say, and I am a step ahead of you." His lips curl.

Uh-oh! I am not sure I like the expression on his face. He seems too confident, too sure of himself. He releases his hold on Aurora only to wrap his arm around her and pull her close.

"Nonna," He tilts his head, before he locks his gaze with Michael's. "Don Sovrano," his smile widens, "meet the woman who is going to be my wife."

To find out what happens next read Christian & Aurora's story HERE. Karma and Michael's story too continues in this book, and will be told from their point of view. Click HERE

Read an excerpt

Two months later

## Karma

I bend over the ceramic bowl of the commode and throw up the breakfast that I have just eaten. I puke until there's nothing left, then manage to flush away the disgusting mess before I sink back onto the floor. I push my head back into the wall. Holy shit, this is the third morning in a row this has happened. That, combined with my tender breasts, and the period that I have missed, confirms that I am pregnant. Oh, yeah. Also, the pregnancy test with the two pink lines that I took yesterday is an indicator of what my current status is. I stay there for a few more seconds as I will my head to stop spinning. Close my eyes, take in a breath, then another. A few more breaths and I feel slightly better. I push up to my feet, and my knees don't buckle under me. Score!

I walk over to the sink, rinse out my mouth, splash some water on my face and wrists. By the time I leave my room, I feel much better. I walk over to my studio, which is just down the hallway from my bedroom, and push open the door. Andy glances up from his cat cave bed in the corner of the room. He stares at me as I cross over to where I have been drawing my latest creation. It's for a bride in London.

Since the day I had sold my first creations in Camden Market, the orders have kept flooding in. They are growing at such a fast rate, I have had to both hike up my price and turn down a few because I couldn't meet the demand.

Michael suggested it's time I expand. He told me he'll build me a separate studio on the grounds surrounding the house, and I should hire a couple of seamstresses to help me.

I've thought about it, and decided that's not for me.

The Karma label is my first baby, and I want to keep the creativity, the quality, and the attention to detail that it has come to embody as consistent as possible. Which means, I need to be hands-on, for now. Maybe later down the line, I might think of expanding and getting help. For now, I'd rather work on it myself.

It's a good thing Michael has been away on business the last few days, else my morning sickness would have sent him into a tizzy. It'd also have revealed my secret… Something I plan to tell him when he returns. For now though, it feels right that I can hold onto this part of me—this feeling, this sensation of being a mother again—to myself. I flatten my palm against my stomach as I stare at the finished design on the drafting board.

I pull off the paper and carefully place it aside. Just need a little break, before I begin translating that into fabric. Meanwhile… I pick up a pencil and begin to draw again… Something different. Something unlike the designs I have created so far. Something softer, more fragile, smaller in size…

A Peter Pan collar, simple long sleeves, slight gathering at the waist, opening at the back so it's easy to put on and pull off… I step back and glance at what I have drawn. It's a bodysuit for a baby…a new born. Tears prick the backs of my eyes and I wipe them away. Shit, I am not even, like, fully pregnant—is that even a concept? I mean, I just found out I am pregnant, and already, the pregnancy hormones seem to be taking affect.

If Michael were here, he'd probably just wrap me in wool, scoop me up, place me on the bed, and order me not to move until the baby is born. I scowl at the drawing. Not likely.

I intend to work until my last week. I intend to continue to design and sew and ensure that all the orders I have taken are fulfilled with Karma originals. No bride who orders a dress from me is going to be empty-handed. No, siree. I only need to convince my husband of that.

Speaking of—I place my pencil on the table—there's a much bigger discussion I need to broach with my husband. I wince. I've been putting it off for so long, and now, I really need to tell him. And if I don't…

*No.* I shake my head. I can't do this to him. It's bad enough I haven't brought it up with him so far. He deserves to know. It's his right to know.

The sound of footsteps reaches me a second before the edgy scent of testosterone—musky, like leather with a hint of woodsmoke—envelops me. I draw in the fragrance of his aftershave, like fresh snow on earth. The cold rush of a winter's wind, followed by the snap and crackle of a fireplace. The images flow over me, just before his arms wrap around me. Goosebumps pop on my skin and my core trembles. I turn around, tip up my chin, and meet those brilliant blue eyes. Warmth flares in their depths, silver flashes riddled with sparks of gold. The look he only wears when he is around me, as I have learned.

"Don," I murmur, "I wasn't expecting you back until tomorrow."

"I missed you, Beauty," his dark voice flows over me, coils in my chest, sinks into my blood. A cascade of warmth flares out from my core to my extremities. My toes curl. I bite down on my lower lip and he lowers his gaze to my mouth. "I missed my wife." He tilts his head and replaces my teeth with his own. He tugs on my lip and my pussy clenches. Moisture beads my center and my stomach flip-flops. My pulse rate ratchets up. Sweat beads my forehead and I tear my mouth from his. I tip up my chin watch him watch me with a curious gaze.

"Everything all right, baby?" He frowns as he pushes the hair back from my face. He pauses with his palm on my forehead, "Your skin is clammy." The lines in his forehead deepen. He peers into my face, no doubt, taking in my sudden pallor. My stomach ties itself in knots, the wave of sickness pushing up against my breastbone, my throat. Turning, I race to the bathroom.

*To find out what happen next read A Very Mafia Christmas HERE*

Read an excerpt from Aurora and Christian's story

Aurora

"Open the door!" The banging on the main door reaches me. I stare at the coffee-table wedged against it. It'll hold the door, surely, won't it? I glance around the living room space, but can't see any means of escaping. Not that I haven't checked every inch of this house in the last few weeks that I have been held here as a prisoner. Every window is barred and the door to the terrace on the first floor is sealed tight. The only way in or out of this house is through the front door. The door on which the man who is trying to enter is currently leaning his weight.

Shit!" The double doors creaks as he puts his shoulder to it.

"Open the fucking door, Aurora, or else I'm gonna break it down."

"Who—" My voice cracks, and I clear my throat, "Who's there?"

"You know who it is. Who else comes to this house, except me?" Christian's voice lowers to a growl, "When I get through, I am going to teach you such a lesson, you are not going to be able to sit down for days."

"Oh?" My stomach trembles. "OH!" I blink as the full meaning of his words sinks in. My heart rate ratchets up and moisture laces my core. I should not find that so hot. Why do I find that such a turn on?

"How can I be sure who it is, if you don't tell me who you are? Not like I can recognize your voice or anything, you know."

"Is that right?" His tone is almost lazy now.

Like he's realized I am playing a game and has decided to go along with it. My belly twists. I rub my damp hands on my thighs. Why the hell did I decide to stop him from coming in? I should have known it was going to be futile, that nothing I say or do would deter him.

The door creaks again, pushes against the coffee table, which moves forward by an inch.

"Oh, hell!" I race toward the coffee table, push against it to hold it in place. Something slams into the door from the other side, and again. The double doors shudder, the bolt across the door shivers, and the coffee table moves forward by another inch. I yelp, take a step back.

"Don't fucking make me wait, Aurora," Christian growls.

I shiver. Even through the heavy wood of the double doors, the menace rolls off of his voice. Goosebumps pop on my skin. My toes curl. Shit, this should not turn me on so much.

That...that mean edge to his tone, the promise of punishment when he finally gets through... I shouldn't want it so much.

"Last chance, Aurora. Open the door or—"

"Or," I call out, "what are you going to do, eh?"

"Do you really want to find out?" He lowers his voice to a hush, but I can still hear him. "Do you, Aurora?"

Yes.

Yes.

"No," I yell back, "I am tired of being kept a prisoner here. Tired of being held without anyone telling me how long I am going to be here."

There's silence for a beat, then another.

"It's why I've come here," he retorts, "to tell you what's going to happen next."

"Do you think I am going to believe you?"

"I hope you are standing clear, Aurora," he says in a low pitched voice. "I am coming through."

I straighten, stare at the door. He's joking. He's not really going to batter down that door, is he?

"Get back, Aurora!" he growls. "Now!"

I jump, stumble back, just as he smashes into the door. The wood creaks, groans. The coffee table I've wedged against the door screeches forward. I yelp, slide back a few more steps. Just in time. For there's another crash.

The entire door whines, then the doors fly off the hinges.

I scream, turn and race toward the bedroom, then close the door and bolt it. I sink down against it, and my shoulders shudder.

Shit, shit, shit. What is wrong with me? Why did I try to shut him out? I should have known I couldn't win, that he'd find a way to come inside. But the truth is, I am tired of sitting here in this house, trying to figure out what is going to happen to me next. Tired of not knowing my fate. Tired of being punished for helping out my friend Karma. She'd wanted to escape her husband, the then Capo—now Don Michael Sovrano, and of course, I couldn't say no to helping her.

I'd known how dangerous it was to do so. To go against the leader of the Cosa Nostra is to bring death to yourself and to your family... I'd known it, and yet, something in me had not been able to turn her down. I'd recognized another woman in need and something in me had snapped.

Maybe it's all the time spent as a woman in the heart of the Mafia. Knowing that we are often seen as disposable. Interchangeable. Good only to procreate, as wives as mistresses, as objects to be lusted after, but never respected as individuals with our own minds, who could control our own destinies.

And you know what? I, sure as hell, am going to control my future… At least, that's what I had thought… That's what I had aimed for during all of my years growing up. And while the Capo had paid off my father's debts and paid for me to go to medical school in London, and I had accepted it then…because it had seemed like the only way to find my way out of the situation that I had been born into—I don't owe him anything. Right?

Clearly, he'd done it so he could indenture my family, ensure that he'd bought our loyalty and those of any future generations. Only I am not going to accept my fate.

It was this streak of defiance in me that had urged me to help Karma. I had treated her when she'd been brought into the hospital in Palermo. She'd been faking the illness, of course, as she'd warned me she would. I had examined her, nevertheless, so the situation would appear as genuine as possible—and discovered that she was pregnant.

I hadn't been able to stop myself from revealing that to her husband. We had returned to her room and found her gone… And the Capo would have killed me on the spot except… His brother, Christian had intervened. He'd saved my life that day, and I suppose, I should be grateful for it.

Only, I am not sure about his intentions toward me. Since that day, he's shadowed me wherever I go. Oh, he hasn't made a move on me or anything like that… I wish he would. That way, I'd know what he wants from me. No, he simply watches me with that gray-blue gaze of his that seems to peer into my soul.

He's the person who accompanied me when I went to see Karma while she was pregnant.

She'd lost her child in an unfortunate incident when her car had been rigged with a bomb which, luckily for her, had turned out to be a defective. Although it had killed Xander, Christian's twin. Turned out, it was their father who was behind it. Michael had ended up killing his father, and becoming Don, and Christian is now even more firmly entrenched in the inner circle of the leader of the Cosa Nostra. So the question is, why is this man, who can have any woman in the city — hell, on the continent, even — beating down the door to my bedroom?

"Go away," I yell as I slap my hands on my ears. "Get the hell away from me…you…you asshole!"

"Now, play nice, Flower," Christian drawls. I can hear him from the other side of the door. Hell, I can all but feel the heat of his body as it permeates through the wood, which is likely my imagination. But every time I've been near him, it's as if I've stepped past a furnace. The man has so much vitality, he can probably light up an entire Christmas tree by his proximity. I snort.

That's fanciful thinking. Probably because I spent Christmas Day shut up in here, feeling sorry for myself. Hell, even criminals in jails get to celebrate Christmas. I had spent it locked up here, and except for the brief time on Christmas Eve when Christian had come in to check on me and had lent me his phone so I could call Karma, I had been alone. At least, I hadn't starved. The fridge had been full of food, as had the pantry, so there was more than enough to eat. Still, it didn't fill the void left by being alone, on the one day of the year when every family is together.

Karma had wanted to organize a Christmas gathering, but Xander's death, and then her losing her baby, had put paid to that. Christian had updated me that she was spending time in London, had even given me his phone so I could speak with her. A favor I hadn't wanted to accept, but which I didn't turn down, starved of company as I had been.

But everyone has a limit, and I have reached mine. No way, am I going to allow myself to be shut up inside here. I want to leave this prison, go see my family, lead a normal life…or else… I am willing to die. Yeah, not being dramatic here…

When you live in the heart of the Mafia community, death is as much a part of life as going out to dinner is. And I…like it or not, am one of them.

I grew up surrounded by macho guys who think they own the world. And you know what? I have spent enough time among them to be able to play them at their own game. I am not going to let one of them scare me, no matter that he happens to be big, brooding and growly, and sexy and…hot…and that he turns me on by just a glance. I am not going to let my attraction to him get in the way. No. I am going to tell him exactly where he can shove this awareness he seems to have for me, the one which has him pushing his shoulder into the door and applying his weight so the entire barrier shakes.

"Open the door, Flower," he rumbles, "or I am going to break this down and come inside and then you are going to regret shutting me out."

Is that right? I jump up to my feet, tuck my elbows into my side.

"Last chance," he warns. "Open. The. Door."

I spin around, unlock the door and yank it open. Just as he lunges forward.

## Christian

I dive forward just as she pulls the door open. I careen through the doorway and toward her, managing to swerve at the last minute. Still I don't avoid her completely, and my shoulder brushes hers. She yells out in surprise and her body hurtles toward the floor. I grab her, manage to get my body under hers as we hit the floor, with her on top of me.

The back of my head hits the floor and the breath rushes out of me. Or it may be because of the soft curves that tremble against my chest, her breath that shivers against my throat, her sweet scent like honeysuckle and crushed rose petals that teases my nostrils and goes straight to my head. The blood rushes to my groin, my cock thickens. She pushes off of me, or at least tries to, for I've thrown my arm around her waist and held her in place.

"Let me go," she snarls.

"No," I sit up wince when the bump on the back of my head protests. I ignore the pain, push myself up to standing, still holding her close."

"What the hell are you doing?" She hisses as I head further into the house with her in my arms.

"Let me the hell go," she slaps her palm against my chest, "Right now."

"Fine." I lower my arms and she hits the floor on her ass.

"Ow!" She grunts, then stares up at me, a shocked expression on her face. "You... you dropped me?" She stutters, "Like honest to god, you allowed me to crash to the floor?"

"You asked me to let you go," I remind her, "I was only obliging you."

"Asshole," She snaps, then pushes up to stand to her full height, which still means she hits somewhere below my breastbone.

Gesü Christo, but she's tiny, and also very angry right now. Her cheeks are flushed, her hair awry about her features. She pushes a strand away from her face and scowls at me, "you're a dick, you know that?"

"Glad you recognized that."

"Argh!" She makes a noise at the back of her throat, "and insufferable, not to mention you're so full of yourself that if anyone were to prick your skin, you'd take off."

"Take off?"

"Yeah, all that hot air which you carry around would catapult you into the stratosphere, no doubt."

I glare at her, then can't stop the surprised chuckle that rumbles up my chest, "You're funny," I murmur.

"You're annoying."

'You're on my turf."

"You're in my house," She shoots back.

"A house you're in thanks to my having intervened on your behalf. If not you'd be dead by now."

Her features flush further, "should I be grateful to you for that? I bet you have your reasons for having stepped in."

"At least you are smart," I curl my lips, "So you'll realize that I am being very serious when I said that I am going to punish you."

"Whatever," She huffs, "Why are you here anyway?"

"It's my place remember? I can come and go as I want."

She seems like she is about to say something, then changes her mind. She pivots and walks into the room. I shut the door and follow her into the kitchen. She reaches the *Bialetti* - the espresso maker, tops it up with coffee powder and places it on the stove. She reaches for two cups and saucers, places them on the counter, then turns to me. "What do you want from me?"

"Marry me."

"What?" Her gaze widens, "What did you say?"

"Marry me," I allow my smile to widen, "not for real, of course."

"Of course," She nods, "So you want me to pretend to marry you?"

"For 30 days."

"What happens in thirty days?"

"I am able to convince my older brother and my Nonna that we are really serious about each other. After which time, you are free to go your own way."

"So if I leave after that how can you convince them that we are serious about each other."

"You're right."

"I am?" She scowls.

"Sixty days," I cross my arms over my chest.

"What the--!" She gapes, "you added on an entire month?"

I raise a shoulder, "It's going to take that long for us to convince them that we are in love with each other."

"But we are not," she points out.

"Given that I am incapable of falling in love, that's a foregone conclusion."

"Is that right?" Her gaze narrows.

"Which is why when we decide to separate, no one will raise an eyebrow. In fact given that by the we'd have proved to be incompatible it will be all too believable that," I peer into her face, "our marriage was a complete mistake."

"And what's the benefit of that?"

"That they won't bother me about getting married to anyone else for a long time after that."

She purses her lips, "Somehow I can't see you being bothered by anyone about being married."

"Have you met my Nonna?" I tilt my head, "She's been planning our weddings from the moment each of us were born, and now that Michael's married and with Xander's passing…" I firm my lips.

"You were saying?" She prompts.

"Nothing," I straighten my spine, "fake marriage, you and I, that's all you need to know."

"Hmm," She takes in my features, "and what's in it for me?"

I glare at her, "Really?" I snap, "you dare ask me that?"

She pales, but doesn't glance away, "yes," she says in a firm voice, "I need to know what's in it for me."

I take a step toward her and she leans back, only there's nowhere for her to go for she presses back and into the counter. I close the distance between us, plant my hands on the counter and cage her in.

"You were saying?"

"I was asking a question actually," she tips up her chin, "what's in it for me, Christian?"

I peer into her features, and her pupils dilate. Her brown eyes lighten until they seem almost golden in this light. I lean in closer until my breath raises the hair on her forehead. I run my finger down the side of her cheek and she shivers, "Don't," She murmurs, "Don't try to distract me."

"Oh, so I do distract you?"

"Don't change the topic."

I step back and the breath rushes out of her, "your life, Aurora, you get a new lease of life."

"So," she furrows her forehead, "if I acted as your fake wife for sixty days, I'll be free to leaves and live as I want."

No.

No.

I nod, slowly. "If you fulfill all the conditions and if you put up enough of a performance that my Nonna and my brothers are convinced of the veracity of our relationship."

She bites down on her lower lip and hell if my gaze isn't drawn to her glistening flesh. Why the hell does this woman affect me so? She's only a convenience after all? Someone to use and discard. So I can go back to the life I prefer to lead. To be surrounded by enough pussy so I can forget that I lost my twin brother. The other half of my soul. The one who's been with me since before we were born. Xander and I were so different yet so alike. He was the artist, and I was the numbers guy. It's why steering the finances of the Cosa Nostra fell to me.

If there's one thing I am good at, it's getting the numbers to speak to me. Numbers don't lie. They can't hide. They can't hurt you like our father had. After our oldest brother Michael had left to study in the States, my father had turned his anger on our mother, and onto us. Luca our second oldest brother got the brunt of it. Massimo our middle brother was already getting to the big and tall enough that our father didn't dare hurt him. But me and Xander? We were still small and young enough, that he knew he could hurt us without fear of retaliation.

I had been older had tried to protect him from being physically beaten up by our father and I had mostly succeeded. I still had the scars to show for it too... I had saved him then, but when he was targeted by the car bomb that our own father had rigged his car with... I hadn't been able to go to his rescue then. The car bomb had been faulty but a piece of metal had embedded in his chest and killed him on the spot. Michael's wife Karma had been in the car and she had managed to escape, but she had been pregnant and lost her child. We had all suffered... but losing Xander, it was a trauma that haunted me, that stuck to me, that accompanied me day and night like a shadow which refused to peel away from me. I'd never be the same again, never be able to see myself in the mirror without seeing my twin brother. Never be able to experience life without thinking that he'd never be able to see, smell, taste life. It should have been me who died in that incident, not him.

Me who was buried under the earth, not him.

I didn't deserve any happiness, not when Xander wouldn't get to experience it.

I should turn away from life itself... except that's not Xander would have wanted. It's for him that I will continue living... didn't mean I had to let myself feel though. It's for him that I would support my family, help Michael consolidate his position as the new Don of the Cosa Nostra. Michael had killed our father... too bad I hadn't had the opportunity to do so. I should have felt some level of satisfaction considering it was our father who had been behind rigging the car, the reason that Xander had died... but all I feel is a numbness. Like I am not in my body. Like nothing else matters except, trying to get through life. Trying to swallow down the grief the threatens to overwhelm my every waking moment. And her... how dare she try to infiltrate the nothingness that I have surrounded myself in since Xander died? Why is it that thoughts of her occupy my mind when I should have only space to mourn Xander?

"And if I don't?" She tips up her chin. "What if I disagree?"

I move so fast that she flinches. I wrap my fingers around her throat and haul her up to her toes. "I don't recall giving you a choice, Flower."

She swallows and I feel the movement against my fingers. Such a slender throat. How would it feel to have my cock sliding down it, hmm?

I tighten my grip and the color fades from her cheeks. A soft sound emerges from her mouth. She parts her lips and I take in her flushed features, the contours of her pouty lower lip and my balls throb. Fuck this, why the hell should I deny myself when I am going to marry her anyway... only temporarily of course. Still... soon she will be my wife and I am going to take full advantage of it. I pull her even closer until her breasts are flush against my chest, then I lower my mouth to her's.

*To find out what happens next read Christian and Aurora's story in A Very Mafia Christmas HERE*

*Want to be the first to find out about L. Steele's new release? Join her newsletter here*

READ AN EXCERPT FROM *SUMMER & SINCLAIR'S* STORY IN THE *BILLIONAIRE'S FAKE WIFE*

## Summer

"Slap, slap, kiss, kiss."

"Huh?" I stare up at the bartender.

"Aka, there's a thin line between love and hate." He shakes out the crimson liquid into my glass.

"Nah." I snort. "Why would she allow him to control her, and after he insulted her?"

"It's the chemistry between them." He lowers his head, "You have to admit that when the man is arrogant and the woman resists, it's a challenge to both of them, to see who blinks first, huh?"

"Why?" I wave my hand in the air, "Because they hate each other?"

"Because," he chuckles, "the girl in school whose braids I pulled and teased mercilessly, is the one who I—"

"Proposed to?" I huff.

His face lights up. "You get it now?"

*Yeah. No.* A headache begins to pound at my temples. This crash course in pop psychology is not why I came to my favorite bar in Islington, to meet my best friend, who is—I glance at the face of my phone—thirty minutes late.

I inhale the drink, and his eyebrows rise.

"What?" I glower up at the bartender. "I can barely taste the alcohol. Besides, it's free drinks at happy hour for women, right?"

"Which ends in precisely" he holds up five fingers, "minutes."

"Oh! Yay!" I mock fist pump. "Time enough for one more, at least."

A hiccough swells my throat and I swallow it back, nod.

One has to do what one has to do… when everything else in the world is going to shit.

A hot sensation stabs behind my eyes; my chest tightens. Is this what people call growing up?

The bartender tips his mixing flask, strains out a fresh batch of the ruby red liquid onto the glass in front of me.

"Salut." I nod my thanks, then toss it back. It hits my stomach and tendrils of fire crawl up my spine, I cough.

My head spins. Warmth sears my chest, spreads to my extremities. I can't feel my fingers or toes. Good. Almost there. "Top me up."

"You sure?"

"Yes." I square my shoulders and reach for the drink.

"No. She's had enough."

"What the —?" I pivot on the bar stool.

Indigo eyes bore into me.

Fathomless. Black at the bottom, the intensity in their depths grips me. He swoops out his arm, grabs the glass and holds it up. Thick fingers dwarf the glass. Tapered at the edges. The nails short and buff. *All the better to grab you with.* I gulp.

"Like what you see?"

I flush, peer up into his face.

Hard cheekbones, hollows under them, and a tiny scar that slashes at his left eyebrow. *How did he get that?* Not that I care. My gaze slides to his mouth. Thin upper lip, a lower lip that is full and cushioned. Pouty with a hint of bad boy. *Oh!* My toes curl. My thighs clench.

The corner of his mouth kicks up. *Asshole.*

Bet he thinks life is one big smug-fest. I glower, reach for my glass, and he holds it up and out of my reach.

I scowl, "Gimme that."

He shakes his head.

"That's my drink."

"Not anymore." He shoves my glass at the bartender. "Water for her. Get me a whiskey, neat."

I splutter, then reach for my drink again. The barstool tips, in his direction. This is when I fall against him, and my breasts slam into his hard chest, sculpted planes with layers upon layers of muscle that ripple and writhe as he turns aside, flattens himself against the bar. The floor rises up to meet me.

*What the actual hell?*

I twist my torso at the last second and my butt connects with the surface. *Ow!*

The breath rushes out of me. My hair swirls around my face. I scrabble for purchase, and my knee connects with his leg.

"Watch it." He steps around, stands in front of me.

"You stepped aside?" I splutter. "You let me fall?"

"Hmph."

I tilt my chin back, all the way back, look up the expanse of muscled thigh that stretches the silken material of his suit. *What is he wearing? Could any suit fit a man with such precision?* Hand crafted on Saville Row, no doubt. I glance at the bulge that tents the fabric between his legs. *Oh!* I blink.

*Look away, look away.* I hold out my arm. He'll help me up at least, won't he?

He glances at my palm, then turns away. *No, he didn't do that, no way.*

A glass of amber liquid appears in front of him. He lifts the tumbler to his sculpted mouth.

His throat moves, strong tendons flexing. He tilts his head back, and the column of his neck moves as he swallows. Dark hair covers his chin—it's a discordant chord in that clean-cut profile, I shiver. He would scrape that rough skin down my core. He'd mark my inner thigh, lick my core, thrust his tongue inside my melting channel and drink from my pussy. *Oh! God.* Goosebumps rise on my skin.

No one has the right to look this beautiful, this achingly gorgeous. Too magnificent for his own good. Anger coils in my chest.

"Arrogant wanker."

"I'll take that under advisement."

"You're a jerk, you know that?"

He presses his lips together. The grooves on either side of his mouth deepen. Jesus, clearly the man has never laughed a single day in his life. Bet that stick up his arse is uncomfortable. I chuckle.

He runs his gaze down my features, my chest, down to my toes, then yawns.

*The hell!* I will not let him provoke me. Will not. "Like what you see?" I jut out my chin.

"Sorry, you're not my type." He slides a hand into the pocket of those perfectly cut pants, stretching it across that heavy bulge.

Heat curls low in my belly.

Not fair, that he could afford a wardrobe that clearly shouts his status and what amounts to the economy of a small third-world country. A hot feeling stabs in my chest.

He reeks of privilege, of taking his status in life for granted.

While I've had to fight every inch of the way. Hell, I am still battling to hold onto the last of my equilibrium.

"Last chance—" I wiggle my fingers, from where I am sprawled out on the floor at his feet, "—to redeem yourself..."

"You have me there." He places the glass on the counter, then bends and holds out his hand. The hint of discolored steel at his wrist catches my attention. Huh?

He wears a cheap-ass watch?

That's got to bring down the net worth of his presence by more than 1000% percent. Weird.

I reach up and he straightens.

I lurch back.

"Oops, I changed my mind." His lips curl.

A hot burning sensation claws at my stomach. I am not a violent person, honestly. But Smirky Pants here, he needs to be taught a lesson.

I swipe out my legs, kicking his out from under him.

## Sinclair

My knees give way, and I hurtle toward the ground.

What the—? I twist around, thrust out my arms. My palms hit the floor. The impact jostles up my elbows. I firm my biceps and come to a halt planked above her.

A huffing sound fills my ear.

I turn to find my whippet, Max, panting with his mouth open. I scowl and he flattens his ears.

All of my businesses are dog-friendly. Before you draw conclusions about me being the caring sort or some such shit—it attracts footfall.

Max scrutinizes the girl, then glances at me. *Huh?* He hates women, but not her, apparently.

I straighten and my nose grazes hers.

My arms are on either side of her head. Her chest heaves. The fabric of her dress stretches across her gorgeous breasts. My fingers tingle; my palms ache to cup those tits, squeeze those hard nipples outlined against the—hold on, what is she wearing? A tunic shirt in a sparkly pink... and are those shoulder pads she has on?

I glance up, and a squeak escapes her lips.

Pink hair surrounds her face. *Pink? Who dyes their hair that color past the age of eighteen?*

I stare at her face. *How old is she?* Un-furrowed forehead, dark eyelashes that flutter against pale cheeks. Tiny nose, and that mouth —luscious, tempting. A whiff of her scent, cherries and caramel, assails my senses. My mouth waters. *What the hell?*

She opens her eyes and our eyelashes brush. Her gaze widens. Green, like the leaves of the evergreens, flickers of gold sparkling in their depths. "What?" She glowers. "You're demonstrating the plank position?"

"Actually," I lower my weight onto her, the ridge of my hardness thrusting into the softness between her legs, "I was thinking of something else, altogether."

She gulps and her pupils dilate. *Ah, so she feels it, too?*

I drop my head toward her, closer, closer.

Color floods the creamy expanse of her neck. Her eyelids flutter down. She tilts her chin up.

I push up and off of her.

"That... Sweetheart, is an emphatic 'no thank you' to whatever you are offering."

Her eyelids spring open and pink stains her cheeks. Adorable. Such a range of emotions across those gorgeous features in a few seconds? What else is hidden under that exquisite exterior of hers?

She scrambles up, eyes blazing.

*Ah!* The little bird is trying to spread her wings? My dick twitches. My groin hardens, *Why does her anger turn me on so, huh?*

She steps forward, thrusts a finger in my chest.

My heart begins to thud.

She peers up from under those hooded eyelashes. "Wake up and taste the wasabi, asshole."

"What does that even mean?"

She makes a sound deep in her throat. My dick twitches. My pulse speeds up.

She pivots, grabs a half-full beer mug sitting on the bar counter.

I growl, "Oh, no, you don't."

She turns, swings it at me. The smell of hops envelops the space.

I stare down at the beer-splattered shirt, the lapels of my camel colored jacket deepening to a dull brown. Anger squeezes my guts.

I fist my fingers at my side, broaden my stance.

She snickers.

I tip my chin up. "You're going to regret that."

The smile fades from her face. "Umm." She places the now empty mug on the bar.

I take a step forward and she skitters back. "It's only clothes." She gulps, "They'll wash."

I glare at her and she swallows, wiggles her fingers in the air, "I should have known that you wouldn't have a sense of humor."

I thrust out my jaw, "That's a ten-thousand-pound suit you destroyed."

She blanches, then straightens her shoulders, "Must have been some hot date you were trying to impress, huh?"

"Actually," I flick some of the offending liquid from my lapels, "it's you I was after."

"Me?" She frowns.

"We need to speak."

She glances toward the bartender who's on the other side of the bar. "I don't know you." She chews on her lower lip, biting off some of the hot pink. How would she look, with that pouty mouth fastened on my cock?

The blood rushes to my groin so quickly that my head spins. My pulse rate ratchets up. Focus, focus on the task you came here for.

"This will take only a few seconds." I take a step forward.

She moves aside.

I frown, "You want to hear this, I promise."

"Go to hell." She pivots and darts forward.

I let her go, a step, another, because... I can? Besides it's fun to create the illusion of freedom first; makes the hunt so much more entertaining, huh?

I swoop forward, loop an arm around her waist, and yank her toward me.

She yelps. "Release me."

Good thing the bar is not yet full. It's too early for the usual officegoers to stop by. And the staff...? Well they are well aware of who cuts their paychecks.

I spin her around and against the bar, then release her. "You will listen to me."

She swallows; she glances left to right.

*Not letting you go yet, little Bird.* I move into her space, crowd her.

She tips her chin up. "Whatever you're selling, I'm not interested."

I allow my lips to curl, "You don't fool me."

A flush steals up her throat, sears her cheeks. So tiny, so innocent. Such a good little liar. I narrow my gaze, "Every action has its consequences."

"Are you daft?" She blinks.

"This pretense of yours?" I thrust my face into hers, "It's not working."

She blinks, then color suffuses her cheeks, "You're certifiably mad—"

"Getting tired of your insults."

"It's true, everything I said." She scrapes back the hair from her face.

Her fingernails are painted... You guessed it, pink.

"And here's something else. You are a selfish, egotistical jackass."

I smirk. "You're beginning to repeat your insults and I haven't even kissed you yet."

"Don't you dare." She gulps.

I tilt my head, "Is that a challenge?"

"It's a..." she scans the crowded space, then turns to me. Her lips firm, "...a warning. You're delusional, you jackass." She inhales a deep breath, "Your ego is bigger than the size of a black hole." She snickers, "Bet it's to compensate for your lack of balls."

A-n-d, that's it. I've had enough of her mouth that threatens to never stop spewing words. How many insults can one tiny woman hurl my way? Answer: too many to count.

"You—"

I lower my chin, touch my lips to hers.

Heat, sweetness, the honey of her essence explodes on my palate. My dick twitches. I tilt my head, deepen the kiss, reaching for that something more... more... of whatever scent she's wearing on her skin, infused with that breath of hers that crowds my senses, rushes down my spine. My groin hardens; my cock lengthens. I thrust my tongue between those infuriating lips.

She makes a sound deep in her throat and my heart begins to pound.

So innocent, yet so crafty. Beautiful and feisty. The kind of complication I don't need in my life.

I prefer the straight and narrow. Gray and black, that's how I choose to define my world. She, with her flashes of color—pink hair and lips that threaten to drive me to the edge of distraction—is exactly what I hate.

Give me a female who has her priorities set in life. To pleasure me, get me off, then walk away before her emotions engage. Yeah. That's what I prefer.

Not this... this bundle of craziness who flings her arms around my shoulders, thrusts her breasts up and into my chest, tips up her chin, opens her mouth, and invites me to take and take.

Does she have no self-preservation? Does she think I am going to fall for her wide-eyed appeal? She has another thing coming.

I tear my mouth away and she protests.

She twines her leg with mine, pushes up her hips, so that melting softness between her thighs cradles my aching hardness.

I glare into her face and she holds my gaze.

Trains her green eyes on me. Her cheeks flush a bright red. Her lips fall open and a moan bleeds into the air. The blood rushes to my dick, which instantly thickens. *Fuck.*

Time to put distance between myself and the situation.

It's how I prefer to manage things. Stay in control, always. Cut out anything that threatens to impinge on my equilibrium. Shut it down or buy them off. Reduce it to a transaction. That I understand.

The power of money, to be able to buy and sell—numbers, logic. That's what's worked for me so far.

"How much?"

Her forehead furrows.

"Whatever it is, I can afford it."

Her jaw slackens. "You think… you—"

"A million?"

"What?"

"Pounds, dollars… You name the currency, and it will be in your account."

Her jaw slackens, "You're offering me money?"

"For your time, and for you to fall in line with my plan."

She reddens, "You think I am for sale?"

"Everyone is."

"Not me."

Here we go again. "Is that a challenge?"

Color fades from her face, "Get away from me."

"Are you shy, is that what this is?" I frown. "You can write your price down on a piece of paper if you prefer," I glance up, notice the bartender watching us. I jerk my chin toward the napkins. He grabs one, then offers it to her.

She glowers at him, "Did you buy him too?"

"What do you think?"

She glances around, "I think everyone here is ignoring us."

"It's what I'd expect."

"Why is that?"

I wave the tissue in front of her face, "Why do you think?"

"You own the place?"

"As I am going to own you."

She sets her jaw, "Let me leave and you won't regret this."

A chuckle bubbles up. I swallow it away. This is no laughing matter. I never smile during a transaction. Especially not when I am negotiating a new acquisition. And that's all she is. The final piece in the puzzle I am building.

"No one threatens me."

"You're right."

"Huh?"

"I'd rather act on my instinct."

Her lips twist, her gaze narrows. All of my senses scream a warning.

No, she wouldn't, no way—pain slices through my middle and sparks explode behind my eyes.

*To find out what happens next get The Billionaire's Fake Wife HERE*

*Read about the seven in the Big bad Billionaires series*

*US*

*UK*

*Other countries*

*Join L. Steele's Newsletter for news on her newest releases*

*Claim your FREE copy of Mafia Heir the prequel to Mafia King*

*Claim your FREE billionaire romance*

*Claim your free paranormal romance*

*Follow L. Steele on AMAZON*

*Follow L. Steele on BookBub*

*Follow L. Steele on Goodreads*

*Follow L. Steele on Facebook*

*Follow L. Steele on Instagram*

*Join L. Steele's secret Facebook Reader Group*

*More books by L. Steele HERE*

# FREE BOOKS

Claim your FREE copy of Mafia Heir the prequel to Mafia King

Claim your FREE billionaire romance

Claim your FREE paranormal romance book HERE

More books by L. STEELE

More Books by Laxmi

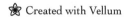 Created with Vellum

www.ingramcontent.com/pod-product-compliance
Lightning Source LLC
Chambersburg PA
CBHW072151210225
22349CB00011B/1026